14/11/17

DEATH'S DARK SHADOW

Recent Titles by Sally Spencer from Severn House

THE BUTCHER BEYOND
DANGEROUS GAMES
THE DARK LADY
DEAD ON CUE
DEATH OF A CAVE DWELLER
DEATH OF AN INNOCENT
A DEATH LEFT HANGING
DEATH WATCH
DYING IN THE DARK
A DYING FALL
THE ENEMY WITHIN
FATAL QUEST
THE GOLDEN MILE TO MURDER
A LONG TIME DEAD
MURDER AT SWANN'S LAKE
THE PARADISE JOB
THE RED HERRING
THE SALTON KILLINGS
SINS OF THE FATHERS
STONE KILLER
THE WITCH MAKER

The Monika Paniatowski Mysteries

THE DEAD HAND OF HISTORY
THE RING OF DEATH
ECHOES OF THE DEAD
BACKLASH
LAMBS TO THE SLAUGHTER
A WALK WITH THE DEAD
DEATH'S DARK SHADOW

DEATH'S DARK SHADOW

A DCI Paniatowski Mystery

Sally Spencer

Severn House Large Print
London & New York

This first large print edition published 2017
in Great Britain and the USA by
SEVERN HOUSE PUBLISHERS LTD of
19 Cedar Road, Sutton, Surrey, England, SM2 5DA.
First world regular print edition published 2013 by
Severn House Publishers Ltd.

British Library Cataloguing in Publication Data
A CIP catalogue record for this title is available from the British Library.

ISBN-13: 9780727895882

Severn House Publishers support the Forest Stewardship Council™
[FSC™], the leading international forest certification organisation. All
our titles that are printed on FSC certified paper carry the FSC logo.

Typeset by Palimpsest Book Production Ltd.,
Falkirk, Stirlingshire, Scotland.
Printed and bound in Great Britain by
T J International, Padstow, Cornwall.

In later years, when Detective Chief Inspector Monika Paniatowski thought about the two particularly brutal killings she'd investigated in Whitebridge, back in November 1975, she would never fail to reflect that, but for a seemingly innocuous suggestion she'd made to her adopted daughter, Louisa, there would have been no murders to investigate.

One

It was a Saturday morning in late October. At one end of the back parlour-study, Monika Paniatowski was sitting at her desk and attempting to scale the mountain of paperwork she had allowed to build up. At the other end, her adopted daughter, Louisa, was sitting at her desk and wrestling with French irregular verbs.

The arrangement had been Louisa's idea.

'I'd rather work in there than in my bedroom,' she'd explained to Monika. 'The study's got a more businesslike atmosphere – and since I'm in the "business" of passing exams, it's ideal for my purposes.'

'Of course it is, sweetheart,' Monika had agreed, doing her best to hide her smile.

'Besides,' the girl had continued, 'even when you're home, you're always working . . .'

'Not always!' Monika had protested.

'No, not always,' Louisa conceded, trying to be fair, 'but certainly a good deal of the time.'

'True,' Paniatowski accepted.

'So it would be nice, wouldn't it, if we were working together?'

'Yes, it would.'

And it was nice, Paniatowski thought, as she watched Louisa put her French book to one side, and reach for her writing pad.

'Who are you writing to?' she asked.

1

'Tía Pilar.'

A couple of years earlier, Louisa hadn't even known she had an Auntie Pilar, but then she'd joined the Whitebridge Hispanic Circle, and Robert Martinez – who'd been running it at the time – had suggested she trace her Spanish relatives, if only as a way of improving her own Spanish. The idea had been a great success, and now Louisa wrote regularly to her great-aunt, as well to several cousins of her own age.

'I've been looking at the map of Spain,' Paniatowski said tentatively, 'and it seems your great-aunt lives just outside Calpe, not far from where your Uncle Charlie and Auntie Joan live.'

'I know,' Louisa agreed.

'And your Uncle Charlie is always asking us to go and stay with them,' Paniatowski said, in a rush. 'So I was thinking . . . you've got a half-term holiday coming up, and I've got some leave owing which they're pressuring me to take soon, so why don't we go and stay with Uncle Charlie, and you can meet all your grandmother's family?'

Louisa noted her choice of words – 'your grandmother's family', not 'your mother's family'. And she was right, of course, because while Louisa had no doubt that the person who had given birth to her had been a wonderful woman – and even found herself missing her sometimes – there was no question about who her actual mum was.

So Monika was right to phrase it like that – but even so, Louisa couldn't help wishing that her mum was confident enough of their relationship to say something like 'your natural mother'.

'Would you like that?' Paniatowski asked.

Louisa wasn't sure. Writing to them was really nice – but meeting them seemed a rather daunting prospect.

'Would you like to do it, Mum?' she countered, to buy herself time.

'Yes,' Paniatowski said. 'I do miss seeing Charlie now he's retired, and I think it would be very good for you to get to know a little something about your Spanish heritage.'

Which was all well and good in theory, Louisa thought, but it was precisely her largely unknown Spanish heritage – which was so different to her familiar English heritage – that frightened her.

'Suppose we *didn't* go to Spain over half-term,' the girl said. 'What would we do instead?'

'Oh, I suppose we could go somewhere else,' Paniatowski said vaguely.

It wouldn't work out like that at all, Louisa told herself – because even though her mum so desperately needed a break, some problem with the Mid-Lancs Constabulary would get in the way, as it usually did, and whatever plans they'd made would be cancelled. But she couldn't cancel Spain – not if she'd already promised Uncle Charlie and Auntie Pilar that they were going.

It is a far, far better thing that I do, than I have ever done, Louisa thought, quoting one of Uncle Charlie's favourite books.

Indeed, the thought of going to Spain was not dissimilar to the thought of climbing the steps to the guillotine – and just as Sydney Carton had done the latter for his love of Lucie, so she would do the former for the love of her mum.

'Yes, I'd really like to go to Spain,' she said.

The office – which in its previous incarnation had been a bar's storeroom, and still looked like one – could only be entered through a door which opened on to an alley, but the splendid brass plate on the door would not have looked out of place on a much grander entrance.

The plate read:

Ojos y Oídos
Agencia de detectives

And underneath, in much smaller letters, were the words, 'Eyes and Ears Detective Agency'.

The two owners of the agency – Paco Ruiz and Charlie Woodend – had chosen the name because they'd thought it would sound intriguing, but it was also a reflection of their division of labour, since Paco's eyes were not quite as sharp as they had once been, and Charlie – having only lived on Costa Blanca for a year and a half – had not yet mastered enough of the language to be able to conduct independent interviews in Spanish.

Business at the agency had been quiet for a while, but that morning they had a new client, a sharply dressed man of around forty-five.

'Sr Garcia says that he mainly sells hi-fi systems and tape decks,' Ruiz was explaining.

'That'd be like gramophones, would it?' asked Woodend, who tried his best to be forward

4

looking, but was still in mourning over the virtual demise of the steam locomotive.

Paco grinned. 'Yes, that would be like gramophones,' he agreed. 'Sr Garcia says that, over the last few years, the business has grown and grown. This is partly because the government has become more relaxed about what can be imported into Spain, and partly because, with the increased tourist trade, the locals now have more money to spend.'

'So what's his problem?' Woodend asked.

'He's losing a great deal of stock, and he has no idea how that's happening,' Paco said. 'His storeroom is at the back of his shop. The only door to the storeroom – which is made of solid steel – is through the shop itself, and he swears that he would know if the lock had been tampered with.'

'Is there a window in the storeroom?'

Ruiz consulted the client.

'He says that there is a window, but it is a very small one, and there are bars on it.'

'Who locks up at the end of the day?'

Ruiz spoke to the client again.

'He says he always does it himself.'

'And does anybody else have a key?'

'During the working day, the manager, Luis Ibañez, has one, but he hands it back to Sr Garcia when the shop closes.'

'Interesting,' Woodend mused. 'We'll need to look at the scene of the crime, of course, but I think it might be wise to wait until all the assistants have gone home for the day.'

* * *

5

'Well, that's it then,' Paniatowski called from the kitchen to Louisa, who was in the dining room, laying the table for tea.

'That's what?' her daughter asked.

'That's all the arrangements made for our trip to Spain. The first thing I did was to ring the Woodends. Your Uncle Charlie wasn't there – he's out on a case, apparently – but your Auntie Joan said they'd both be delighted to put us up for a few days.'

Louisa felt her stomach tighten. 'Are you sure you don't want a bit more time to think about it, Mum?' she asked, laying the knife and fork, with geometric precision, each side of her mother's plate.

'You're not listening, Louisa,' Paniatowski said. 'All the arrangements have been made – I've rung the travel agency and booked the flights.'

'So . . . so we're really going?'

'Yes, we really are going. And you know what you need to do now, don't you?'

'No, I . . .'

'You need to ring your Auntie Pilar and let her know the family can expect a visit.'

Louisa's stomach tightened even more.

Oh dear, she thought.

The main shopping street in Calpe was lined with orange trees. It began at the edge of the old town – located at the top of the hill, through fear of pirates – and gently sloped down to the sea.

Sr Garcia's shop was halfway up the hill. It had a double frontage, and – perhaps as a reaction to

6

a government which had deliberately kept the country isolated from the fashions and trends of the rest of Europe for so long – it was conspicuously and aggressively modern.

The storeroom, on the other hand, was still very much a part of old Spain. It was a large, rectangular room, full of crude shelving which was crammed with music centres and tape decks, and – as Sr Garcia had promised them – there was only one door and a small, barred window opening to the outside.

'If they didn't come through the door – and having seen it, I'm almost sure they didn't – then they must have entered through the ceiling, the floor or one of the walls,' Woodend said.

But the floor was solid concrete, and the ceiling and the walls showed no signs of having been breached.

'I had a very interesting murder involving a locked room, once . . .' Woodend began. And then he stopped himself.

That kind of reminiscence was fine when he and Paco were sitting on his terrace (a bottle of Veterano brandy between them), and were reliving Ruiz's time as a homicide inspector in Madrid and his own as a DCI in Whitebridge, but when they were on a case – even a simple robbery like this one – they needed to keep themselves professional.

'Maybe the goods went out through the window,' Ruiz suggested.

'To pass them out through the window, they'd first have had to get into the storeroom through the window themselves,' Woodend said, 'and

7

even a small kid couldn't squeeze through that space.'

'So maybe it was an inside job,' Ruiz suggested. 'Maybe one of the employees came into the storeroom during working hours, and passed the equipment to an accomplice who was waiting outside.'

That would be rather risky, Woodend thought – but it would certainly be possible.

'What's the smallest thing that went missing?' he asked.

Ruiz consulted his notes.

'A tape deck.'

'See if you can find one.'

Ruiz handed Woodend a box, and Woodend took it over to the window, but before he even tried to push it through, he could see that it would never fit.

'There's a lot of packing in that box,' Ruiz said. 'Perhaps, if we removed that, we could slide the tape deck through.'

Woodend opened the box. The deck had come all the way from Japan, and in order to ensure its safe arrival in Calpe, the manufacturers had encased it in polystyrene blocks, and filled what little space was left with shredded packing.

Woodend stripped it all away, and held the deck up to the barred window. It still wouldn't fit.

'They must have removed the bars,' he said.

Ruiz shook his head. 'Whoever did it would be taking a big enough chance just passing the equipment through the window during working hours,' he said. 'It would be impossible to remove

8

the bars – and then put them back in place again – without being noticed.'

From a logical point of view, Paco was right, Woodend thought, but murder – crime, he corrected himself, not murder, bloody crime! – did not always conform to the rules of logic.

'Let's go and look at the window from the outside,' he said.

The *cabaña* had been built close to the port. Its original purpose was to store fishermen's nets, but ever since she had lost her job, it had been Elena's home.

And as a home, it was not so bad, she told herself. True, it was only one room, but why would a woman like her need more than one room? True, too, it had no windows at all – just gaps in the brickwork to let air in – but if she wanted more light, she had only to step outside on to the quay, where there was the sun in daytime and street lamps by night. And so what if she had to fetch all her water from the stand-pipe next to the harbour master's office – that was good exercise.

All in all, it was perfectly satisfactory. She had a bed, she had a table and chair, hooks on which to hang her few clothes, enough crockery and cutlery for her simple needs, and a small paraffin heater for when the weather turned cold. She had the friendship of the fishermen, who would sometimes give her something from their catch. She had the support of the local communist party, which had recently done her the honour of electing her its secretary. And while any woman might want more – that was only natural – none had the right to expect more.

Yet even though she truly did believe all this, she still felt a little awkward when Doña Pilar paid an unexpected call on her that afternoon, because she had been a guest in Doña Pilar's home, and knew that it was a fine farmhouse which had its own bathroom.

'The reason that I have called is to tell you that I have just had a phone call from my English great-niece, Doña Elena,' Pilar said. 'You will have heard me talk about her.'

'I have indeed,' Elena agreed.

'It seems that she will be coming to visit me soon, and I thought it would be nice to have a party for her.'

'Is it wise to have a party – of any kind – while the Caudillo is still so ill?' Elena asked.

Pilar frowned with a gravity which only the matriarch of a large family can ever carry off successfully.

'I understand why you are careful when you are speaking to most people, Doña Elena, but, knowing me as you do, I am a little offended that you should exercise such caution now,' she said.

'I apologize, Doña Pilar,' Elena said, looking down at the cobblestones. Then she raised her head again, and said, 'Let me phrase it another way – one that might be more acceptable to you. Is it wise to have a party while that *hijo de puta* Francisco Franco is dying?'

Overhead, a seagull screeched loudly, and Pilar felt a shiver run through the length of her body.

'He has been ill so many times,' she said. 'Do you think he is actually dying this time?'

'I do,' Elena confirmed.

And she was right. The old man had held in his hands the power of life and death over every man and women in Spain for thirty-six long years. He had made full use of that power, ordering the execution of thousands after the Civil War had ended. And though his lust for blood had slowed down as the years went by, he had not stopped. Five men had been executed only months earlier, despite pleas from other heads of state – and even the pope himself – that they should be shown mercy.

But just as he had refused to grant a reprieve to others, so he could not grant one for himself. Despite the fact he had thirty-two doctors in constant attendance, despite the complicated medical machinery which helped support his failing organs and the tubes which led in and out of his body – despite, even, the mummified arm of St Teresa of Avila, which was believed to have miraculous powers, and which always travelled with him – he was dying.

That was why, for days, the radio had played only solemn music, and the newspapers had produced long and elaborate reports in which each of his decaying organs had become a celebrity in its own right.

'Perhaps it might not be wise to have a party, but it is the right thing to do,' Pilar said firmly. 'The whole family will be there to welcome little Louisa – and I would like you to be there, too.'

'I am not family,' Elena pointed out.

'I have taken you to my heart, Doña Elena and that makes you family,' Pilar said.

'You're very kind,' Elena said humbly.

'And you,' said Pilar passionately, 'are my inspiration.'

The storeroom window overlooked an alley – just as Woodend and Ruiz's own office did – making it easy for someone standing in that alley to be handed the stolen goods with little chance of being seen.

The only problem with that theory was that, rather than there being indications that the bars had been tampered with, there was very clear evidence that they hadn't. The screws were rusted, the screw heads showed no signs of being turned since the day they had been installed. And when Woodend grabbed hold of the bars and shook them, they didn't move at all.

'The stuff has to have come through the window,' Woodend said. 'They couldn't possibly have got it out any other way.'

But they hadn't used the window, because if they had . . .

It was then that he noticed the small pieces of white material on the ground, and bending to pick one up, discovered they were tiny bits of polystyrene.

He straightened up again.

'When is Sr Garcia expecting his next delivery, Paco?' he asked.

'Not until the middle of next month,' Ruiz replied.

'Then there's nothing more that we can do until the middle of next month,' Woodend told him.

'Nothing?' Paco repeated, astonished.

'Nothing,' Woodend confirmed.

'So we'll just let the thief carry on stealing the goods for another three weeks, will we?' Paco asked.

'Nothing more will be stolen in the next three weeks,' Woodend said confidently. 'Nothing can be stolen – not until Sr Garcia signs the manifest for the next delivery.'

Paco grinned. 'You know how it was done, don't you?' he said.

'Yes,' Woodend agreed. 'I know how it was done.'

Two

The Woodends' main terrace looked out towards the sea at one end, and back towards the mountains at the other, but Paniatowski, who kept striding up and down it, didn't seem to be really appreciating either of the views.

'For God's sake, Monika, calm down,' Woodend said. 'It's only an hour since we dropped Louisa off at her Auntie Pilar's place, and you've already walked miles. Carry on like this, and you'll have worn a hole in the terrace by the time we pick her up this evening.'

'I can't help worrying about how she's getting

13

on,' Paniatowski replied. 'It's the first time she's ever met any of her Spanish relatives, you know – and she's only fifteen. She's bound to find the whole experience completely intimidating.'

'No, she won't,' Woodend reassured her. 'That Doña Pilar will take care of her. You could tell just by looking at the woman that she's got a heart the size of a double-decker bus, and that she loves kids.'

'She seemed quite formidable to me,' Paniatowski said doubtfully.

'She is that,' Woodend agreed. 'In fact, she scared the hell out of me – but then I'm not a pretty fifteen-year-old blood relative, am I? – and I guarantee that when Louisa comes back, she'll be babbling on for days that Auntie Pilar said this, or Auntie Pilar said that.'

'Yes, she might well be,' said Paniatowski, looking even more unhappy.

'Ah, so that's it!' Woodend exclaimed. 'You're not so much worried that Louisa won't like them, as you are that she'll like them too much.'

Paniatowski shuddered.

Yes, there was something to that, she admitted to herself. The girl was only her adopted daughter, and though Louisa's real mother – Maria – had been murdered when she was small, she was still Spanish. And perhaps the idea of being constantly surrounded by a large, loving family – a family to whom she was actually biologically connected – would start to seem appealing.

'You're an idiot,' Woodend said – though not unkindly.

'I'm *what*?'

14

'An idiot. You're the most important person in the world to your daughter, and that's not going to change until she falls in love, when – quite rightly – you'll be demoted to the number two position.'

'I know all that, but . . .' Paniatowski said helplessly.

'How's *your* love life?' Woodend asked, changing the subject.

Paniatowski shrugged. 'What with the job and Louisa, I don't seem to have much time for one,' she admitted.

'Love isn't just going to fall into your lap, you know,' Woodend said, a little sternly. 'If you want a feller, then you're going to have to make just a little bit of an effort yourself.'

'Where does this sudden urge to start poking your nose in my private affairs come from?' Paniatowski demanded – and though she was angry, she knew that at least part of it was defensive anger.

'You're right, it's none of my business,' Woodend admitted. 'But I'm only asking because I care about you,' he added. 'And I *do* care about you, Monika – you know that, don't you?'

'Of course I know it,' Paniatowski replied, calming down a little.

There was the sound of the phone ringing inside the villa, and for a moment, it looked as if Woodend would use that as an excuse to escape.

Then he sank back into his chair, and said, 'But if I am interfering where I'm not welcome, it's only because I'd like to see you settled before . . . before . . .'

'Before I get too old?' Paniatowski asked, feeling her anger return. 'Before I become a piece of mutton that no man will even look at – before I find myself left on the shelf?'

'No, I wasn't going to say that at all,' Woodend replied, sounding uncomfortable.

'Maybe you wouldn't have used those exact words – but that was certainly the general idea,' Paniatowski countered.

'I've not handled this well, have I?' Woodend asked.

'No, you bloody well haven't!' Paniatowski agreed.

'Am I interrupting something?' asked a voice from the doorway, and Woodend and Paniatowski turned to see Joan standing there.

'No, you're not interrupting, lass,' Woodend told her. 'We were just chatting about things in general.'

'I'm pleased to hear that,' Joan said, 'because it sounded to me like an argument.'

'It wasn't!' Woodend and Paniatowski replied simultaneously.

Joan nodded. 'Good. Anyway, what I came to tell you was that that was Paco on the phone, and he says that the van's arrived, and the driver's just ordered his lunch at the Playa y Mar.'

Woodend stood up. 'I'd better get down there, then,' he said, his relief at escaping from the earlier conversation evident in his voice. 'Would you like to come along for the ride, Monika?'

'I'd love to,' Paniatowski replied – and she sounded relieved, too.

* * *

16

Everyone back home would be walking around in overcoats, and wearing mittens and scarves, Louisa thought, but here it was so warm that just a cardigan would do – and when you were in the sun, you didn't even need that!

She looked around her – at the old stone farmhouse, at the groves of lemon and orange trees, and the women standing over the open wood fire on which the paella was being slowly brought to perfection – and, with her earlier trepidation now quite vanquished, she sighed with contentment.

She had been introduced to so many aunts and great-aunts, uncles and great-uncles, cousins and second-cousins – all of whom had given her such an enthusiastic welcome that her head was swimming.

'What are you thinking about, little Louisa?' asked a voice to her left.

The speaker was Tiá Pilar, and though no one had actually said she was the matriarch of the family, it was obvious from the deference paid to her that that was exactly what she was.

'I was thinking how nice it is here – and how very nice all of you are,' Louisa said. 'And I was also wondering,' she added tentatively, 'why all the older women here are dressed in black.'

'It shows we are in mourning for a loved one,' Doña Pilar said. 'I first put on my mourning clothes when my father died, and before my period of mourning for him was over, my mother died. Then an uncle passed away, then a cousin, and eventually, my dear husband, Curro. That is the way life goes. There is always someone to

17

mourn. But you must not think we are unhappy with our lives, child – it is simply that we are brought up to show respect.'

'I see,' Louisa said dubiously.

'They tell me you were not brought up speaking Spanish,' Doña Pilar said in a puzzled voice, as if it were inconceivable to her that anyone in the whole world could have been raised in such strange circumstances.

'No, I wasn't,' Louisa agreed. 'But my mother – my adoptive mother – has always believed that I should learn to speak the language, and I've been having lessons since I was quite small.'

'Why isn't she here with you now?' Doña Pilar asked.

'She thought it would be easier for me if she stayed away the first time I met the family,' Louisa said, 'but I will bring her with me next time.'

There was the sound of a cowbell being struck from somewhere close to the paella pan.

'Lunch is ready,' Doña Pilar said.

The Playa y Mar was a very popular place at lunchtime, and since all the tables were already taken, Woodend and Paniatowski sat at the bar.

'That's the driver who'll be delivering Sr Garcia's latest order of music centres in an hour or so,' said Woodend, gesturing discreetly at a man in a boiler suit who was sitting alone, and had already started on the dish of meatballs in tomato sauce, which was his second course.

'And why are we watching him?' Paniatowski wondered.

'Because this is where we think Luis Ibañez, Sr Garcia's manager, will pay him off.'

'You're sure Ibañez is the man you want?' Paniatowski asked.

'Yes, because he's the only one in the whole shop, apart from the owner, who has a key.'

'But I thought you told me that he has to hand his key in to the boss at closing time.'

'He does. But it's during the day he needs it – because he has to lock himself inside.'

'You're being deliberately mysterious,' Paniatowski said.

'That's one way of looking at it,' Woodend said. 'Another way is to see it as me testing you, to see if you're as good a detective as you used to be.'

'All right, I'll play along with it,' Paniatowski said, with a theatrical sigh. 'Why will the driver be getting his pay-off now? Shouldn't he have to wait until after the robbery?'

'Of course – but, you see, the robbery's already taken place.'

'Before the goods have even been delivered?'

'Yes,' Woodend said. 'Maybe things will become clearer to you when I tell you that I found flakes of polystyrene in the alley.'

Paniatowski thought about it.

'Ah!' she said.

'Got it now?'

'I think so.'

'And just in time – because here comes Ibañez.'

The manager entered the restaurant and took a quick look around him, then walked up to the bar and ordered a black coffee.

'Since the van driver is sitting midway between the bar and the toilets, my guess is that Ibañez will suddenly feel the need to take a pee,' Woodend whispered to Paniatowski.

The manager drained his coffee and headed towards the gents. As he passed the delivery man's table, he dropped an envelope on it, and the delivery man swept it up and put it in his boiler suit pocket. The whole exchange had taken only a couple of seconds, and anyone who had not been looking specifically at the table would have missed it completely.

'Right,' Woodend said, 'now we move into phase two.'

There were thirty to lunch, and they ate it at a long table on the terrace in front of the farmhouse. The youngest guests were three or four, and could only reach the table by sitting on a small mountain of cushions. The oldest were Doña Pilar and her surviving sisters – all of them widows, and all dressed in black.

The meal began with bread, garlic butter and olives, followed by several kinds of cold meat and cheese. And then the paella – a magnificent concoction of rice, rabbit, chicken and seafood – was served.

Doña Pilar sat at the head of the table, with Louisa to her left and Uncle Jaime – her son – to her right. As they ate, Aunt Pilar treated Louisa to a potted history of everyone present.

That middle-aged man was Cousin Antonio, who had worked in the Continental Tyre Factory in Germany for a number of years, and been so

20

successful at making tyres that he had saved up enough money to buy his own small bar.

The man next to him had been a bullfighter in his youth. He should have risen to the top of his profession, but he was so good that the more famous matadors – envious of his talent – had conspired to keep him from making an appearance in any of the more important rings, like the ones in Madrid or Seville, and he had been forced to make a living performing at village fiestas.

The women with a large mole on her cheek, Cousin Teresa, had once been courted by a count, but had turned her back on a life of luxury and chosen to marry a poor wine press mechanic instead.

Uncle Jaime listened to his mother's stories with a smile on his face which said that while there was certainly an element of truth in all of them, the old lady was – at the very least – guilty of a little light embroidery.

'And you see the woman at the end of the table?' Aunt Pilar asked.

Louisa saw she was pointing to a woman in her early sixties, who must once have been very handsome, but whose face now wore the marks of intense suffering.

'Yes, I see her,' she said.

'That is Doña Elena,' Aunt Pilar said. 'She is not a part of this family – she is not even from our village – but when I heard her story, I clasped her to my bosom, and she has remained there ever since.'

'Tell me about her,' Louisa said.

'She was still a young woman when the Civil

War ended, but when the fascists marched into her village . . .'

'Be careful what you say, Mother,' Uncle Jaime cautioned her, with a hint of panic in his voice.

Doña Pilar gave him a look which could have frozen blood.

'I am an old woman, in the midst of my own family, and I will not pretend to have anything but contempt for that butcher who lives in Madrid and calls himself our Caudillo,' she said.

'But Mother . . .' Jaime said.

'You will say no more,' his mother told him. 'Is that clear?'

Don Jaime bowed his head like a guilty five-year-old, and mumbled, 'Yes, Mother.'

'Now where was I?' Doña Pilar asked, turning back to Louisa.

'You were saying that Doña Elena was a young woman when the Civil War ended,' Louisa prompted.

'Ah yes. When the fascists marched into her village, she did not pretend – as many of us, to our eternal shame, did – that she thought of them as conquering heroes. And when their officer offered her extra rations if she would . . .'

'Mother, please!' Don Jaime said.

'This time, you are right to stop me,' his mother said. She thought for a moment, before continuing, 'This officer made a suggestion to her that no decent man should ever make to a respectable woman – and she spat in his face.'

'And . . . and what happened to her?' Louisa gasped.

'They had already locked up her husband, and now they took her baby son from her,' Doña Pilar said. 'Then the officer took from her what she would not give freely, and when he had had his way, he locked her up, too. They said she had insulted an officer – it didn't matter to them why she had done it – and they kept her in prison for ten years. She was lucky she was not shot,' tears began to form in Doña Pilar's eyes, 'although perhaps she does not think she was lucky at all, and would have seen a bullet as a merciful release.'

'What happened to her husband and baby?' Louisa asked.

'She never saw either of them again,' Doña Pilar said, wiping away a tear with her handkerchief. 'But enough of that – let me tell you about cousin Mauricio, who once shook hands with a big American film star.'

The first customer who came into the shop after Luis Ibañez returned from his coffee was an old man who was looking around in amazement, as if he had suddenly and unexpectedly found himself in an alien world.

But as out of his depth as he might be, he probably had a fat wallet – Luis could smell money at a hundred metres – and when Antonio, one of the junior salesmen, started to approach this new customer, the manager quickly cut in ahead of him.

'How can I help you, sir?' he asked.

'I want to buy a gramophone for my grand-daughter,' the old man said uncertainly. 'It's for her birthday, and I want the best you have.'

Oh, he'd certainly get the best they had, Luis promised, already calculating how much extra commission he could make from the little 'add-ons'.

And then, much to his disgust, he saw that the delivery man had finished his lunch earlier than expected, and had entered the shop with a trolley packed high with music centres.

'Excuse me,' he said to the customer, turning and intercepting the ever-helpful Antonio before he had time to reach the delivery man.

'I will assist with unloading the new stock,' the manager said to the young salesman.

'But you've got a customer,' Antonio pointed out.

'You deal with the customer,' Luis said, 'and . . .' he swallowed hard, 'you can have the commission.'

'All of it?' the assistant asked, open-mouthed.

'All of it,' Luis snapped. 'Well, get on with it, then.'

The assistant went over to the customer, and launched straight into his sales patter. A Dolby unit was a must, he said. He had one himself, and the sound filled the room.

The customer was not really listening. Instead, he was watching as the delivery man and the manager pushed a cart containing the new equipment across the shop floor to the cash desk, where Sr Garcia carefully counted the boxes before signing the invoice.

'So what do you think, sir?' the young salesman asked eagerly.

24

'Do you know, I think I've rather lost interest in the whole idea,' Paco Ruiz replied.

The last of the paella had been eaten, and the plates cleared away. Now, everyone was sipping coffee, and most of the men had a brandy as well.

'Louisa has brought us some pictures of her life in England, Mother,' Don Jaime said. 'Do you think that this would be a good time to look at them?'

'It would be an excellent time,' Doña Pilar said.

Louisa reached under the table for her satchel.

She had thought long and hard about which postcards and photographs to include in what her mother had, slightly sarcastically, called her 'Welcome to Sunny Whitebridge Package'. The problem was that she did not want to paint a rosily dishonest picture of a town which was in industrial decline, but nor did she want to besmirch the place which was her home, so in the end she had chosen a selection of pictures, and left it to those viewing them to reach their own conclusions.

She opened the satchel and took her carefully selected exhibits out.

Aunt Pilar liked the pictures of the moors which surrounded Whitebridge.

'Good for sheep,' she said approvingly.

But she was not at all impressed by the factory chimneys.

'We Valencianos have too much respect for good clean air to allow such monstrosities in our

25

region,' she commented, with some disdain. 'We leave that sort of thing entirely to the money-grabbing Catalans and the Basques.'

'We mostly leave it to them,' Don Jaime said in fairness – and almost under his breath, 'but there are factories in the Valencia region.'

'But not in Calpe,' his mother countered.

'No,' Don Jaime agreed, 'not in Calpe.'

'Well, there you are, then,' his mother said, as if she had just demolished his argument.

Doña Pilar showed great interest in Louisa's personal photographs.

'Now that is a fine figure of a man,' she said, looking at a picture of DI Beresford. 'Do you like him, little Louisa?'

'Yes, I call him Uncle Colin.'

'Then your mother should marry him.'

The picture of DS Meadows did not meet with the same approval.

Doña Pilar ran her eyes over the short skirt and the pixie haircut, and then said, 'This one could learn a little modesty from the women of Spain.'

One of the last of Louisa's exhibits was a newspaper article which had a photograph of three people in it. Two of them were men – and the third was Louisa herself. She and the younger of the two men were in the foreground, and smiling self-consciously at the camera. The older man was standing a little behind them, and if he was aware he was being photographed, it didn't show in his expression.

Louisa had been in two minds about whether to bring the article with her. On the one hand, she had argued with herself, it did seem just a little like showing off. But on the other hand, she had never had her picture in the paper before, and she was secretly quite proud of it.

'This is a newspaper story about the Whitebridge Hispanic Circle,' she explained. 'It's only a small group of people, but we manage to do all sorts of interesting things.'

'Such as?' Uncle Jaime asked.

'If there's an exhibition of Spanish paintings, or a concert of Spanish music, we organize a trip to go and see it. And we have a stall at the Whitebridge May Fair, which sells Spanish food.'

'What is wrong with buying the food from ordinary shops?' Aunt Pilar asked, puzzled.

'Nothing,' Louisa said. 'But you can't buy Spanish food in the ordinary shops.'

'You're being silly, child,' Doña Pilar said. 'You can buy *chorizo* and *morcilla* everywhere.'

'Not in Whitebridge.'

'I don't believe that,' Aunt Pilar said firmly. 'Even just after the war – at the time of the great hunger – there was still *chorizo* and *morcilla*. If you look hard enough, you will find it.'

Uncle Jaime gave Louisa a smile which said that she should understand that his mother had very definite views which were based on very limited experience.

'Who are the other two people in the picture?' he asked.

'That's Mr – I mean, Sr – Martinez and his father,' Louisa said. 'The younger Mr Martinez was the founder and president of the Hispanic

Circle, but now he's been elected as our member of parliament, he's had to give that up.'

'Your member of parliament!' Don Jaime said, clearly impressed. 'You see, Mother, England is such a land of opportunity that even a foreigner – a Spaniard – can become part of the government.'

'I spit on all politicians,' his mother replied.

It was time to put her photographs away, Louisa thought, but when she turned to where she had carefully placed them, she saw that they had vanished. Then she realized that they had not disappeared at all, but were being passed around the table.

Her Uncle Jaime smiled again. 'In this family, when one person hears or sees something, everybody else has to hear and see it,' he said. 'It is something about us that you will just have to get used to.'

Three

It was late afternoon, and the inside of Paco Ruiz's little car – which was parked out on the street, opposite Sr Garcia's electrical shop – was thick with the smoke of black tobacco.

'The longer Luis Ibañez waits before making his move, the more risk he runs,' Woodend said, 'so my guess is that he'll do it as soon as the boss goes out for his next coffee.'

As if he was waiting for just this cue, Sr Garcia

came out of the shop and started to walk down the street.

A minute passed, and then three young men in boiler suits appeared out of nowhere, one of them carrying a large, empty sack in his hands. Two of the men immediately disappeared into the alley at the side of the shop, but the third remained at the head of it.

'That's the lookout,' Paco said. 'How long do you think we should give them?'

'Two minutes at the most,' Woodend replied. 'They'll have got this whole process down to a fine art by now, and if we leave it any longer, we might not actually catch them in the act.'

It was exactly two minutes later when Paco Ruiz strode to the head of the alley, only to find his way blocked by the lookout.

'You don't want to go down there, Grandad,' the youth said, shifting every time Paco did, in order to stop the older man from looking down the alley. 'There are some men at work, and you might get hurt.'

'Hurt?' Paco repeated, mystified. 'How could I possibly get hurt?'

'Ah, well, you see, these men I told you about are handling some heavy materials.'

'Heavy materials?'

'That's what I said. Are you deaf or something?'

'No, I'm not deaf – and I wouldn't have described polystyrene and cardboard as heavy materials,' Paco said mildly.

'How did you . . .?' the young man asked,

shocked. 'I mean, I've no idea what you're talking about.'

'The game's up, son,' Paco said. 'So now you've only two choices – you can stand here and wait for the police to arrive, or you can run away. Not that I think running away will do you much good, because I've been studying Luis Ibañez, and I imagine that the moment the cops start questioning him, he'll rat on the lot of you, without a second's thought.'

Luis Ibañez was hard at work in the storeroom when he heard the loud banging on the steel door.

'Go away, whoever you are!' he called, as he ripped another box to pieces. 'I'm busy.'

And then he heard the key turn in the lock.

But that was impossible, he thought. There were only two keys to this door. He had one himself, and the boss – who had gone out for a coffee, and was never away for less than half an hour – had the other one.

And yet, as impossible as it might seem, the door swung open, and he found himself looking in horror at a very big man in a hairy sports coat, and a blonde woman with a figure that – at any other time – he would have given his entire attention to.

'It was a clever idea,' Woodend said. 'You couldn't get the music centres out of the window, but if you flattened the boxes they came in, you could get *them* out. So all you had to do was arrange with the delivery man to remove the machines from the boxes before delivery. It looked like they'd arrived – they were signed for as if they'd arrived – but they were already being stored somewhere else, waiting for you to sell them on later.' He paused. 'You haven't understood a single word I've said, but you still know what I mean, don't you?'

And Luis Ibañez – who did know what he meant – merely nodded.

The police had already taken Ibañez away. There was nothing more for the private detectives to do now but collect their money, and as Sr Garcia was writing out the cheque, he delivered a monologue which sounded to Woodend suspiciously like a speech.

'Our client thinks you have done a brilliant job,' Paco translated, when Garcia finally finished talking.

'I can't claim all the credit,' Woodend said awkwardly. 'You and me are a team.'

'He knows that, but he also knows that you were the one who spotted the vital clue lying beneath the window,' Paco replied, 'and he said that even if he'd seen that clue himself, it would have meant nothing to him. In conclusion, he thinks you are a great detective.'

Woodend sighed. 'Maybe I was once,' he said.

Almost as soon as the words were out of his mouth, he started to feel a little ashamed of himself, because – even to him – they sounded a little self-pitying.

And he didn't need pity – from himself or anyone else. He enjoyed his life in the sun – the walks in the mountains, the drinks in bars overlooking the beach, the games of dominoes with the local domino sharks. And he had been right to retire when he had – while he was still among the best – rather than clinging on and slowly sliding into decline.

And yet . . .

And yet he couldn't help wishing that someone would hand him just one more juicy murder.

Garcia spoke again, and this time he was looking directly at Monika, and smiling warmly and enticingly.

'Our client would like to show you the town's nightlife, and wonders if you are free this evening,' Paco translated, deadpan.

'Is he married?' Monika asked.

'I believe he is,' Paco answered.

Monika turned her fullest and most promising smile on Garcia.

'Tell him I'd love to see the nightlife with him,' she said to Paco, 'but unfortunately, it can't be tonight, because my husband's having a bare-knuckle fight with the local champion, and I've promised I'll attend. Ask him if we can do it tomorrow night, instead.'

As Paco translated, the smile on Garcia's face quickly disappeared, and when he replied, there was a hint of both disappointment and concern in his voice.

'He says he's busy tomorrow night,' Paco told her. 'In fact, now he's had time to think about it, he realizes, he's busy tonight too – and every other night for the next three weeks.'

'Now that is a shame,' Paniatowski said.

Paco pocketed the cheque, and everyone shook hands.

As they walked to the door, Woodend, Paco and Monika had their arms around each others' shoulders. They were feeling good, and well they might – they had solved the case, got their money, and had a little well-deserved fun at Sr Garcia's expense.

Then they stepped out into the street, and what they saw there made all feelings of well-being evaporate.

Some people were standing on street corners, engaged in earnest, whispered conversations. Others were wandering around aimlessly, as if they had quite forgotten why they had come into town. Several cars had pulled into the side of the road, and their drivers just sat there, staring at their steering wheels. And even the cars which were still moving were doing so at a snail's pace.

'He's dead,' Paco said heavily. 'General Francisco Franco y Bahamonde, Caudillo of Spain by the grace of the devil, is dead.'

Ted Melly was surprised when Elena turned up at his hotel that afternoon, and positively shocked at the state she seemed to be in.

'Forgive me for coming here, Don Eduardo,' the woman said, as they stood in the lobby next to the reception desk where she had once worked. 'Believe me, I do not wish to get you into trouble with the authorities, but . . .'

'Now just calm down, Elena,' Melly said soothingly. 'And don't worry about the authorities. If they want to cause me trouble over seeing an old friend, then let them – because I can only be pushed so far.'

'You are a good man, Don Eduardo,' Elena said.

'And you are a good woman,' Melly told her. 'What can I do to help you, Elena?'

'I need some money,' the woman said. 'I will pay you back – I promise I will pay you back.'

'I know you will,' Melly said. 'How much do you want?'

When Elena told him, Melly whistled softly.

'That is rather a lot,' he said.

'I know it is,' Elena replied miserably, 'but I have added up how much it will cost me, and I cannot do it for any less.'

'Can't do what for any less?' Melly wondered.

'Leave the country.'

'Is this all to do with the fact that Franco died this afternoon?' Melly asked. 'Because if that is the reason, then you're panicking unnecessarily. You've no cause to run away. You'll be safer here now that he's gone than you ever were when he was alive.'

'It is nothing at all to do with Franco,' Elena said. 'No,' she corrected herself, 'it *is* to do with Franco, but not in the way that you seem to think. Please do not ask me any more.'

'Have you even got a passport?' Melly asked.

'No, I have not, but my comrades in the party will provide me with one,' Elena said.

'A false one?'

'Yes, it will be a false one, but it will be good enough to fool the immigration police.'

'It seems to me that you should wait a few

34

days before doing anything, just to give yourself time to think this through properly,' Melly said, 'then if you still want the money . . .'

'I have been waiting for thirty-six long, bitter years,' the woman said desperately. 'A few more days would seem like a lifetime to me. A few more days would kill me.'

'It all sounds very mysterious, and I really would like more details before I make a decision,' Melly said.

Elena looked up at him through tear-filled eyes.

'I am asking you to trust me, Ted,' she said. 'I am asking you to give me the money because you know me and because you have faith in me.'

Melly sighed. 'Let's go into the office and see how much cash there is in the safe,' he suggested.

The three of them were sitting on Woodend's terrace. Woodend and Ruiz were drinking beers with brandy chasers; Monika Paniatowski – as always – was sticking to vodka.

'I suppose I should have been expecting that Franco would die today,' Paco said.

'Why is that?' Woodend wondered.

'Because it's the twentieth of November, the date on which José Antonio Primo de Rivera – the leader of the fascist movement – was executed by the Republicans in 1936. It's widely believed that Franco could have saved him through a prisoner exchange, but his death ensured that all the power went to the Generalissimo, so it is hardly surprising the exchange did not take place.'

'I still don't see. . . .' Woodend began.

'Though they disliked each other intensely while José Antonio was alive, it was convenient – once he was dead – for Franco's propaganda machine to turn him into a martyr of the fascist cause. So it is not surprising that Franco's doctors kept him alive until this symbolic date. Or maybe,' Paco shrugged, 'he has actually been dead for days, and they have only just announced it.'

'Out on the street, it looked as if everyone was in a state of shock,' Woodend said.

'There are many Spaniards – I think easily the majority – who are glad he is dead,' Paco said reflectively. 'The shops all ran out of *cava* days ago . . .'

'*Cava*? What's that?' Paniatowski asked.

'Spanish champagne,' Woodend explained.

'. . . because people have been stockpiling it for just this moment,' Paco continued. 'Yet,' he added, in a slightly bemused voice, 'it still feels strange that the old man is gone, and even I – who hated him more than most – am a little unnerved.'

'What will happen now?' Woodend asked.

'Initially, on the grand scale of things, very little,' Paco said. 'Prince Juan Carlos will be sworn in as king and caudillo, and then everybody will wait to see what he does next. The army will not attempt to take over unless they consider it is absolutely necessary. The communist party and socialist party will remain hidden until they are sure they can emerge without being immediately crushed. It will be months – perhaps even years – before it becomes clear what direction Spain will take.'

'So that's the grand scale,' Woodend said. 'What will happen on the small scale?'

'On the small scale, there are people who will take advantage of the uncertainty to settle old scores,' Paco told him.

'And will they try to settle them violently?' Woodend asked.

'Oh yes, people who have been subject to state violence for thirty six years might well decide it is time to exercise a little of their own,' Paco said.

Four

The hawthorn bushes had been unusually heavy with berries that autumn, and though most people dismissed, as an old wives' tale, the belief that it signalled a hard winter ahead, the old wives had been proved right, and by the middle of November, the cold had begun to set in.

The canal which ran through the centre of the old industrial part of Whitebridge had started the freeze several days earlier – the water closest to the bank icing over first. Now, on the last Saturday in November, it was entirely covered with a thin sheet of ice, and was the focus of attention of the five boys standing on the towpath.

'I bet you could skate on that,' said Tommy

Maddox, who was twelve, and, by unspoken agreement, the leader of the gang.

'I bet you couldn't,' said Robbie Nelson.

This had been happening a lot recently, Tommy thought – he'd say something, and Robbie would automatically say the opposite. Maybe it had something to do with Robbie being almost three months older than he was. Maybe Robbie thought, by virtue of his age, he should be the one who was leading the gang.

'You know nothing, you, Robbie Nelson,' Tommy said. 'That ice has been freezing over for three days. You could drive a car on to it now – and that's a scientific fact!'

The moment the words were out of his mouth, he realized that he had gone too far – that he had turned his earlier tentative statement into a strong assertion – but it was too late to back down.

'I'll bet you fifty pee it isn't strong enough to skate on – never mind holding the weight of a car,' Robbie said.

'You haven't got fifty pee!' Tommy jeered – and felt his heart sink when Robbie reached into his pocket and produced the coin.

'Well?' Robbie asked.

'I'm a bit short of money, just at the moment,' Tommy said weakly. 'If I lost the bet – and I'm sure I wouldn't – I couldn't pay you till the end of next week, at the earliest.'

That should have been enough to settle matters, because although all the members of the gang had become blood brothers in a ceremony of Tommy's own devising – a ceremony in which each had sworn to give up his own life to save the others – that sacred oath had not gone quite so far as to oblige them to grant each other credit.

Robbie Nelson smirked. 'Let's not call it a bet at all, then, Tommy,' he suggested. 'If you can skate across the ice – which you say is no problem – I'll *give* you the fifty pee.'

It was a clear challenge to his leadership, and he should have seen it coming, Tommy thought.

But he hadn't seen it coming – and now he had no choice but to do what Robbie asked.

'I will skate across the ice,' he said, sounding as resolute as he could manage. 'But I don't want your money – I'll do it just to show everybody how bloody thick you are!'

He placed one foot on the ice. It held – but he was still not happy about testing it with his entire weight.

'Not so sure of yourself now, are you?' Robbie mocked.

Tommy put his second foot on the ice. There was no cracking sound.

'There you are,' he said.

'That's not skating,' Robbie said. 'That's just standing there.'

'Yeah, that's just standing there,' echoed Jed Rawlings, who seemed to have decided to give his backing to Robbie's tentative *coup d'état*.

There really was no choice, Tommy told himself. He put his left foot in front of him, kicked off with his right, and began to glide slowly towards the centre of the canal.

It was working! The ice held, and he was starting to feel just like one of them skaters he'd seen on the telly. He gave another push – harder this time – and reached the middle.

'You're bloody brilliant, Tommy!' shouted Jed Rawlings, already starting to compensate for having backed the wrong horse.

Yes, he was brilliant, wasn't he, Tommy thought.

A twirl would really impress them, he decided. A twirl would be the cherry on the cake.

But as he twirled, the ice began to crack beneath him, and though he stopped moving immediately, the crack got wider, until it became a hole and he sank into the chilly water.

There was panic on the towpath, rapidly followed by recrimination.

'This is all your fault,' screamed Jed Rawlings at Robbie Nelson, as both gazed in horror at the hole in the ice. 'You'll have to go in and get him.'

'I can't swim,' Robbie moaned. 'You know I can't swim.'

Bubbles were rising from the spot where Tommy had disappeared, but whether these were caused by his immersion or were being pumped out from his lungs, none of them were sure.

It was then that Harry Dobson – a fourth, hitherto silent, member of the gang – proved his mettle. Turning from the canal, he looked around for something that could be used as part of a rescue, and his eyes fixed on a dead hawthorn bush just a little further down the bank.

Tommy's head appeared in the hole in the ice. His eyes were wide with terror, his mouth gasping for air like a landed fish's.

'Swim, Tommy,' Jed screamed. 'Swim for the side.'

But all Tommy did in response was to sink again.

Harry tugged at a branch of the hawthorn, and heard it crack. He twisted, and it came away in his hand.

He had just had time to return to the bank when Tommy came up for a third time.

'Grab this, Tommy!' he shouted, laying the branch across the ice.

Tommy managed to get a grip with one hand, and then with the other. The boys on towpath pulled the branch slowly back towards them, and Tommy ploughed a path through the thin ice.

Once he was close enough, the other boys reached out and pulled him on to the bank. His skin was as pale as a ghost's, his teeth were chattering, and his eyes – not yet registering the fact that he had been saved – were still full of fear.

'You'll be all right,' Robbie gabbled, almost hysterically. 'You'll be all right. No harm done at all. And even though I won the bet, you can still have the fifty pee, my old mate.'

Tommy was trying to speak, though with his teeth chattering so much, and the cold still squeezing his lungs, it was hard for him to get the words out.

'Deba boduy dun dare,' he said finally.

'What was that, my old mate? What were you trying to say?' Robbie Nelson coaxed.

Tommy made another attempt.

'There's a body down there,' he gasped.

* * *

The road which led to the canal bridge had been closed in both directions, but the constables manning the road block recognized the bright red MGA, and waved it through.

Paniatowski parked on the bridge itself, next to the other official vehicles, and realized that, despite a week in the sun, it felt as if she had never been away.

The fierce wind hit her the second she stepped out of the car. It was one of those winds which were not content merely to rattle hanging pub signs and swirl abandoned sheets of newspaper crazily through the air. No, this wind – this bloody-minded wind – had insisted on first sweeping across the moors, where it had acquired an extra level of cold from the newly fallen snow.

Paniatowski shivered, turned up the collar of her coat, and walked over to the parapet.

The scene which greeted her on the canal towpath was pretty much what she might have expected. Several uniformed constables were already on the scene, two police divers were leaning against the wall of the disused factory on the other side of the canal, smoking cigarettes, and Colin Beresford, her right-hand man, was staring down into the icy water. There was no sign of the ambulance men or the police doctor yet, but they would be arriving soon.

Beresford turned, saw her, and waved. She waved back.

It had been nice being in Spain, she thought, as she made her way carefully down the steep and slippery path which led to the canal. The air had been caressingly warm, the sky had been brilliantly blue, and the fresh local food had been truly delicious. But this was where she really belonged – under grey skies, on a dilapidated canal bank, investigating a murder.

'When did you get back, boss?' Colin Beresford asked, as she drew level with him.

'The night before last,' Paniatowski replied. 'Officially, I'm still supposed to be on leave until Monday, but . . .'

'But you were already starting to get bored,' Beresford said, completing the sentence for her. 'How's Mr Woodend?'

'He's on great form.'

'And did Louisa like Spain?' Beresford asked.

'She did,' Paniatowski replied. And she thought, *Perhaps she liked it just a little too much.*

Beresford nodded sombrely, as if, instead of just thinking the words, she'd actually said them out loud.

'When it came on the news that Franco had died, we were a bit worried about you,' he said. 'Was there any trouble?'

'Not really,' Paniatowski replied.

True, there seemed to have been more policemen on the streets of Calpe after Franco's death than there had been before it, and true, there had been a military checkpoint on the road to the airport, but other than that, it seemed as if Paco had been right, and everybody was just watching and waiting.

Beresford looked down at the canal again.

'Well, another day, another body,' he said.

'There actually *is* a body down there, I take

43

it,' Paniatowski said. 'It's not just some old fridge or a battered pram?'

'Oh, there's a body all right,' Beresford confirmed. 'The divers say it's a woman, but they'll not be bringing her up until Dr Shastri arrives.'

Paniatowski allowed herself a small sigh of contentment. It was good that Shastri was back from her sabbatical in India – the mortuary had seemed a much less cheerful place without her!

'We're not likely to find much evidence on the ground,' Beresford said. 'It's been frozen for the last few days.'

'Well, we never like it when our job's made too easy, do we?' Paniatowski asked.

And she was surprised to discover that what had been meant as a joke was, in fact, true. Of course, murder was a terrible thing, and her job was to get the murderer off the streets as quickly as possible, but a straightforward case simply didn't give her the rush that the more complex ones did.

'The doc's coming now,' Beresford said.

And so she was. Wearing her heavy sheepskin jacket over her gossamer-light sari, Dr Shastri was just approaching them.

'I would appreciate it if you could arrange that the next victim I am called out to examine has been murdered somewhere with central heating,' the doctor said. 'Of course, that has its drawbacks, too. The heat makes the body decompose much more quickly, and often I find that the moment I make an incision . . .'

'Would it be all right if we got the body out

of the water now?' Paniatowski interrupted, before Shastri had time to reveal some of the more gory details of her trade.

'But of course,' Shastri said, and once Beresford had waved the instruction to the divers, she continued. 'So how did Louisa like Spain, Monika?'

'She thoroughly enjoyed herself,' Paniatowski said.

'Ah!' Shastri said, reflectively.

Could everyone read her mind? Paniatowski wondered.

No, of course they couldn't. Shastri could read it, and Woodend, and Beresford, and possibly Sergeant Meadows . . .

The divers emerged from the water, towing the body between them. Once they reached the edge of the canal, they stood on the narrow shelf which ran along it, and gently lifted the corpse on to the side.

The dead woman was somewhat bloated, but otherwise, decay seemed hardly to have set in at all. She was of late middle age, and was wearing a long skirt, blouse and heavy cardigan. Her body was criss-crossed with cords, which, at their ends, had bricks tied to them.

Shastri knelt down and took the woman's head in her hands.

'Could be a suicide, I suppose,' Beresford said. 'A very determined suicide, I'll grant you, but we've come across them before.'

Shastri looked up. 'Unless you can explain to me how she smashed in the back of her own head with a blunt object, Inspector Beresford, I think we can safely rule suicide out,' she said.

The divers, who seemed impervious to the cold, were still standing on the ledge.

'Can you go down again and see if you can find a coat or a handbag, lads?' Beresford asked.

The divers nodded, and disappeared beneath the surface again.

'There is nothing in her pockets,' said Shastri.

So whoever she was, her killer didn't want her identified in a hurry, Paniatowski thought.

'Could you spend some time with the police artist, and see if you can produce a sketch of what the victim probably looked like before she went into the water, Doc?' she asked Shastri.

'Of course,' the doctor agreed. 'Such an exercise would fill my morning beautifully. And if I happen to have a little time free when I have finished with the artist, I could always do a post-mortem.'

Paniatowski grinned. 'It's really good to have you back with us, Doc,' she said.

'It's really good to be back,' Shastri told her.

Charlie Woodend had once told Paniatowski that when you'd got a good team together – by which he meant a team that was loyal, could use its own initiative, and didn't always agree with you – then you had a pearl beyond price.

Paniatowski believed him. She cherished her team, and when they met in the public bar of the Drum and Monkey that lunchtime – as was their habit at the start of a new investigation – she reminded herself how lucky she was to have them working for her.

46

Aside from herself and Beresford, there were two other members of the permanent team.

One of them, Sergeant Kate Meadows – her bagman – could, if she'd chosen, have been a fashion model, and had probably (given her general approach to life) already been many other things in pre-police life that Paniatowski thought it wisest not to find out about.

The other member – DC Jack Crane – was a handsome young university graduate who was heading for great things, but for the moment was prepared to learn from Monika as she had learned from Charlie Woodend.

'So where are we?' Paniatowski asked, when the waiter had delivered the drinks and gone away again.

'At the moment, we're nowhere at all,' Beresford admitted. 'We haven't got Dr Shastri's estimate of the time of death yet, but we know that the victim must have been killed at least three days ago.'

'Because of the ice?' Paniatowski asked.

'That's right,' Beresford agreed. 'She was under the ice, which means she must have been dumped in the canal before it froze over – and that means a minimum of three days. Yet despite that, nobody's reported her missing.'

'That would suggest she doesn't have a job,' Meadows said.

'She certainly looks old enough to be retired,' Beresford replied. 'And if she's divorced or widowed, it's perfectly possible that nobody's noticed that she's not around.'

Yes, it was, Paniatowski thought. But friendless

47

widows and divorcees weren't found at the bottoms of canals with bricks tied to them. Their bodies were discovered in their own homes, after they'd been robbed or raped by complete strangers.

The very fact that someone had gone to so much trouble with this woman suggested that the murderer had both known her and wanted her death kept quiet for as long as possible. And the latter was a smart move on his part, because it was an article of faith in most police forces that the most crucial time in any investigation was the first forty-eight hours after the murder – and this woman had been dead for at least seventy-two.

'The victim's picture will be on the lunchtime news and in the evening papers, but in addition to that, I want a door-to-door canvas of the areas she was likely to have lived in,' Paniatowski said to Beresford.

The inspector nodded. 'I've already put a team of eager young DCs and fresh-faced PCs together,' he said. 'Based on what she was wearing, I assume you want me to canvass areas that are neither too posh nor too poor.'

'Exactly,' Paniatowski agreed.

'Even by limiting it to them, that's a lot of doors to have to knock on,' Beresford pointed out.

'Do the best with the manpower you have available,' Paniatowski told him. 'I also want you to interview anybody who regularly visits the area around that section of the canal.'

'That'll be a handful of people, at best,'

Beresford said. 'Most of the factories and mills have been derelict for years, and since the boot factory closed down, hardly anybody has any reason to be in that vicinity.'

Which was probably exactly why the killer chose it as a place to dump his victim, Paniatowski thought.

And that argued at least some local knowledge.

'It's unlikely there'll be many possible witnesses, but there might be a few,' she said. 'I've seen men fishing in that canal – though what they expect to catch is anybody's guess. Then there are people who use the canal towpath as a short cut. If you can find out who they are, we might be getting somewhere. And I want the motorists who drive across the canal bridge on a regular basis stopped and questioned as well.'

'I'll get right on to it,' Beresford said.

'As for you two,' Paniatowski continued, turning towards Crane and Meadows, 'there's bugger all for you to do at the moment.'

'I could always help out with the door-to-door inquiries, boss,' Jack Crane suggested.

'Yes, you could,' Paniatowski agreed, 'but when this investigation really starts moving, I want your mind fresh and your feet clear of blisters – because if we're not all completely on the ball, we'll lose this one. And we don't want that, do we? Not with the chief constable breathing down our necks.'

The rest of the team nodded, because the chief constable *was* breathing down their necks – or, more specifically, down DCI Paniatowski's neck – and they all knew exactly why that was.

Dr Shastri had been a stunningly beautiful woman when she was younger, Paniatowski reminded herself – and the passing of the years had done little to rob the doctor of her looks. In fact, she seemed hardly to have aged at all – which didn't seem quite fair when everyone around her was acquiring wrinkles and putting on the pounds.

'You are wondering about the secret of my youth, aren't you?' Shastri asked, with a smile.

'No – I don't need to wonder, because I've seen the picture in your attic,' Paniatowski replied.

Shastri laughed, and it was like the tinkle of delicate temple bells.

'I am no Dorian Grey,' she said, 'and my secret is really very simple – I eat sensibly, drink in extreme moderation, and I do not smoke at all. Would that you yourself, and the rest of your team – or Monika's Marauders, as I like to call them – followed the same regime.'

'Can we talk about the body now?' Paniatowski asked, starting to feel slightly uncomfortable.

'Certainly,' Shastri agreed. 'Your victim – Madame X – appears to have followed the same philosophy as I have.'

'She wasn't young and beautiful,' Paniatowski said.

'No, she wasn't – on the outside,' Shastri agreed, 'but her organs are in excellent condition for a woman of her age. I doubt she ever ate a bag of chips or a steak and kidney pie in her entire life – and which of the Marauders can say that? I suspect – though I cannot be sure – that she ate a lot of fish, and cooked with oil, rather than lard. It is what is becoming known as the Mediterranean diet.'

'Are you saying that she originally came from one of the countries on the Mediterranean?'

'It is more than possible. Certainly, her skin seems to have had more exposure to the sun than you would expect from a native of Whitebridge.'

'What else can you tell me about her?' Paniatowski asked.

'Always so demanding,' Shastri said. 'You are quite as bad – in your own way – as Chief Inspector Woodend used to be.' She paused. 'How is Mr Woodend, by the way?'

'He's fine – as happy as a pig in shit,' Paniatowski said.

But she had to admit that in the week or so that she and Louisa had stayed with him and Joan, there had been moments when he seemed to be fretting for something – and she had a good idea what that something was.

'To return to the question of your cadaver,' Shastri said. 'She was in her mid-sixties, I would estimate. From the condition of her hands, I would say that she had been used to manual labour of some kind. She had no distinguishing marks, nor had she undergone any major operations. Her teeth were in good condition for a woman of her age, but I would say it is a long time since she visited a dentist.'

'How did she die?' Paniatowski asked.

'She was killed by a single – very violent – blow to the back of the head. The murder weapon was very likely a ball-peen hammer or something similar. Death would have been almost instantaneous, and there is no evidence of any other damage of either a physical or a sexual nature.'

'And how long has she been dead?'

'Given that the cold water prevented some of the natural processes of decomposition from taking place, it is difficult to pinpoint it exactly,' Shastri admitted, 'but I would say that death occurred approximately three days ago.'

'In other words, she probably went into the water on Wednesday night or Thursday morning.'

'Yes,' Shastri agreed, 'and given that most people don't like disposing of bodies in broad daylight, I would suggest that Wednesday night was more likely.'

'What can you tell me about her clothes?'

'The skirt, blouse and cardigan are all mid-market brands which could have been bought from any of a dozen shops in Whitebridge and from thousands of shops elsewhere. None of them are new. In fact, I would guess they are all at least two years old. The underwear, on the other hand, is brand-new, and I'd say it has never been washed.'

'Is there anything unusual about the underwear?' Paniatowski asked.

'Nothing at all,' Shastri replied. 'It is just as sensible as the rest of her clothes, and quite appropriate to a woman of her age.'

So did it mean anything that the underwear was new, while the rest of her clothes weren't? Paniatowski wondered.

Probably not, she decided.

'Is there anything else you'd like to know?' Shastri asked.

'Her address would be nice,' Paniatowski said, 'but I don't suppose even a miracle worker like you can provide me with that.'

'Alas, no,' Shastri agreed. 'But I am sure the estimable Inspector Beresford will soon provide you with that information.'

Yes, she could only pray that he would, Paniatowski thought – because the clock was ticking.

Five

There was a brilliantly blue sky that Sunday morning, and the winter sun – while not exactly aggressively hot – did at least give the impression that it was prepared to make some effort to warm the town up.

And slowly but surely, Whitebridge did begin to feel a little less chill. Icicles, hanging from roof guttering, dripped, quivered and then fell; pavements and roads became a little less lethal; and at the scene of the crime – if the crime had, actually, been committed there – a channel of greenish water ran through what had been the middle of Tommy Maddox's defective skating rink.

Tommy Maddox had inadvertently handed them a break, Paniatowski thought, as she sat at her

53

desk, smoking her sixth cigarette of the day. If the boy hadn't been foolhardy enough to try and skate across the frozen canal, the body could have lain there until the ropes finally rotted away, and the lump of decayed meat – hardly recognizable as a human being at all by that time – had been allowed to rise to the surface.

Yes, that had certainly been a lucky break, but they didn't seem to have had much luck since. The door-to-door inquiries had turned up nothing positive, and though there'd been a fair number of responses to the newspaper and television reports, these had all proved, on further investigation, to have been filed by the lonely, the loony and the merely confused.

She was dreading her next meeting with the chief constable. In the old days, those meetings had, on the whole, been very productive, for though they had once been lovers, they had mostly managed to put that fact to one side, and behave like professionals.

But everything had changed since his wife's suicide.

His wife's accident, Paniatowski corrected herself – the coroner had ruled it an accident.

George Baxter blamed himself for his wife's death, but he also blamed his ex-lover – even though their affair had been long over before he had ever met Jo.

It wasn't logical of him, of course, but you couldn't really blame a man consumed by grief and guilt for not being logical, Paniatowski told herself.

But whether she understood his situation or

54

not – and she did understand it – it didn't make those meetings any easier.

Beresford appeared in the doorway, but it was clear from the expression on his face that he had nothing positive to tell her.

'I've managed to scrounge up a few more officers from the other divisions,' he said. 'Do you want me to use them to widen the scope of the door-to-door inquiries?'

'Do you really need to ask?' Paniatowski replied.

It was impossible for anyone to be invisible in a close-knit and downright nosy town like Whitebridge, she thought, so there would be people who knew the dead woman.

But maybe some of those people didn't read the newspapers, watch television, or live in an area that had already been canvassed. Maybe some of them were away on business, or visiting family in another town.

The victim would be identified eventually, Paniatowski was sure of that. But the problem was, the longer it took, the colder the trail grew.

At lunchtime the team all came together at their usual table in the Drum and Monkey.

'I'd like to start by hearing your theories on why it's proving so difficult to identify our victim,' Paniatowski said.

'Maybe she's agoraphobic,' Beresford suggested. 'She never left the house, so nobody recognizes her.'

'Surely, there'd be friends and family who'd know who she was,' Paniatowski argued.

55

'Not necessarily,' Beresford countered. 'Agoraphobia is a mental illness, and some people are unenlightened enough to consider mental illness shameful.'

Like I did, he thought. *When my mother's Alzheimer's got bad, I was ashamed of her – and it wasn't her fault.*

'Go on,' Paniatowski encouraged gently, sensing his pain.

'If she was ashamed of it – or if her husband was ashamed – it's very unlikely she would have had any contact with other people. And perhaps her husband had finally had enough of the strain of it all, and decided to kill her.'

'Another possibility is that she belonged to some strict sect or other religious group which believes that women should never be allowed to leave the house,' Crane said.

'If that was the case, she'd at least have had contact with other members of the sect,' Paniatowski pointed out.

'Yes, but she may have done something which so offended the other members that they were complicit in her murder,' Crane said.

But it was hard to see how a seemingly harmless old woman could have done something so offensive that it merited her death, Paniatowski thought.

'What do you think, Kate?' she asked her sergeant.

'The problem with those two theories is that they're both based on the assumption that no one – or at least very few people – could identify her,' Meadows said.

'And despite the newspaper reports, the television appeals, and the door-to-door canvassing, no one *has* identified her,' Beresford said, in the aggressive–defensive tone he sometimes adopted when he suspected that Meadows was getting at him. 'So doesn't that suggest we may be thinking along the right lines?'

'No,' Meadows countered, 'because if the killer thought she couldn't be identified, he wouldn't have gone to such lengths to hide the body.'

Whatever direction they went in, they always came back to the same point, Paniatowski thought.

This was anything but a random killing, and it seemed as if the murderer was convinced that when the body was identified, the motive would be clear – and that once the motive was clear, the man who had that motive would find himself firmly in the spotlight.

Louisa was eating her afternoon tea at the kitchen table when she heard the key turn in the front door, and looking up at the clock was surprised to discover that it was still not quite half-past five.

'You're home early, Mum,' she shouted.

'It's been a quiet day at the office,' Paniatowski said from the hallway.

'It's been a quiet day at the office?' Louisa repeated with mock-incredulity. 'How can it have been quiet, Mum, when you're in the middle of a murder investigation?'

'The truth is that there's not much I can do, because the case is in the doldrums for the moment,' Paniatowski admitted, entering the kitchen and sitting down opposite her daughter. 'What's that you're eating?'

'It's called *pan con tomate*,' Louisa said. 'You get a piece of French bread, cut it down the middle, toast it, pour olive oil over it, and then rub it with sliced tomato. Tía Pilar showed me how to do it.'

Her Auntie Pilar seemed to have shown her quite a lot in a very short time, Paniatowski thought – and, worryingly, Louisa seemed to have embraced it all very enthusiastically.

Taking her daughter to Spain had been her idea, she reminded herself, and it had been a good thing – the *right* thing – to do.

She became aware that Louisa had said something to her, but she had no idea what it was.

'Sorry, love,' she said. 'Could you repeat that?'

'I've been thinking about the sketch, Mum,' Louisa said.

'What sketch?'

'The one that's been in all the papers – the one of the dead woman who was fished out of the canal.'

'You shouldn't be bothering yourself with that kind of thing at your age,' Paniatowski said, with just a hint of disapproval in her voice.

'If I'm going to be a detective, then it's never too early to start,' Louisa countered.

If I'm going to be a detective, Paniatowski repeated silently.

When Louisa had first mentioned the idea of joining the police force, she had thought it was no more than a whim – something that would quickly fade away when some more glamorous

58

profession presented itself to her – but it had been over a year now, and the girl still seemed quite determined.

It's not that I don't want her to be a bobby, Paniatowski told herself regularly. *It's flattering, in a way, that she wants to follow in my foot-steps. But I could never be a brain surgeon or a famous writer – and I really do believe that Louisa could be either of those things.*

But at least there was some consolation to be drawn from the fact that if Louisa became a police officer, she'd stay in England, rather than following a completely new life in a foreign country.

Paniatowski felt a wave of shame wash over her. She had always said that all she ever wanted was for Louisa to be happy – and if Louisa could be happier in Spain than she was in England, then that was just fine.

Honestly it was.

'You're off picking daisies again, Mum,' Louisa said.

'You're right, I was,' Paniatowski agreed. 'You're determined to talk about the sketch what-ever I say, aren't you?'

'Well, I do think it's quite important,' Louisa said seriously.

'All right, let's have it,' Paniatowski said, lighting up a cigarette and giving in to the inevitable.

'I'm not absolutely sure about it, but I think that I may have met her,' Louisa said.

'It is only a sketch, you know, Louisa,' Paniatowski pointed out. 'It's meant to be a memory jogger, rather than an accurate portrait.'

'What do you mean?'

'What normally happens is that people look at the picture and say to themselves, "That's a bit like Mrs Smith." And then they think, "Where is Mrs Smith? I haven't seen her around recently." And that's when they contact us. Sometimes it *is* Mrs Smith, and sometimes it turns out to be someone quite different. As I said, it's only a sketch.'

'Could I see the photograph of her?' Louisa asked.

'I don't have a photograph of her,' Paniatowski replied. 'She didn't have a handbag, and since we have no idea where she lives . . .'

'Ah!' Louisa interrupted – and it was a very significant 'ah' – 'you don't know where she lives.'

'And what's that supposed to mean?' Paniatowski asked.

'I really would like to see the photograph, Mum,' Louisa said insistently.

'I've told you, we haven't got one.'

'Not one of her alive, no,' Louisa agreed. 'But you'll have one – probably several – of her dead.'

'Yes, I do have photographs of the body – but I've no intention of showing it to you.'

'You let me see Grandad and Granny, when they died,' Louisa pointed out. 'You let me look right down into their coffins – and I was much younger then than I am now.'

'That was entirely different,' Paniatowski countered. 'They were your Spanish family, and it was the proper thing to do. You were paying them your respects. This woman, on the other

60

hand, is a murder victim who was in the water for at least three days . . .'

'Don't you harbour a secret ambition that I might eventually decide to become a doctor?' Louisa asked cunningly.

'What makes you think that?' asked Paniatowski, who thought she'd been very discreet about her flights of fancy.

'Don't you?' Louisa persisted.

'I've considered the possibility that your thoughts might turn in that direction eventually,' Paniatowski said, suddenly on the defensive.

'So if I do decide to become a doctor, you'll have no objection to me cutting up bodies in three years' time – but you won't even show me a picture of a dead woman now,' Louisa said.

Paniatowski sighed and opened her briefcase. 'Here you are,' she said, laying the photograph on the table. 'And I hope that makes you happy!'

Louisa examined the picture from one angle, and then from another.

'She's rather puffed up,' she said.

'I did warn you it wouldn't be pleasant,' Paniatowski said. 'So if you're upset now, you've only yourself to blame.'

But Louisa didn't actually seem as if she was upset – in fact, she seemed to be rather enjoying herself.

'Yes, she doesn't look quite right, but I'm certain it's Doña Elena,' the girl said.

'Who?'

'Doña Elena. I don't know her other name. I met her at Tía Pilar's lunch party.'

'Remind me when that party was,' Paniatowski said.

Louisa counted back on her fingers. 'It was eleven days ago.'

'And so you're asking me to believe that seven days after you see this woman at a party on the Costa Blanca, she turns up dead – under the ice – in a Whitebridge canal?' Paniatowski asked.

'It doesn't seem likely,' Louisa admitted.

'No, it doesn't.'

'But it's her. I know it's her. I paid special attention to her at the party, because Tía Pilar said she was a true heroine.'

Dr Shastri had said the dead woman hadn't been living on a typical northern diet – no chip butties or steak and kidney pies. In fact, she'd gone so far as to suggest that the woman might have been following a 'Mediterranean diet', Paniatowski thought. And Shastri had also said that she appeared to have had more exposure to the sun than most people in Lancashire would have.

So maybe it was just possible that . . .

'You're starting to think that I just might be right, aren't you?' Louisa asked gleefully.

'We're trained not to overlook any possibility, however unlikely it might seem,' Paniatowski replied.

Louisa grinned. 'And now you're going to ring Uncle Colin and ask him to check it out,' she said.

Paniatowski stood up. 'Smart arse!' she said.

And then she walked into the hallway, dialled

62

the number of Whitebridge CID, and asked to be put through to DCI Beresford.

'I thought you were making an early night of it, boss,' Beresford said, when he came on the line.

'I was,' Paniatowski agreed. 'Have you checked the railway station and bus station?'

'I'm sorry, boss?'

'Have you shown the sketch to everyone who works at the railway station and the bus station?'

'Well, no,' Beresford admitted. 'There didn't seem much point in that, since we'd established that our victim lived in Whitebridge.'

But they hadn't established that at all, Paniatowski now realized.

What they had established was that she probably knew her murderer, and that he probably had reasons for not wanting her to be identified – and that wasn't the same thing at all.

'We've probably spoken to some of the railway and bus staff in the course of the door-to-door inquiries,' Beresford continued. 'I can check through the records, if you like.'

'Bugger that for a game of soldiers,' Paniatowski said. 'I want your lads to interview all railway and bus station employees – and I want it done now! Have you got that?'

'Got it,' Beresford agreed.

The row of cottages behind the railway station was – accurately, if a little prosaically – called Railway Row. They were solid, two-up, two-down houses, and each one had a small garden

63

at the front, and backed on to an alley at the rear.

The gardens of the houses were neat and tidy, the paintwork on the windows and doors bright and fresh, Beresford noted, as he walked along the row. If he had to guess, he would say that most of the people who lived there were young couples who planned eventually to move up the housing ladder, but in the meantime were determined to show pride in their modest little homes.

Number Eleven, Railway Row, was a marked contrast to the other houses – the garden overgrown, the dark brown paintwork cracked and peeling, and when Beresford opened the gate, it squeaked an exhausted protest.

The man who answered his knock was in his mid-fifties, and had a pencil-thin moustache, a weak jaw and resentful eyes.

'Mr Higgins?' Beresford asked. 'Mr Ben Higgins?'

'Who's asking?' the other man replied.

Beresford produced his warrant card. 'Are you Ben Higgins?'

'Yes.'

'Then I'd like to ask you a few questions, sir, if you wouldn't mind.'

'All right,' Higgins agreed, though his tone said that he certainly did mind.

'You're a baggage porter on Whitebridge Railway Station, aren't you?' Beresford said.

'What if I am?'

'We're trying to trace the movements of a woman who may have arrived here by train,'

Beresford said, unfolding the sketch. 'This woman, to be precise.'

'Never seen her,' Higgins replied, barely glancing at the sketch.

'I'd like you to take a closer look,' Beresford said firmly.

The second glance was longer than the first – though not by much.

'Don't know her,' Higgins said dismissively.

Behind him, the gate creaked again, and Beresford turned to see a middle-aged woman struggling with three heavy carrier bags full of groceries. Higgins had seen her too, but it was plain from his unaltered stance that he had no intention of abandoning his position on the doorstep.

Beresford turned around, met the woman halfway up the path, and relieved her of two of the bags.

'Well, that is kind of you, young man,' the woman said, 'but if you're hoping that by helping me you'll persuade that miserable old bugger to buy whatever it is you're selling, you're due for a disappointment.'

'I'm not selling anything,' Beresford said, as they reached the front door. 'I'm a police officer, conducting inquiries.'

'Well, I have to say, you certainly took your time getting here,' the woman said. She looked up at her husband. 'When was it exactly that you called the police station, Ben?'

'I don't remember,' Higgins said, looking distinctly unhappy.

'Well, I do. It was Sunday morning, on your way to the pub,' Mrs Higgins said.

'I . . . er . . . might have forgotten to ring,' Higgins said.

'That's not what you told me when you got back from the boozer, smelling of beer and expecting your Sunday dinner to be waiting for you on the table,' his wife countered.

'What was the call about?' Beresford asked.

'Why, that woman whose picture was in the paper, of course,' Mrs Higgins said. 'He was looking through the *Whitebridge Sunday Post*, and he said to me, "I've seen that woman," and I said, "Have you? Then you'd better report it," and he said, "I will."'

'Look . . .' Higgins began.

'So why didn't you report it?' Beresford interrupted him.

'Like I said, I forgot.'

'And why did you tell me just now that you didn't recognize her?'

'You never could keep your mouth shut, could you?' Higgins said, glaring at his wife. 'It's like this,' he continued, turning back to Beresford, 'I'm a busy man, and I knew if I reported it, I'd have to go down to the station and you'd keep me there for hours.'

'A busy man!' his wife said, with obvious contempt. 'The only thing you're ever busy doing is sitting on your big fat backside.'

'Besides, I knew I couldn't be the only one who'd seen her, so I didn't think there was any point in bothering you,' Higgins continued.

But no one else had seen her, Beresford thought – and why was that?

'Am I in trouble?' Higgins asked, sounding rather worried now.

'Undoubtedly,' Beresford lied, 'but things might go a little easier on you if you were to tell me exactly what you saw.'

The first words that Beresford said when Paniatowski answered the phone were, 'How the bloody hell did you know, Monika?'

'I take it that means that somebody recognized her,' Paniatowski replied.

'A railway porter called Higgins. He says he saw her get off the train from Manchester last Wednesday.'

'That was the day on which we think she died!'

'Exactly!'

'Why didn't he contact us before?'

'Because he's an idle bastard?' Beresford speculated, his voice tinged with anger. 'Because he's got about as much a sense of civic responsibility as a corporation lamp-post has?'

'Was there anything else that he could tell you, apart from when she arrived in Whitebridge?'

'He thinks he remembers that she was carrying a small bag or suitcase, but he can't remember what colour it was.'

'And we still haven't found that, have we?'

'No. We haven't found the coat she was wearing, either.'

'I'll meet you at headquarters in half an hour, Colin,' Paniatowski said, and hung up.

When she returned to the living room, she saw that her daughter was grinning again.

'Well?' Louisa asked.

'Thank you for your help, darling, I really appreciate it,' Paniatowski said. 'But do you have to look so bloody smug?'

Louisa gazed down at the table. 'I'm sorry, Mum,' she said, in a little girl voice.

'No, you're not,' Paniatowski said.

Louisa raised her head again, and the grin was still in place. 'No, I'm not,' she agreed. 'Is there a reward?'

'Indeed there is,' Paniatowski told her, 'the reward of knowing that you've done your duty as a responsible citizen.'

'I'm not old enough to be a citizen,' Louisa pointed out. 'But I am old enough to be given a record voucher.'

'Well, you've earned it,' Paniatowski conceded. 'In fact, if I'm honest, you've more than earned it.'

'Glad to oblige,' Louisa said.

It was relatively easy for the switchboard in Whitebridge police headquarters to make contact with the headquarters of the Cuerpo de Policía Armada in Madrid, but rerouting the call to their office in Alicante took over half an hour, and it was another twenty minutes before anyone who spoke English could be found to deal with the inquiry.

The man who eventually came on the line said that his name was Captain Muñoz.

'Never been to Britain, but I spent a few years in the States,' he told Paniatowski. 'So what can I do for ya, Chief Inspector?'

'We have a murder victim – a woman – here

in Whitebridge who we believe may recently have come here from Calpe, or one of the outlying villages,' Paniatowski explained.

'Oh yeah?' Captain Muñoz replied, but there was no real interest behind the question.

'We were wondering if you could find out something about her background for us,' Paniatowski said.

'We can look through the files and see what we've got on her,' Muñoz suggested.

'Is she likely to be on your files?' Paniatowski asked.

'Sure, if she was a subversive,' the captain replied, 'and since she was in England when she got hit, I'd guess there's a pretty good chance that's exactly what she was.'

'Would you care to explain the reasoning behind that?' Paniatowski asked cautiously.

Muñoz sighed at her obvious stupidity.

'Most Spanish women would never even think of leaving Spain unless they'd got something to hide,' he explained.

She and the captain clearly had very different ways of looking at the world, Paniatowski decided.

'The victim in the case was quite an old woman,' she said, hoping the information would make a difference to his attitude.

'There's no age limit for people who are intent on destroying the fatherland, lady,' the captain said.

'Maybe there is a file on her,' Paniatowski conceded in an attempt to meet him halfway, 'but since I don't even know her surname . . .'

'Jeez, if you don't know her name, then how do you expect us to look her up?' Muñoz interrupted.

'I don't know her surname, but I have the name and address of someone who I think will know it,' Paniatowski said.

'I don't get it,' the captain said. 'If you've got a murder on your hands, why don't you just pull in the usual suspects and give them the third degree until one of them either confesses or rats out one of the others.'

'It doesn't quite work like that over here,' Paniatowski said patiently. 'What we like to do during an investigation is build up a profile of the victim, and see where that leads us.'

'Weird,' the captain said. 'Listen, I'll tell you my problem, lady. The Generalissimo has just died, and now that he's gone, all kinds of low-life have taken their opportunity to come creeping out of the woodwork. There's murderers, rapists, child molesters, homosexuals, communists – you name it, we've got it – all trying to get their dirty business done before we're organized enough to clamp down on them again. And you want me to waste my men's time chasing up the details on some old broad who may not even have been a subversive?'

'Exactly,' Paniatowski agreed.

'No can do,' Muñoz said – and hung up.

Six

The Spanish Consulate in Manchester was located midway between the Central Reference Library on Albert Square and the Piccadilly bus station, and when it opened its doors for business that Monday morning, Paniatowski was already waiting outside.

Establishing her credentials with her warrant card was enough to get her inside without a prior appointment, and ten minutes later she found herself sitting across a desk from the deputy vice consul, a man in his middle-thirties who looked as if he regarded his present position as no more than a step on the ladder to future diplomatic eminence.

'We are always willing to cooperate with the English police, Detective Chief Inspector Paniatowski,' he said, 'but I am still unclear how we can help you.'

'I have some questions I need answering about a woman who was found dead in Whitebridge, but who we suspect may have come from the Costa Blanca,' Paniatowski told him.

'Then I would suggest that you contact the Cuerpo de Policía Armada in Alicante.'

'I've already done that. They say they haven't got the available manpower to make any inquiries.'

The deputy vice consul nodded. 'Yes, it's probably true that they haven't,' he said.

71

It was time to turn up the bullshit meter, Paniatowski decided.

'I don't suppose there's a police force in the world that doesn't feel it's short of manpower,' she said, 'so it's usually a case of setting out your priorities. Now you can't expect the local police on the Costa Blanca to see my investigation as important. Their work, by its very nature, is bound to be parochial. But surely someone with a much wider view of the world – like yourself, for instance – can see the benefits of international cooperation, and could suggest, through the proper channels, that it might be to their long-term advantage to assist us.'

Not bad, she thought, awarding herself a mental pat on the shoulder. Not bad at all!

And then she saw the sanctimonious look which had appeared on the deputy vice consul's face, and realized it had been a waste of effort.

'You have heard, have you not, that our great leader – the man who has steered Spain through stormy waters of both national and international affairs for almost forty years – passed away last week?' the man asked.

The conversation was probably being taped, Paniatowski thought, and when it was over, the deputy vice consul would play it back to his superiors, to prove what a good boy he'd been.

'Yes, I have heard that,' she agreed.

'Well, there you have it,' the deputy vice consul said, spreading his hands in a gesture of helplessness.

'There I have what?' Paniatowski wondered.

72

'The Spanish people are in a very disturbed and distressed state. Cruelly robbed of their leader, they are wandering around like lost sheep. They need the police to guide them.'

The game was lost, and she should leave it right there, Paniatowski told herself.

And then she thought about what Paco had told her of his own experiences – and those of his comrades – after the war had ended, and she heard herself say, 'So it's because the people are all so upset over Franco's death that the police have their hands full, is it?'

'Certainly.'

'Not because they're expecting any kind of trouble?'

'Why would there be any trouble? The whole nation admired and respected the Caudillo.'

'I got a very different impression when I was over in Spain recently,' Paniatowski said.

'You must have been talking to some of the very few malcontents who live in my country, then,' the deputy vice consul said. He paused for a moment, before continuing with fake casualness, 'Who were these people who gave you such a distorted view of Spain?'

'Why would you want to know that?'

'Is it not obvious?'

'No, not to me.'

'If they are unhappy, it is either because they have a genuine grievance or because they have been misinformed about the true state of affairs. Whichever the case, they must be contacted, so that their grievances can be addressed and their misconceptions corrected.'

'I must say, you take your job very seriously,' Paniatowski said.

'Thank you. I certainly like to think that is the case.'

'I can't imagine an English deputy vice consul in Spain having so much concern for the people back home.'

'Perhaps not, but we Spaniards are very much one big family,' the deputy vice consul replied. 'Now, if you could just give me the names . . .' he pressed her.

Paniatowski frowned. 'Let me see . . . one of the people who seemed particularly unhappy was called Miguel.'

'Do you happen to know what his second name is?' the deputy vice consul asked.

'I think his second name was El Raton,' she said.

'Miguel el Raton,' repeated the deputy vice consul, glaring at her. 'That is what we call Mickey Mouse in Spanish. Do you think that is amusing?'

'No,' Paniatowski said, 'but I don't think it's particularly funny, either, that you're trying to pump me for the names of people who are not happy with your government.'

'This meeting is over,' the vice consul said coldly.

'Yes,' Paniatowski agreed, 'I rather think it is.'

George Baxter, the chief constable, had always reminded Paniatowski of a huge ginger teddy bear, but since his wife's death, that resemblance had all but melted away. In the days between

74

Jo's car crash and her funeral, his shock of red hair had turned completely white, and whilst he was still a big man, he no longer seemed as solid as he once had. But it was his eyes that told the story best. For most of the time, they were like huge swimming pools of guilt and grief, and when they did express another emotion, that emotion was usually anger.

He was angry with Paniatowski at that moment, and part of the anger – but only part – was as a result of her early-morning trip to Manchester.

'I don't know what you think gave you the right to enter the Spanish consulate and interrogate the deputy vice consul, Chief Inspector,' he said, 'but let me tell you, here and now, it was a completely unacceptable action.'

'With the greatest respect, sir, I didn't go there to interrogate him, I went to ask him for help,' Paniatowski replied.

'That is certainly not the impression the vice consul gave me over the telephone,' Baxter countered. 'He says you were rude and threatening.'

'And you automatically assume he was telling the truth, do you, sir?' Paniatowski asked. 'There was a time when you wouldn't have done – a time when you would have accepted the word of one of your officers over that of a minor official from a fascist dictatorship.'

'You're verging on insubordination with that comment, Chief Inspector,' Baxter said.

But it was clear from the new expression in his eyes that he was remembering the time to which she'd referred.

'I will make further inquiries about this

morning's incident, and then inform you if you will be subject to disciplinary proceedings,' he continued, 'but in the meantime, I would be grateful if you would tell me why you thought it necessary to ruffle the feathers of the Spanish government.'

'I think my murder victim may be Spanish, sir,' Paniatowski said. 'I think that, until recently, she may have lived on the Costa Blanca.'

'Do you have any evidence to back that up?'

'Not direct evidence, no.'

'You've suddenly become psychic, have you?'

'No, sir,' Paniatowski replied.

And told him how she'd reached that conclusion.

'So you're basing your whole investigation on the fanciful and over-imaginative speculations of a fifteen-year-old girl who happens to be your daughter?' Baxter asked.

'Don't attack Louisa,' Paniatowski said, with a sudden ferocity. 'Say what you like about me, but leave her alone!'

Baxter blinked. 'You're right,' he agreed. 'That was uncalled for, and I apologize. But you still can't go basing your investigation on the word of one girl, however sensible she is, Monika.'

'That's why I want confirmation,' Paniatowski said, 'and since the Spanish police and the Spanish consulate refuse to cooperate with me, I'll just have to go to Spain myself.'

'That's out of the question,' Baxter said, hardening again. 'You're supposed to be leading your team, not swanning off to the Costa.'

'In that case, do I have your permission to

76

send one of the team instead?' Paniatowski asked.

'No, you do not,' Baxter said. 'The link you have established is far too tenuous to justify the expense.'

'Please don't punish my team, and the investigation, because you've got something against me, sir,' Paniatowski said, almost desperately.

'You may go now, Chief Inspector,' Baxter said.

Charlie Woodend, a glass of beer in one hand and a cigarette in the other, was contemplating the blue Mediterranean Sea from his terrace when he heard the phone ring in the living room.

'It's Monika, Charlie,' Joan called. 'She wants to have a quick word with you.'

She wanted to have a quick word with him!

It was probably just a social call, Woodend thought, as he headed for the living room.

But his gut instinct – which was not quite ready to retire yet – told him it was more than that, and his heart began to beat a little faster.

'I need your help, Charlie,' Paniatowski said, when he'd picked up the phone in his big hand, 'but before I tell you what it is that I'd like you to do, I want to make it quite clear that I'm only turning to you because I've tried everything else, and you're my last resort.'

'You certainly know how to win a man over with flattery,' Woodend said dryly.

'That came out all wrong,' Paniatowski said, sounding flustered.

'You think so?' Woodend asked, smiling.

'What I meant to say was, I don't want to get you involved, but I don't seem to have any choice.'

'Better and better,' Woodend said.

'Please, Charlie, this is serious,' Paniatowski said.

'Aye, I can tell that now,' Woodend replied, chastened. 'I'm sorry I was flippant. What is it you want me to do?'

'The thing is – the reason I've got qualms about asking you – is you have this habit of treading on other people's toes,' Paniatowski said.

She was not so much speaking to him as trying to talk herself out of asking the favour, Woodend thought. And he also knew that whatever it was she wanted him to do, it was real police business – and he desperately wanted to do it.

'I used to tread on people's toes when I was a bobby back in Lancashire,' he said, 'but that's all over and done with now, and – like a good brandy – I've been maturing with age.'

'I don't want you getting yourself in trouble with the authorities,' Paniatowski agonized, 'especially since the situation over there in Spain is rather delicate at the moment.'

He could picture her in his mind, pacing up and down the office which used to be his.

'Don't you go worrying yourself about me getting myself into trouble,' he assured her. 'Remember, I've not just got my new-found maturity to keep me on the straight and narrow, I've also got Paco Ruiz.'

'It's precisely because of Paco that I'm so

concerned about the whole business,' Paniatowski admitted.

'What do you mean?'

'Paco's a lovely man, just as you're a lovely man, but each of you on his own is a bit of a loose cannon – and together you're a small war.'

'I don't know whether to take that as an insult or compliment,' Woodend said. 'I think, on reflection, I'll take it as a compliment.'

'I mean it, Charlie,' Paniatowski said. 'I'd just hate to see you being deported from Spain – apart from anything else, Joan would kill me if that happened – and I break out into a cold sweat just thinking about the possibility of Paco going back to gaol.'

'We'll be careful,' Woodend said. 'If there's even a whiff that things are about to go pear-shaped, we'll pull back.'

And he was thinking, *What is it that you want us to do? I'll have a heart attack if you don't tell me soon.*

'You promise?'

'I promise,' Woodend said – and even as he spoke the words he was promising himself that he really would try to keep his promise to Monika, even though he knew that when he was elbow-deep in an investigation, such promises usually counted for nothing.

Paniatowski sighed. 'All right, here's what I want you to do,' she said.

Seven

Hillton Rise was considered by most people to be one of the better areas of Whitebridge, and Ashton Avenue was one of the better parts of Hillton Rise. All the houses on Ashton Avenue had double frontages, attached garages, and large gardens both front and back, and the people who lived in them employed cleaners and part-time gardeners, and really considered themselves rather posh.

But it was on Tufton Court – a cul-de-sac which ran off Ashton Avenue – that the real wealth was on display. People there didn't manage large factories, they owned them. And if any of the inhabitants happened to work in a bank, then it was a merchant bank, rather than one of the common-or-garden high-street variety.

Paniatowski parked her MGA in front of number seven, Tufton Court, got out of the car, lit up a cigarette, and reviewed what little she knew about Robert Martinez MP.

Most of the information, she quickly realized, came either from the newspapers or from Louisa.

From the newspapers, she had learned that Robert was the son of a political refugee called Javier Martinez, who had arrived in Whitebridge in the late thirties, and had built up his luxury coach business from scratch. The papers had also informed her that Robert had been running the family business for a number of years, and had only stepped down when he'd been elected as the Member of Parliament for the Whitebridge constituency. Furthermore, they went on to claim, there was strong circumstantial evidence to suggest that he regarded his constituents as more than just a ticket to Westminster, and was actually prepared to fight hard for their interests whether they'd voted for him or not – a trait that was unlikely to gain him preferment within his party, but had certainly earned him the grudging respect of some of his political enemies locally.

Louisa had a slightly different take on things. According to her, Sr Roberto was clever, witty and enthusiastic, and – taking into account the fact that he was quite old – really rather handsome. He played the Spanish guitar beautifully, and knew a lot about flamenco dancing. It was he – and he alone – who had created the Whitebridge Hispanic Circle, and when he had announced that he would have to give it up, there had been a universal wailing and gnashing of teeth from the members.

Though the house itself looked quite grand, the Martinez residence had a relatively low wall running around its boundary, and the front gates were no more impressive than those of the less imposing houses on Ashton Avenue.

The gate had a notice attached to it which read:

Robert Martinez's office is to be found around the left-hand side of the house. The gate is not locked, so just push it open and walk in. Constituency surgeries

are normally held every Saturday from 9 to 3, but if I'm here in the week, I'll see you at any time, if you consider it urgent.

Hanging from the big notice was a smaller one which announced, **Robert Martinez is in/is not in**, and had an arrow pointing to the 'is in'.

Paniatowski pushed open the gate. A broad path led to the front door, and a narrower path branched off it and led around to the side of the house. She followed this smaller path and found herself looking at an annex which had probably once been a garage. The annex had a large picture window, and through it, she could see an efficient-looking woman in her late thirties, who was pounding away at a typewriter as if she hated the machine.

When Paniatowski knocked at the door, the woman called out, 'It's not locked – it never bloody is!'

Paniatowski opened the door and stepped inside.

'I'd like to see Mr Martinez,' she said.

The woman stopped typing, and looked up at her.

'I don't suppose you'd believe me if I said he was in London, would you?' she asked.

'I might, but for the fact that his London office has told me he's here, and that's confirmed by the notice on the gate,' Paniatowski said.

The other woman shrugged. 'Oh well, it was worth a try. How about if I asked you whether whatever you've come about could wait for a few days, because we're already running late?'

'I'm afraid it can't wait,' Paniatowski told her.

'That's probably just as well,' the secretary said, philosophically. 'If I had succeeded in turning you away, I'd only have got into trouble for it – again!'

'You get into trouble, do you?' Paniatowski asked, smiling.

'Constantly,' the secretary replied. '"Now that's not how we deal with our constituents, is it, Marjory?"' she said, in a much deeper voice than her natural one. '"No, Robert, it isn't,"' she continued, in a meeker version of her own voice. She grinned. 'I'm sorry, but he drives me insane. I'm supposed to be his gatekeeper – that's what he said I'd have to be when he gave me the job – but every time I close the gate, he bloody opens it again.'

'It must be difficult for you,' Paniatowski said.

'Difficult,' Marjory repeated. 'It's bloody near impossible. He should be in London today, and the party whips – who have a big say in who gets promoted and who doesn't – will be very cross that he isn't. And do you know why he's in Whitebridge instead?'

'No,' Paniatowski confessed, 'I don't.'

'He's arranged a meeting with some businessman, to discuss the possibility of opening a new factory in the town. I told him it wasn't his job. "That sort of thing is the responsibility of the town council," I said. "It's the responsibility of everybody who cares about the future of Whitebridge," he said. Well, you can't argue with that, can you?'

'I suppose not,' Paniatowski agreed.

'You really do have to see him, do you?' Marjory asked.

'Yes, I do,' Paniatowski replied, producing her warrant card.

The secretary clicked on the intercom. 'I've got a Chief Inspector Paniatowski out here,' she said. 'Can you see her?'

'Of course,' replied a slightly tinny voice from the machine.

'Of course the answer's "of course" – it's always "of course",' Marjory said, with resignation. She pointed to a door in the far wall. 'You'll find him the other side of that.'

'Thank you.'

'And if you could find an excuse to get him banged up on some bogus charge for a few days, I'd really appreciate it – because we could both do with the rest,' the secretary said, grinning again.

Robert Martinez was at his desk, flanked by mountains of documents, and when Paniatowski entered the room, he stood up.

'You must be Louisa's mother,' he said, shaking her hand and then gesturing her to sit down, 'but since you mentioned your rank to my secretary, I assume this is an official, rather than a social visit.'

'Yes, it is,' Paniatowski agreed.

'What a pity,' Martinez said – and sounded as if he meant it. 'But before we get down to whatever business brought you here, would you mind if I asked you how Louisa is getting on?'

'Not at all,' Paniatowski said.

84

He'd got very nice eyes, she thought – dark, heavy, Latin eyes. And Louisa was right – he was rather handsome.

'So how is she getting on?' Martinez asked, with a slightly awkward note in his voice.

She realized she must have been staring at him.

'Louisa's fine,' Paniatowski told him. 'She's enjoying school – and doing rather well. And, as a matter of fact, we've just got back from Spain, where she met her Spanish relatives for the first time.'

'Lucky girl,' Martinez said wistfully. He paused. 'I miss running the Whitebridge Hispanic Circle, you know. Of course, I know the work I'm doing now is more important and can change more lives for the better, but the Circle wasn't just worthy – it was fun.'

'And parliament isn't?'

'Parliament is a grind, full of people who like the sound of their own voices too much,' Robert Martinez said, 'and if I could find someone who I thought could represent Whitebridge better than I do, I'd gladly surrender my seat to him – or her – tomorrow.'

He took a packet of Ducados out of his pocket, and offered them to Paniatowski. When she declined, he lit one up himself.

'Do you prefer black tobacco?' Paniatowski asked, reaching into her handbag for her own cigarettes.

'Yes, I do,' Martinez replied. 'I left Spain when I was a baby – and given my father's political background, I imagine I would be far from welcomed back – yet I smoke Spanish cigarettes,

85

drink Spanish wine, know how to cook a very decent paella, and am an almost fanatical supporter of Valencia Club de Fútbol.' He grinned suddenly. 'I am also, of course, a fanatical supporter of Whitebridge Rovers – it would be political suicide not to be.'

'Yes, it most certainly would,' Paniatowski agreed.

'Yet sometimes, I worry about being so attached to a country I left so long ago,' Martinez said, frowning slightly. 'You know what it's like when you hear some people talking about the good old days?'

'Yes.'

'I think those good old days can only seem quite that good when viewed from a distance, and through rose-coloured glasses. So is my attachment to Spain – my equivalent of the good old days – more to do with the fact that I'm dissatisfied with the life I've got now? I don't think so – but how can I be sure?' He paused for a moment. 'How do you feel about Poland?'

It was a complicated question, Paniatowski thought. To her, Poland was her father, and her father was dead – mown down in the last foolish-heroic cavalry charge against German machine guns – and she was not sure she would feel quite comfortable talking about it to a man she had only just met.

'I like the vodka,' she said.

Martinez laughed, then seemed to sense her dilemma and said, 'I'm sorry, I should never have put you on the spot like that.'

86

'That's all right,' she told him, appreciating his sensitivity.

'So, shall we get on to the real purpose of your visit?' Martinez suggested.

Paniatowski nodded, and took the sketch of the dead woman out of her handbag. She would have laid it down on the desk, but with all Martinez's papers, there really wasn't room, and so she just held it up for him to look at.

'It's about this woman,' she said.

'Ah, yes, I saw that picture in the paper,' Martinez said, 'but she's a complete stranger to me, and I don't really see how I could help you.'

'What we didn't know until last night is that there's a strong possibility she was Spanish,' Paniatowski told him.

'Ah!' Martinez said.

'And we also think that until a few days ago, she was living in Spain, and only arrived in Whitebridge shortly before she was murdered.'

'You think she came here to visit someone?' Martinez guessed.

'Exactly,' Paniatowski agreed.

'And you think that person murdered her?'

'Not necessarily,' Paniatowski said cautiously, 'but if we could identify her, we might have a better idea of why someone would want to kill her.'

'And you've come to see me not because I'm your MP, but because you think that since I used to run the Whitebridge Hispanic Circle, I know more about the Spaniards in Whitebridge than anyone else?'

'Yes,' Paniatowski said.

And she was thinking, *Please give me something I can use, so I can call Charlie off the investigation before he gets himself into trouble.*

'There aren't actually that many Spaniards living here, you know,' Martinez told her. 'I haven't done the calculation, but I doubt the number even reaches treble figures.'

'Then it should be easy to track them down,' Paniatowski said. 'Do you have a list?'

'Not as such,' Martinez admitted, 'but from the information I have collected from various sources on other matters, I'm sure I could get Marjory to compile one for you.'

The door from the outer office opened, and a man entered. He was around seventy, Paniatowski guessed, and the expression on his face could only have been described as stern.

'They told me you were talking to a policeman,' he said to Robert Martinez, and looked sweepingly around the room as if he expected to find one lurking in a corner.

'For "they" read "Marjory",' Robert Martinez said to Paniatowski. 'She'll have sent my father here to chase you out as soon as possible. She thinks I spend too long with my visitors.'

'She is the policeman?' Javier Martinez asked, examining Paniatowski critically, as if he suspected someone was playing a trick on him.

'She is the police officer – DCI Paniatowski,' Robert Martinez replied.

'When you are talking to the police, it is always wise to have witnesses,' the older man said.

Robert Martinez laughed uncomfortably. 'My father has lived in this country for nearly forty years,' he said to Paniatowski. 'He has run a successful business, and has dined at the mayor's table at official banquets on numerous occasions.' He turned to the older man again. 'How are Valencia CF doing this season?' he asked.

'How would I know that?' Javier Martinez replied indifferently.

'Then let me ask you another question, Father,' Robert suggested. 'Do you agree with me that Whitebridge Rovers are likely to be relegated at the end of this season?'

The older man snorted with contempt at the very idea.

'Of course not!' he said. 'We have had a few poor results – that is true – but the team is coming together, and the new centre forward has not yet shown half his talent.'

'You see?' Robert Martinez asked, smiling at Paniatowski. 'My father is, in many ways, as English as the people who were born here. He likes warm beer, and adores steak and kidney pie. Yet a police officer – any police officer – is always, to him, just a member of the Cuerpo de Policía Armada in disguise.'

Robert had delivered the whole argument light-heartedly, and most people in Javier Martinez's situation would have laughed – perhaps a little embarrassedly – at the way his son had exposed his inconsistencies. But Javier did not laugh – he didn't even betray the slightest flicker of amusement.

Unlike his son, he seemed a very cold man, Paniatowski thought.

'You did not know the Policía Armada as I

did,' the old man said. 'If you had known them, you would never again . . .' He stopped suddenly, and squared his shoulders. 'You are right, Roberto,' he continued. 'Wariness of the police is no excuse for being discourteous to a lady.' He bowed to Paniatowski. 'I apologize, madam, for ever seeming to question your integrity.'

'Apology accepted,' Paniatowski said.

'DCI Paniatowski would like to know if we recognize this woman,' Robert Martinez said, holding up the sketch.

'When I saw that in the newspaper, I thought, for a second, that I might possibly recognize her,' Javier Martinez said. 'But when I looked closer, I saw that she was just like the old women I pass on the street every day.'

Paniatowski checked her watch.

'I have to go,' she said. 'Could you get that list to me as soon as possible, Mr Martinez?'

'Marjory will probably demand her pound of flesh for it, but I'll see you get it within the hour,' Robert Martinez promised.

The front parlour of Doña Pilar Crespo Torres' farmhouse had exposed roof beams made of olive wood, and a floor paved with heavy stone slabs. The furniture was handmade, rustic, and smelled of beeswax, and the room was dominated by a huge stone fireplace – on which there was a spit for roasting meat – and the large wooden crucifix that hung to the left of it.

It was in this parlour that Doña Pilar had chosen to receive Woodend and Ruiz. And receive was the right word to describe it, Woodend thought,

90

because sitting there, bolt upright, dressed entirely in black, and resting her old hands on her carved walking stick, she made it seem as if, after this experience, an audience with the pope would be an absolute doddle.

The old woman scrutinized the two men thoroughly, and then spoke to Paco in rapid Spanish.

'Doña Pilar says she has seen you before,' Paco translated.

'That's right,' Woodend agreed. 'I was the one who brought Louisa here for the party.'

More rapid Spanish followed, of which the only words Woodend could catch sounded like tío Echarlee.

'She didn't know who you were at the time, but she realizes now that you must be the Uncle Charlie who Louisa spoke of,' Paco explained. 'She says she is pleased to discover that Louisa had such a manly man in her adopted family.'

'Ask her about this Elena woman,' Woodend said, starting to feel a little hot under the collar.

Paco did.

'She says the woman's full name is Elena Vargas Morales,' he told Woodend, when the old woman had finished speaking. 'She comes from a village in the mountains called Val de Montaña, and until a few years ago, she worked in Melly's Hotel, which is on the seafront.'

'I know it,' Woodend said. 'Ask her if Elena seemed in any way strange at the lunch that she and Louisa went to.'

Another conversation followed, in which Doña Pilar lifted one of her hands from her stick in order to make extravagant gestures with it.

91

'She says that Elena was behaving perfectly normally at first, but when she saw the photographs, a sudden change came over her.'

'What photographs?'

'Louisa brought some photographs with her, to show her Spanish family what her life was like in Whitebridge. The photographs were passed around the table. When they reached Elena, she seemed very shocked by them.'

'Shocked? How?'

'She went pale, and there was one particular picture that she appeared to be unable to tear her eyes away from.'

'Who was in the picture?'

'Doña Pilar does not know that, because Elena was right at the other end of the table from her. But she has absolutely no doubt in her mind that Elena was very upset by them.'

'What happened next?'

'Doña Pilar determined to have a quiet word with her friend – to find out what had upset her – but she did not want to appear rude to her other guests by ignoring them, and she decided to wait until lunch was over.'

'But by then, Elena had gone,' Woodend guessed.

'Yes, that's just what happened. Elena left without even thanking her hostess, which is both very discourteous in Spain, and very unlike Elena, who has impeccable manners. Doña Pilar sent her son – Don Jaime – round to Elena's cottage the next morning, but she wasn't there, and no one has seen her since.'

'Ask Doña Pilar if she knows if Elena has done much travelling,' Woodend told Paco.

The old woman laughed at the apparent absurdity of the question that *tío Echarlee* had put to her.

'She says that women from Elena's background don't travel,' Paco translated. 'The men sometimes travel – to find work, or because they have been called up to serve in the army – but the women live their whole lives within a few miles of where they were born. They might perhaps visit Alicante, or even Valencia, once or twice, but for most of them, even that is too great an adventure.'

The old woman spoke again.

'Besides,' Paco continued, 'she couldn't leave the country without the permission of a male relative. And even if a male relative could have been produced from somewhere, the authorities would never have issued a passport to someone with her political background.'

If it had been anybody but Louisa who had made the identification, Woodend would already have started thinking that she must have been mistaken. But Louisa had been playing observation games with her Uncle Charlie since she started primary school, and she had one of the sharpest pairs of eyes – and best recalls – of anyone he had ever come across.

'Thank Doña Pilar for seeing us, and tell her that she's been very helpful,' Woodend said to Paco.

'*De nada!*' said Doña Pilar, who clearly understood his tone.

'She says it's nothing,' Paco translated.

'I know,' said Woodend, who understood hers.

* * *

93

'If Louisa is right about it being Elena who was found dead in Whitebridge – and I'm sure she is – then it must have been her photographs that were the catalyst,' Woodend said to Ruiz, as they walked back to Paco's car. 'But that doesn't make any kind of sense, does it?'

'Not a great deal,' Paco admitted. 'Perhaps we would be able to make the connection if we saw the photographs ourselves.'

'I'll ask Monika to post them to us,' Woodend said. 'But what are we going to do in the meantime?'

'It might be useful if we found out more about Elena's background,' Paco suggested.

'Just what I was thinking,' Woodend agreed. 'So first we'll go to the village she came from, and then the hotel where she worked.'

'That's not a good idea,' Paco said. 'They would not trust you – a foreigner – in the village, and the owner of Melly's Hotel would probably be much more comfortable talking to a fellow Englishman than to the Englishman and his Spanish associate.'

'So you take the village, and I take the hotel?'

'Yes, I think that would work best.'

They were dealing with the case of a woman who had never travelled before in her life, but had gone to England on the basis of a photograph shown to her by a girl she had only just met, Woodend thought, as he squeezed his large body into the passenger seat of Ruiz's small car.

That same woman had been murdered in Whitebridge for reasons completely unknown, and her killer had attempted to hide her body, even though it was unlikely that anyone but he would recognize her.

If there was ever a case that was head-bangingly complicated, it was this one.

His knees jammed hard against the dashboard of Paco's car, Woodend sighed contentedly.

It was starting to feel just like old times!

Eight

Paco hit the roadblock just after he turned off the N332. It was manned by young soldiers – probably conscripts – who were all attempting, with various degrees of success, to grow their first moustaches. The sergeant in charge of them was a middle-aged man with a hard, square body. He had no moustache – but then he had nothing to prove about his masculinity, either.

'Identification card!' the sergeant demanded, when Paco had wound down his window.

Paco handed it to him.

'So you are Francisco Ruiz?' the sergeant said.

'Yes.'

'And where are you going?'

Since the road he was about to take led to the village of Val de Montaña – and to nowhere else – there didn't seem to be much point in lying.

'I'm going to Val de Montaña,' Paco said.

'And why are you going there?'

'May I ask why you want to know that?' Paco said.

'Why would you want to know why I want to know?' the sergeant countered suspiciously.

'Merely for professional curiosity,' Paco replied.

'Professional curiosity?' the sergeant repeated, with a frown. 'What do you mean by that?'

'When I was a sergeant myself – in the Army of Africa – I, too, manned roadblocks with my lads,' Paco explained. 'But I could never really see the point of them. Nobody I knew could see it either. So if there is a point – and you know what it is – I would be grateful if you could explain it to me.'

The sergeant frowned again. He was well aware that he didn't have to answer questions put to him by an aged civilian, but he was also aware that if he didn't answer this particular question, then his men – who were listening carefully to the conversation – might start to think that this roadblock was equally as pointless as the ones Paco had manned.

'We are here, my men and I,' he said, his chest expanding as he spoke, 'to defend Spain.'

'And am I a threat to Spain?' Paco wondered.

'You might be,' the sergeant said. 'An old man – especially an old man who has served as a sergeant in Morocco – can plant a bomb quite as well as any young man.'

'I am flattered that you think that at my age, I might still be dangerous,' Paco said.

The sergeant smiled indulgently. 'Just tell me why you're going to Val de Montaña, *abuelo*,' he said.

96

'I am going to see my mistress,' Paco replied.

The young conscripts, who were standing just behind the sergeant, began to giggle.

'Your mistress?' the sergeant repeated, incredulously.

'That's right.'

'And how old is this mistress of yours?'

'Sixty-six,' Paco said – and the young conscripts thought this was really hilarious.

'That is very old for a mistress,' the sergeant said

'How old are you?' Paco asked.

'Forty,' the sergeant said – and then looked surprised at himself for answering the question.

'And if you had a mistress who was only thirty, wouldn't you be proud of yourself?' Paco asked.

'Well, yes, I suppose I would,' the sergeant admitted.

'And my mistress is ten years younger than me, so I, too, am proud,' Paco said.

The sergeant grinned. 'All right, it wouldn't do to keep her waiting, so you'd best be on your way.'

As Paco slipped his little car into gear, the conscripts banged on the roof, and one of them shouted, 'Good luck, old man – I hope you can find what you're looking for among all the wrinkles.'

Arrogant little shit, Paco thought, as he pulled away.

The sergeant was laughing along with the rest of the soldiers, but that still did not stop him taking out his notebook and writing down the number of Paco's car.

As the sergeant had pointed out, an old man could plant a bomb as well as a young one, Paco thought, as he left the roadblock behind him, but the soldiers had not checked the boot of the Seat 500 to see if there were explosives in it. And the reason for that, he decided, was that their real purpose in being there had nothing to do with checking on anything.

The roadblock was, in fact, like one of those billboards that were placed at the side of trunk roads. It was an advertisement – and that adver- tisement said, *Don't forget that though the Generalissimo has gone, we are still here, and we are more than ready to crush you if you attempt to step out of line.*

And no doubt there were similar roadblocks all over Spain, he told himself, because the army mistrusted the people quite as much as the people mistrusted the army.

As it started to climb, the Seat 500 found the twisty mountain road harder and harder going, but the little car seemed determined not to give up, and slowly but surely it drew closer to the village of Val de Montaña, where a woman called Elena Vargas Morales had once lived.

On one side of the road there was a sheer drop down into the valley. On the other side there were terraces, cut into the steep slope, on which cherry and almond trees were growing.

It must have been back-breaking work to carve out those terraces, Paco thought – and even main- taining them would be no picnic – but the people who lived in these mountains were as tough as the scrawny goats that they drove from thin pasture to thin pasture, and they took hard work in their stride.

It would not be easy to get the villagers to talk, he reflected. Mountain people had always been suspicious of strangers, and after thirty-six years of being continually punished by the Franco regime for being on the 'wrong' side in the Civil War – as so many other towns and villages in Spain had been – they had closed in on themselves even further.

The little car reached the crest of the road, and Paco could see the village spread out in the small valley ahead.

'Well done, Rocinante,' Paco said, and the engine snorted as if to say it was glad it had not let him down.

There were only two people in the Pig and Whistle Bar of Melly's Hotel and Restaurant. One was Ted Melly himself (who was serving the drinks), and the other was Charlie Woodend (who was sinking them).

'I used to have a couple of barrows on the old Petticoat Lane market in London,' Melly was telling Woodend. 'I'd sell anything. One week it would be crockery, the next one clothes, and the one after that, record players. It all depended what I could get my hands on cheap.'

'It was a good business, was it?' Woodend asked.

'It was a great business, especially if you knew how to cook the books – and I was bloody brilliant at that. In fact, I've been told that they only assigned the smartest tax inspectors to my case, and even then, at least three of them found it so frustrating that they ended up taking sick leave.'

'You do know I'm an ex-bobby, don't you?' Woodend asked, just out of curiosity.

'An ex-what?' Melly asked.

'Copper,' Woodend said, translating from Northern English to London English. 'I'm an ex-copper.'

'Oh yes, I knew that,' Melly said easily. 'I wouldn't be talking to you like this if I didn't.'

'You've lost me,' Woodend confessed.

'Well, when you tell some people you've got something a little bit dodgy in your past, they start looking all superior – like they've never done anything bent in their entire lives,' Melly said. 'Coppers aren't like that. They know nobody's all that squeaky clean. In fact, some of the ones I knew in the East End were so bent themselves that they made your ordinary decent criminals look like Mary Poppins.' He held up his hands in front of him, palms outstretched. 'No offence intended – I'm sure that when you were on the job, you were as straight as they come.'

'I was,' Woodend said.

'But you know what I mean, don't you?'

'Yes,' Woodend agreed. 'I know what you mean.' He looked down at his empty pot. 'I think I'll have another one of those.'

'Coming up,' Melly said, reaching for a fresh glass. 'Anyway, as I was saying, I was making

100

good money on the market, but it was so easy that I was getting bored with the whole thing, so when I got the chance to open a hotel in sunny Spain, I jumped at it.'

'When was this?'

'Back in 1962,' Melly said, sliding a newly filled pint pot in front of Woodend. 'I was what I suppose you might call a bit of a pioneer – and like all pioneers, I had my fair share of frustrations. The Spanish government wanted us to come here, of course. They needed the foreign currency that we were bringing in. But they were damned if – just because we were vital to the economy – they were going to make it easy for us. You just can't imagine the number of forms I had to fill in, and even when I'd done that . . .'

'You used to have a woman called Elena Vargas Morales working for you, didn't you?' Woodend interrupted.

'What makes you ask that?' Melly said, with a new note of suspicion entering his voice.

'It seems that Elena's got into a spot of trouble in England,' Woodend told him.

'Oh, so that's where she was go . . .' Melly began, before he realized his mistake and clamped his mouth shut.

'What was that?' Woodend asked.

'Nothing.'

'Anyway, as I was saying, she's got into this spot of trouble, and as a favour to a mate of mine, who's still on the force, I'm doing a bit of background research on her.'

'Well, you've certainly come to the wrong

place if you're looking for somebody to grass Elena up,' Melly said, backing slightly away from the edge of the bar.

'He's not trying to hurt her, this mate of mine – he wants to help her,' Woodend said. 'And nothing you tell me can possibly do her any harm – you have my word on that.'

Melly hesitated for a moment, then, clearly not wishing to offend his customer by doubting his word, he said, 'I've always liked employing women. They're good workers, and, unlike a lot of the men you hire, they don't spend half their time trying to show they're better at doing the job than you are yourself. But it's through that policy that I hit one of my first problems in this country.'

'Go on,' Woodend said encouragingly.

'Apparently, before the Civil War, women had all kinds of jobs. But after the war, Franco and the church soon put a stop to that. Women couldn't be judges – hell, they couldn't even appear as witnesses in court – they couldn't have high-ranking jobs in the civil service, they couldn't . . . well, you get the picture, don't you?'

'Yes,' Woodend agreed. 'I get the picture.'

'But even at the lower levels, they had a very hard time. If a woman was unmarried, she couldn't take any job at all without first getting her father's permission in writing, and if she was married, that permission had to come from her husband. And there was me, a single man in his late thirties – a bloody foreigner – wanting them to give me the right to have their women in my power for eight hours a day.

102

Well, given the macho Shithead attitude they all have here, they weren't going to stand for that, because even if the husband thought his wife would be safe enough with me, he knew his mates would imagine the worst – and nobody wants his mates laughing at him behind his back.'

'But Elena didn't have a father or a husband – or any close relatives for that matter,' Woodend said.

'Exactly,' Melly agreed, 'so nobody kicked up any sort of fuss when I took her on.'

'What kind of work did she do for you?'

'She started in the kitchen, and, by God, that woman could graft. Once she'd learned the ropes, she was doing the work of two men. And not only that, but she had a thirst for learning. She could hardly speak a word of English when she started here, but after a couple of years, she was good enough to take out of the kitchen and put on Reception. And when I expanded, I made her assistant manager – and she was bloody good at that, as well.'

'When did she leave your employment?'

'About three years ago.'

'And why did she leave?'

'She left because I sacked her,' Melly said, slightly shamefaced. 'I had no choice.'

'But if she was such a good worker . . .'

'A couple of plain-clothed policemen paid me a visit out of the blue one day. They had half a dozen free drinks off me, and when they'd finished, they said they thought they should tell me – as friends of the establishment – that it wasn't good to have a suspected enemy of the state working for me.'

'Was she an enemy of the state?'

'Depends how you look at it. She'd spent some time in prison for political crimes after the Civil War. Also, I think the policemen might have suspected she was a member of the local communist party – and since the party is illegal in Spain, that certainly makes her Franco's enemy.'

'And was she a member?' Woodend asked.

Melly grinned. 'Just between you, me and the gatepost, she wasn't just a member – she was the party secretary.'

'So you sacked her.'

'Like I said, I didn't have any choice in the matter. If I hadn't have sacked her, they'd have found some excuse or other to close me down. But I wouldn't want you to think I just cut her adrift.'

'No?'

'Certainly not! I could never have done that. I pay her a small pension. It's not as much as she'd earn if she was actually working for me – I couldn't afford that – but she gets by.'

'Would this pension of hers be enough to get her to England?' Woodend wondered.

'Er . . . no, I don't think it would,' Melly said evasively.

'So how could she afford it?'

'I don't know,' Melly said – and now the shutters had come down over his eyes.

'I told you she'd had a spot of bother in England,' Woodend said, 'but I'm afraid it's a bit more than that. She was murdered.'

'Oh God, no!' Melly gasped, holding on to the bar for support. 'She can't . . . she just can't . . .'

'If you don't mind me saying so, you seem to be very affected by the news of her death,' Woodend said.

'I . . . I wasn't her lover, or anything like that, you know,' Ted Melly said, as his eyes began to fill with tears. 'I don't think – strictly speaking – we could even have been called friends. But I really admired her, and the truth is, I was very fond of her, as well.'

'And you'd like to see her killer brought to justice?'

'Of course I would.'

'So how did she get the money to travel to England?'

'I gave it to her.'

'Why didn't you say that before?'

'She asked me not to.'

'Did she say why she had to go to England?'

'She didn't even say that it was England she was going to.'

'And yet you were prepared to hand over a wad of money without further explanation? I find that rather unusual.'

'You wouldn't say that if you'd known Elena. She never asked me for anything she hadn't earned. I virtually had to twist her arm to make her accept her pension.' Melly gulped. 'Oh, sweet Jesus!'

'What's the matter?'

'If I'd never given her that money, she couldn't have gone to England and she'd probably still be alive.'

'If you hadn't given her the money, it would have made no difference, because she'd have got it from someone else.'

'Are you sure of that?' Melly asked.

'I'm positive,' Woodend lied.

Because what would have been the point in increasing Melly's sense of guilt, when all he'd tried to do was help?

'Yes, she'd have got it from someone else,' Melly agreed, embracing the lie eagerly. He shook his head slowly from side to side. 'Poor bloody Elena.'

Val de Montaña was typical of the settlements to be found up in the mountains. It consisted of around two hundred houses, a church, a town hall, and a main square. The houses were all three storeys tall – the top two being where the people lived, the bottom one used as a storeroom and stable for the animals in the winter. The church and town hall – two of the pillars of Franco's Spain – were grander than the houses (though not by much) and faced each other across the square.

There was a fountain in the centre of the square, and as Paco parked his little car, an unattended donkey – which had been drinking from the fountain – looked up at him with only mild interest.

Paco got out of the car and headed towards the bar he had spotted at the edge of the square. He always walked with a slight limp, but now – aware that he was being observed – he exaggerated it.

106

The bar itself was much as he had expected it to be. A zinc counter ran along one wall, and behind the counter were two large barrels, one containing cheap red wine, and the other holding cheap white. There were shelves behind the counter, too, and on them sat the packets of cigarettes, tins of sardines, bags of rice and electric batteries, which the bar sold as a sideline. On prominent display between two of the sets of shelves was a large framed photograph of General Franco, bordered with a black ribbon.

The barman was in his late fifties, but his only two customers – who were sitting at a rickety table in the corner – were much, much older than that.

'I'd like a glass of white wine, please,' Paco said, placing a peseta on the counter.

The barman poured the wine, and swept the coin up in his hand, all without saying a word or even really looking at his customer.

Paco sipped his wine, and waited.

He did not have to wait long.

'I noticed you were limping badly when you walked across the square,' one of the old customers said, with mountain-man directness. 'Have you perhaps had an accident?'

'You could call it that, if you wanted to,' Paco replied. 'And no doubt that's what he would call it,' he continued, pointing at the picture of Franco.

'What do you mean by that?'

'You ask a lot of questions for a man who has only come out for a drink,' Paco said.

'You are wrong to see me as no more than an ordinary customer. I own this bar,' the old man said with a hint of pride in his voice. 'And, as the proprietor, I am naturally curious about my customers.'

'There are those who would assume that someone who asks so many questions is probably a government spy,' Paco countered.

'If they did make that assumption, I would take it as an insult,' the old man said hotly.

'And yet you display the picture of the Butcher of Asturias in this bar of yours,' Paco pointed out.

'We are sometimes visited by the Guardia Civil patrol,' the old man explained. 'If we were seen not to be paying respect to our "great fallen leader", I would be in big trouble.'

'I don't see any members of the Guardia Civil here now,' Paco said, looking around him.

'True,' the old man agreed. He turned his gaze on the barman. 'Return the general to his rightful position, Antonio.'

'Are you sure, Don Ramon?' the barman asked.

'I'm sure,' Don Ramon said. 'Our visitor is an honourable man. I would stake my life on it.'

The barman reached up and turned the photograph around, so that now it was facing the wall.

'Come and join us,' Don Ramon said to Paco.

Paco walked over to the table – remembering to exaggerate his limp – and sat down.

'So now that old *hijo de puta* Franco is not watching us, you can perhaps tell us how you hurt your leg,' Don Ramon suggested.

'I worked in the Valley of the Fallen, outside Madrid, building that great one-hundred-and-fifty-metre-high cross which is supposed to commemorate all our war dead, but which we know is only there to honour the dead who followed Franco,' Paco said.

'And what happened?'

Paco shrugged. 'I did not matter – I was a political prisoner, and so expendable. I was sent to work where it was not safe to work, and a block of granite fell on me. I was lucky not to lose the leg.'

He took another sip of wine. That, at least, was true, he thought, though what he intended to follow it with would be a pack of lies.

'Can I ask you a question now?' he said.

'It seems only fair.'

'Did you ever know a woman called Elena Vargas Morales?'

'It is quite a common name,' Don Ramon said, with sudden caution. 'Why would you want to know about her?'

'She had a distant relative living in the United States, who has recently died,' Paco lied.

'Was his name Arturo Sanchez?' Don Ramon asked.

'Yes, as a matter of fact, it was,' Paco replied, deciding to take a gamble.

'I remember the day he left the village,' Don Ramon said. 'It was a fresh spring morning in 1916, and . . .'

'It was spring, all right – but it was 1917,' the other old man, whose name was Don Pedro, interrupted. 'I know that, because it was the same year that Maria Teresa broke her leg during the fiestas.'

Don Ramon glared at him, in the way that a man will glare when he realizes that he himself is wrong, but doesn't want to openly admit it.

'It does not matter when Arturo left,' he said. 'What I want to know is why his death has brought our friend here to the village.'

'Arturo Sanchez left Elena a legacy,' Paco said. 'It was, in fact, quite a large one. I have been instructed to find her – and to make a small payment to anyone who assists me in that task.'

'I can tell you where she is at this very moment,' Don Ramon said, with growing interest.

I strongly suspect you can't, Paco thought, *because if Louisa Paniatowski is right – and Charlie seems convinced she is – then Elena's currently lying on the slab in the Whitebridge mortuary.*

'You can tell me where Elena Vargas Morales is to be found,' he said aloud, 'but as you pointed out yourself, it is a common name. To be sure it is the right Elena Vargas Morales, you must tell me a little of her history.'

'Oh, I can certainly do that,' Don Ramon replied, 'and a harrowing tale you will find it.'

Nine

'Do you think I could see the photographs you took with you to your Auntie Pilar's lunch?' Paniatowski asked her daughter, who was sitting at her desk, engaged in a fight to the death with a quadratic equation.

'Sorry, Mum, didn't hear that,' said Louisa, who was still wondering if multiplying both sides by two had been a good idea.

'The photographs,' Paniatowski repeated. 'The ones you took to Spain. Could I see them?'

'Of course,' Louisa said, slightly mystified. 'But why would you want to see them?'

'Your Uncle Charlie thinks that it might have been something that she saw in one of those photographs which made Doña Elena decide to come to England,' Paniatowski explained.

'So I was right,' Louisa said triumphantly.

'I never doubted you for a second,' Paniatowski replied.

'Mum!' said Louisa, giving her one of those looks that made Paniatowski feel – just for a moment – that their roles had been reversed, and she had not only become the child in the relationship, but a rather errant child.

'All right,' she admitted, 'I wasn't quite convinced you were right at first.'

Louisa grinned. 'It was more than that,' she said. 'You thought that I was being naive and unsophisticated.'

'Aren't naive and unsophisticated just two different ways of saying the same thing?' Paniatowski asked, to buy herself time. Then she smiled, and added, 'You're quite right, I did think that. Can I see the pictures now?'

'Of course,' Louisa said, gratefully pushing the quadratic equation to one side.

It was quite a collection that her daughter had

111

presented her with, Paniatowski thought, flicking through the pictures. There were photographs of the house, of Louisa's school, of Louisa's Uncle Colin and Louisa's friends, but there was nothing there that might have inspired Doña Elena to travel to England.

'And you're sure this is everything you took with you?' she asked, trying to hide her disappointment.

'Yes.'

'You're quite certain there isn't something that you've left out?' Paniatowski persisted.

'Quite certain,' Louisa affirmed. She paused for a moment. 'Well, there's the article from the newspaper,' she added.

'What article from the newspaper?'

'The one from the *Evening Telegraph* all about the Whitebridge Hispanic Circle.'

'And why isn't that here?'

'Because it's not a photograph – and what you asked me for was the photographs I took to Spain,' Louisa said, with maddening logic.

'Where's the article now?' Paniatowski asked.

'It's upstairs, back in my scrapbook,' Louisa said. 'Would you like me to bring it down?'

'Very much,' Paniatowski told her.

'Elena married her childhood sweetheart, but then there is nothing unusual in that, because in a village like this, most people marry their childhood sweethearts,' Don Ramon said.

'That was the way in my village, too,' Paco said.

Don Ramon nodded, and then gave a laugh which sounded like a paper bag being crinkled.

'I thought so,' he said. 'You might wear fine clothes now,' he pointed a gnarled finger at Paco's cheap off-the-peg suit, 'but I had you marked down as a country boy the moment that you walked through the door.'

'Tell me more about Elena,' Paco said.

'Her husband had a very good job. He had learned how to repair tractors, and though there were still not many tractors around, there were not many men who knew how to repair them, either. People would come from miles around to ask him to fix their machines. Even the big landowners would treat him with respect, because of his magic hands.'

'He was a genius with engines,' said Don Pedro. 'He could raise them from the dead.'

'When the war broke out in 'thirty-six, he joined the militia immediately,' Don Ramon continued. 'It was a hard war for him, as it was for everyone. He was wounded twice – once in the chest – but as soon as he had recovered from his injuries, he rejoined his unit.'

'They made him a captain,' Don Pedro said.

'Who is telling this story?' Don Ramon demanded.

'I don't see why it should be you, rather than me, who gets to tell it,' Don Pedro said.

'Then let me ask you another question,' Don Ramon countered. 'Who owns this bar?'

Don Pedro sighed theatrically. 'Tell the story, Ramon,' he said.

'The militias fought bravely and hard, but

Franco had German pilots and Italian soldiers and Moroccan cavalry, and he was bound to win in the end. And when it was over, Elena's husband – and all the other men who had survived – came back to the village.' He paused for a moment, and looked Paco straight in the eye. 'And do you know why they did that?' he asked, challengingly.

Paco shrugged. 'Where else were they supposed to go?' he said.

'Exactly, country boy,' Don Ramon agreed. 'Where else were they supposed to go?'

'And why would they even want to go anywhere else?' Don Pedro asked. 'This village has everything a man could possibly need.'

'There are times when you almost seem to be talking sense – and this is one of them,' Don Ramon told his old friend. He turned to Paco. 'The village is not perfect, and only a fool would say it was – but it is better than everywhere else.'

'Tell me the rest of the story,' Paco prompted.

'I have forgotten where I was,' Don Ramon admitted.

'The men came back to the village after the war . . .'

'Ah, yes, and eventually, Franco's soldiers came to the village, too. They were led by a lieutenant, and he was the biggest *hijo de puta* within a hundred kilometres of here. The soldiers immediately rounded up all the younger men, and locked them in one of the bigger barns.'

'Did they arrest you, too?' Paco asked.

'They did not,' Don Pedro said, perhaps a little sadly. 'We were too old for war, even then.'

114

'The lieutenant said each of those arrested would be questioned in turn,' Don Ramon said. 'The ones who could convince him they had not fought for the Republic would be released. Those who had fought for it would either be shot or sent to Alicante to stand trial.'

Paco nodded. 'That didn't just happen here,' he said. 'It was going on all over Spain. It was called Pacification.'

'But that wasn't the main reason that the lieutenant was here,' Don Pedro said. 'He had come for the gold.'

'There was no gold,' Don Ramon said dismissively. 'That was nothing but a fable.'

'Fable or not, the lieutenant believed in it,' Don Pedro said, sticking to his guns.

'Yes,' Don Ramon agreed. 'He did.'

'Where was this gold supposed to have come from?' Paco asked.

'At the start of the war, the government sold a quarter of its gold reserves in France, and sent the rest to Moscow for safe-keeping,' Don Ramon said.

'I know that,' Paco said.

'But what you probably don't know is that – according to the rumours – a few dozen bars of gold were held back, and were given to trusted militiamen, so that they would be able to raise money to carry on fighting even after the Republic was forced to surrender. And Elena's husband was said to be one of those militiamen. As I told you, it is no more than a fable, but Pedro is right when he says that the lieutenant believed it.'

'So they locked all the men in a barn,' Paco said, steering them back on to the story.

'They did, and the lieutenant set up his headquarters in what had once been the priest's house, and so was, of course, the best house in the village. And once he had done that, he began to look around the village for some entertainment, and his eyes rested on Elena.'

'She was a pretty young thing,' Don Pedro said wistfully.

'He said if she would sleep with him, he would see that she was given extra rations – and she spat in his face,' Don Ramon said.

'It's true! I saw it with my own eyes,' Don Pedro said, and chuckled.

'It was a foolish thing to do,' Don Ramon said harshly.

Don Pedro bent his head. 'Yes,' he agreed, 'it was.'

'And what was worse than the spitting – much worse for Javier – was what she said to him,' Don Ramon continued.

'What did she say?' Paco asked.

'She said that her husband had been a captain in the people's militia, and that the lieutenant was not fit to lick his boots. It was a foolish thing to do, but she was very angry, and so perhaps it would be wrong to blame her.'

'But before she said it, the lieutenant had not known that her husband had been a captain!' Paco exclaimed.

'Just so. The lieutenant had Elena arrested and taken to the priest's house, where he raped her. And when he had finished raping her, he told her that she would be sent to prison for a long time, and that her son – little Roberto – would become a ward of the state until more suitable parents could be found for him.'

'That happened a lot, too,' Paco said. 'Many Republicans had their children taken from them and given to childless Nationalists.'

'He had the child taken to the priest's house, and Elena locked up in one of the barns,' Dom Ramon said. 'And then he sent his men to fetch Javier, Elena's husband.'

'He probably intended to use the child to put pressure on the father,' Paco said.

'Yes, that is the sort of thing they did,' Don Ramon agreed. 'The lieutenant only had two of his soldiers with him in the priest's house. I suspect that was because he did not want too many witnesses around when he discovered where the gold was hidden. But three men are more than enough to control one prisoner – or so they thought.'

'Or so they thought?' Paco repeated.

'Bastards like that lieutenant like to do their torturing in the dead of night, and it was just after dark that Javier was taken to the priest's house,' Don Ramon said.

'And it was just after midnight that the fire started,' Don Pedro added.

'We do not know when the fire was started – only when it was noticed,' Don Ramon said witheringly. 'We became aware of the fire just after midnight,' he continued, as if Don Pedro had not already provided this information. 'We tried to get inside – we knew little Roberto was there – but the fire had taken a real hold by then and we were forced back. Fortunately, there was no danger of any of the other houses catching alight – the priest did not want to have to rub shoulders with the likes of us, and so his house stood some distance away from the rest – but it broke our hearts that we could not save the child. When morning came, we raked through the hot ashes, and found the bodies of the lieutenant and his two bodyguards.'

'But you did not find Roberto's body?' Paco asked.

'We did not. Nor did we find Javier's. And so, of course, we knew what must have happened – Javier had found a way to overpower his enemies, and had escaped with his son.'

'The soldiers went mad – they acted as if it was all Elena's fault,' Don Pedro said.

'Yes, they did,' Don Ramon agreed. 'They beat her very badly – she almost died – and then they sent her on the back of an open wagon to the prison in Alicante. It was ten years before we saw her again, and though she was only thirty-two, she looked like an old woman.'

'She came back to the village, did she?'

'Yes, but only because she wanted to know how many of us had survived. She was still a big-hearted woman, you see, even after everything she'd had to endure. We begged her to stay. We told her that she never needed to work again – that, as little as we had, we would support her for as long as she lived.'

'But she wouldn't stay?'

'No. Perhaps she was too proud to accept our

118

charity, or too ashamed that she had been raped. Whichever it was, she was wrong. It was not charity we were offering, and all the shame belonged to the lieutenant. But she would not stay. She moved to Calpe, where, we have heard, she works in a hotel. We have not seen her ourselves for twenty-five years.'

'But one day – and that day may soon be here, now that Franco is dead – this village will put up a monument to Elena and her husband,' Don Pedro said.

'It will,' Don Ramon agreed. 'We have been planning it for years, and we know exactly what it will be like.'

'And what will it be like?' asked Paco, because he knew that was what was expected of him.

'It will be a simple stone tablet,' Don Ramon told him, 'and it will say, "This tablet stands as a monument to the two heroes of Val de Montaña – Elena Vargas Morales and Javier Martinez Blanco".'

The short article on Whitebridge Hispanic Circle was dominated by a large photograph, and the caption underneath it read: *The picture shows Mr Robert Martinez, the president of the Hispanic Circle, Mr Javier Martinez, his father, and Miss Louisa Paniatowski, the junior secretary.*

'Don't all Spaniards have two surnames?' Paniatowski asked.

'Yes, they do,' Louisa agreed.

'So what's Mr Javier Martinez's second surname?' Paniatowski said, opening her notebook, and skimming through the information that Woodend had given her over the phone.

'I don't know,' Louisa admitted.

'But after all the time you've spent with Mr Robert Martinez, you surely know his second surname, don't you?'

'Yes.'

'Well, then, silly, his father will have the same name, won't he?'

'No,' Louisa said. 'He won't.'

'Why not?'

'Because Spaniards take one of their surnames from their mother, and the other one from their father, so Mr Robert is called Martinez after his dad, and Vargas after his mother – which is why he's Robert Martinez Vargas.'

Paniatowski glanced down at her notes again.

'Well, I'll be buggered!' she said.

'You shouldn't be swearing, Mum!' Louisa said, with mild disapproval. 'You should be setting a proper example for your impressionable daughter.'

'Who would have bloody thought it?' Paniatowski asked, reading the notes for a second time.

'It cannot be my wife,' Javier Martinez muttered, as Paniatowski led him into the mortuary. 'The fascists will have killed her as soon as they realized I had escaped.' He turned to his son, who was walking beside him. 'Tell them, Roberto. Tell them it cannot be her.'

'We'll have to wait and see, Father,' Robert Martinez said softly.

'And even if – by some miracle – she had

120

survived, why would she come to England now, after all this time?' Javier Martinez moaned.

Dr Shastri was waiting for them in the viewing room. 'When the curtain is drawn back, you will see the body of a woman in the next room,' she said to Javier Martinez. 'Once you have seen enough, tell me, and the curtain will be closed again. Are you ready?'

Javier Martinez took a deep breath and straightened his shoulders.

'No!' he said.

'You will have to look at her sooner or later, Father,' Robert told him. 'It's your duty.'

'Do not try to lecture me on what is or is not my duty,' Javier Martinez said. 'I did not say that I would not look at her – I only meant that I will not look at her through a window.'

'People often find it more of a strain to be close to the body than they ever imagined it would be, Mr Martinez,' Dr Shastri said, in a soothing tone. 'Perhaps the best idea might be for you to look through the window first, and then if you decide that you want to . . .'

'I am no stranger to death,' Javier Martinez said. 'I was a militia man, fighting an enemy which had no heart – an enemy which had no pity. I have seen dead women before. I have seen dead children, too – many, tiny, dead children.'

'That was a long time ago, when you were a much younger man,' Robert Martinez said.

'A long time ago?' Javier Martinez repeated incredulously. 'Do you think all that is behind me now? Do you think I don't still see them?'

'Of course I don't think that,' Robert replied. 'And that is why you should just look through the window.'

'I know it will not be her,' Javier Martinez said. 'But if I look through a pane of glass and say that, the police will not believe me. I need to be close enough to touch her, and then perhaps they will accept that I know my own wife, and that this woman is not her.'

'We won't let you do it, Father,' Robert Martinez said, turning to Shastri for support.

'It must be your father's decision,' the doctor said.

'Then let us get this pantomime over with, so we can all go home,' Javier Martinez said.

The cadaver was lying on a trolley, covered with a white sheet, and when Shastri gave the signal, her young assistant folded back the sheet just far enough to reveal the dead woman's face.

'It's not her,' Javier Martinez said. 'I told you right from the start that it wasn't her.'

'If you could just take a second look, just to make absolutely sure,' Shastri suggested.

'There's no need,' Javier Martinez said angrily. 'I have already told you that it is not her.'

There was no point in pressing him any further, Dr Shastri decided. She gave the briefest of nods to her assistant, and the assistant folded the sheet back over the face.

They were almost at the door when Javier Martinez stopped and turned around.

'I . . . I will take one more look,' he said, with a catch in his throat.

He reached into his inside pocket, and took out his wallet. With trembling hands, he opened the wallet and took out a sepia photograph, and when the sheet was folded back again, he held the photograph next to the dead woman's head.

'It's her,' he sobbed. 'It's my Elena.'

Ten

It was incredible the change that had come over Javier Martinez in the hour since he had identified the body, Paniatowski thought.

He had entered the mortuary a worried man – though still a vigorous one – but the sight of his wife lying there seemed to have drained all energy from him. Now, back in his own home – and sitting in an armchair which looked as if it had been bought to accommodate someone much bigger – there was an almost ghostlike quality about him.

'My comrades and I fought long and hard against the fascists, but in the end, we lost,' he said in a thin voice, 'I went back to my village – which was called Val de Montaña. I had given up all my hopes of seeing a fairer society in which the poor no longer went to bed hungry. All I wanted . . .' He began to cough violently, and for well over a minute he could not speak. 'All I wanted,' he continued with some effort, 'was to survive long enough to see my son grow up.'

'Perhaps we should leave this until the morning, Father,' Robert Martinez said.

'I may be dead in the morning, and then my story will never be told,' Javier Martinez said. He looked across at Paniatowski. 'You want to hear it, don't you, Chief Inspector?'

'Yes, I do,' Paniatowski agreed. 'But if you start finding it too much of a strain . . .'

'When the fascists came to the village, I denied I had ever been a militiaman,' Javier Martinez interrupted her. 'I was not alone in that. Every man there denied he had been in the militia. We knew, even as we were telling those lies, that they would shoot some of us as a matter of course, but we also knew that they could not shoot us all, because now that the war was over, they would need people to work the land – and each of us prayed that we would be one of the lucky ones who was spared. It was a cowardly thing to do, to pray for the death of someone else, so that you might live yourself, but . . .'

'It wasn't cowardly at all, Father,' Robert Martinez said sympathetically. 'In your situation, any man would have thought the same.'

'You were not a man in the village at that time, so you cannot possibly know,' Javier said harshly.

'The soldiers locked you all up in one of the village barns, didn't they?' Paniatowski said.

'How did you know that?' Javier Martinez asked, suspiciously.

'I asked a Spanish friend of mine to talk to some of the old men who still live in the village.'

'Is he a fascist, this friend of yours who went to the village?' Javier Martinez demanded.

'No,' Paniatowski assured him. 'He fought on the Republican side for the whole of the war.'

Javier Martinez gave a slight nod. 'Then he is a man of honour, and the villagers will have told him the truth,' he said. 'You are right, they locked us in the barn, but just after dark, two soldiers came and took me to the priest's house. That was where I met the lieutenant. He was in the priest's library, and he had a pistol held in his hand. I thought he might shoot me, then and there, but he merely pointed the pistol at me and told the two soldiers to go downstairs.'

'Are you sure that you're strong enough for this, Father?' Robert Martinez asked.

'I'm strong enough,' the old man said, and he did sound stronger – almost as if he were drawing some strength from the memory of the man he used to be. 'This lieutenant said that he knew who I was, because my wife had informed on me. I told him I did not believe it – that I knew my wife would never betray me. But he said it was quite true. He said she went to see him, and offered to sleep with him if he would give her extra rations, and that he turned her down. I did not believe that either. I think that he was the one who offered the rations. He said that she spat on him, and screamed that her husband was a captain in the militia. And that I did believe – because Elena always had a fiery temper.'

'You were right to have faith in your wife,' Paniatowski said. 'Half an hour ago I was talking to my friend who went to the village, and he told me that what you thought happened was exactly what did happen.'

'The lieutenant said that he had had her locked up for daring to insult him, and that he hadn't yet decided whether to have her shot or not. And then he asked me to tell him about the gold . . .' The old man paused. 'Do you know all about the gold, too, Chief Inspector?'

'Yes, I know about the gold.'

'He said I could buy my freedom – and that of my wife and child – if I could lead him to the gold.'

'He was lying, of course,' Paniatowski said.

'Naturally he was lying,' Javier Martinez agreed. 'If there had been any gold, and I'd told him where it was, he would have shot me immediately, and if I had told him there was none, he would have got his men to shoot me. So I played for time. I said there was gold – ten bars of it – and that it was hidden in that very room, behind the bookcase. I have never seen a man lose control of himself so quickly. He laid the pistol he had been pointing at me on the desk, and rushed over to the bookcases, and began pulling them away from the wall. If my hands had been tied behind my back, there would have been nothing I could have done to take advantage of the situation. But they weren't – they were tied in front of me – and while he was pulling the bookcase away, I grabbed the big crucifix which was hanging on the wall, and struck him on the back of the head with it.'

'Did the blow kill him?'

'No, but it knocked him unconscious. The two soldiers who were down below had heard the sound of the bookcase falling, and were running up the stairs. I picked up the lieutenant's pistol from the desk, and when they came through the door, I shot them both dead.'

'Did anyone outside hear the shots?'

'No, the house had very thick walls, and anyway, all the other soldiers were billeted near the barn in which we were being held prisoner.'

'What did you do next?'

'I found a knife in the kitchen, and cut through my bonds. I had decided that I would find out where Elena was being held, and do all I could to free her, even if it cost me my own life. And that was when I heard a baby crying.'

'Your son?'

'My little Roberto. I found him in one of the bedrooms. And I knew, at that moment, that I had to choose between saving my wife and saving my son, because I could not do both. I chose my son.'

'Did you kill the lieutenant before you left?' Paniatowski asked.

'No.'

'Why not?'

'Because he was still lying unconscious where he had fallen – and I could not bring myself to kill an unconscious man, however wicked he had been. It was a matter of honour.'

You might have killed him if you'd known he'd raped your wife, Paniatowski thought.

'He died anyway – in the fire,' she said aloud.

'What fire?' Javier Martinez asked.

'You didn't set the house alight before you left?'

'No.'

'Then why did it burn down?'

Javier Martinez gave a weak shrug. 'Maybe the fire had been started during the struggle – the house was lit by oil lamps, we did not have electricity in the village, not even the priest – but only really caught after Roberto and I had left. I wasn't there, so I cannot say.'

'What did you do after you left the village?'

'We made the long and terrible journey north. We lived off roots that even the pigs would have rejected.' Javier Martinez turned to his son. 'I am thankful that you were too young to remember it.'

'Perhaps I do remember it – or at least, a part of it,' Robert Martinez said. 'Sometimes in the middle of the night, when I'm not quite asleep, I feel a terrible coldness coming over me, and suddenly everything around me seems to have become perfectly white.'

The old man nodded. 'You are remembering crossing the Pyrenees, which was the worst part of it all,' he said. 'But we survived, and we got to France. There were some kind people on the other side of the mountains, and they cared for us until we had regained our strength. I wanted to stay with them, but they said that if Hitler invaded – and they feared that he might – we would be sent back to Spain. They gave me a little money, and Roberto and I came to England. And that is the end of our story.'

'You never tried to contact your wife?' Paniatowski asked.

'No, I did not.'

'Why not?'

'I believed that she was probably dead. And if she was not dead – if she had somehow managed to survive – I would only have been putting her life in danger by trying to get in touch with her.'

'The retribution went on long after the war ended,' Robert Martinez explained. 'People were executed just for having been friendly with someone else who had been executed. If my mother had received a letter from England – written by a known rebel – it would have been as good as a death warrant.'

'And perhaps,' Javier Martinez said, with a tremble in his voice, 'perhaps I did not want to get in touch with her. Perhaps there was a part of me that began to feel that the lieutenant had been right, after all, and she had betrayed the family.'

'In what way did you feel she'd betrayed the family, Don Javier?' Paniatowski asked.

'This part of me kept whispering Elena's first duty was to protect little Roberto – that she should have undergone any indignity that the lieutenant chose to inflict on her, as long as it meant she could keep her baby by her side. But she chose instead to make the grand gesture, and if I had not rescued Roberto, who knows where he might have been now?' The old man bowed his head. 'That is what part of me said, but it was the unworthy part of me. It was Elena's spirit that I fell in love with – the spirit which made her the woman she was. And I can no more blame her for spitting in that *hijo de puta*'s face than I can blame myself for leaving my family in the village and going off to fight the fascists.'

'Father . . .' Robert Martinez said with growing concern.

'When I looked down at that body in your mortuary – when I finally really looked – I did not see an old woman who bore all the scars of the life she had led,' Javier Martinez said fiercely. 'I saw a young woman – a beautiful, wonderful young woman – and my heart was broken all over again.'

Paniatowski stood up.

'I'd better go,' she said. 'I want to thank you, Sr Martinez, for telling me your story. I know it can't have been easy.'

But the old man had a glazed look in his eyes – as if he were no longer in his living room in Whitebridge, but back in Val de Montaña – and he didn't even seem to realize she'd spoken.

'I'll see you to the door, Monika,' Robert Martinez said, standing up.

Paniatowski followed him into the hallway. 'You can get grief counselling for your father, you know,' she said. 'I have some telephone numbers, if you'd like me to give them to you.'

'And what about counselling for me?' Robert Martinez said.

He sounded angry, she thought. And then she realized that it wasn't anger she was hearing.

'You're crying!' she said.

'Yes, I'm crying,' he admitted. 'I'm a grown man – and I'm crying. Isn't that the stupidest thing you've ever heard?'

'No, of course not,' Paniatowski said

130

soothingly. 'You don't like to see your father so upset . . .'

'It's not my father I'm crying for – I'm crying for myself,' Robert Martinez said.

And now there *was* anger in his voice, though whether that anger was directed at her for failing to understand, or at himself for seeming so weak, she wasn't quite sure.

'I . . . I haven't seen my mother since I was a baby,' Robert said. 'I thought I had no real memory of her at all. Yet tonight, looking down on her cold, stiff body, I realized that I had always loved her. And now she's gone forever. Now she's never coming back.'

Paniatowski put her hands on his shoulders to console him, and suddenly they were kissing.

This was insane, she told herself – yet she did not want to let go.

The kiss continued, and it felt wonderful and natural – as if it had always been meant to be.

Someone outside rang the doorbell, and as the chimes reverberated down the hall, she forced herself to break away from him.

'I'm sorry,' she said.

'It's as much my fault as it is yours,' Robert Martinez said.

The doorbell rang again, more insistently this time.

'It won't happen again,' Monika told Martinez. 'I promise it will never happen again.'

'But I want it to happen again,' Robert said. 'I so desperately want it to happen again.'

'For God's sake, you're part of my investigation,' Paniatowski told him.

'But once the investigation's over . . .' he said hopefully.

The doorbell rang for a third time.

'Who is it?' Robert Martinez called out.

'Courier service,' said a voice from the other side of the door.

'It'll be my House of Commons mail,' Martinez told Paniatowski. 'When I'm away from London for any length of time, I always have it couriered up. It won't take a minute for me to sign for it, and then we can . . .'

'I have to go,' Paniatowski said.

'But there's so much we have to say to each other. Just give me another five minutes,' Robert pleaded.

'I can't,' Paniatowski told him.

She reached for the latch, and flung the door open. The courier, surprised by the sudden violence of the move, instinctively sidestepped, and thus avoided her crashing into him.

Paniatowski strode quickly down the path. By the time she reached her car, she had calmed down a little.

She had been saved by the bell, she thought – by God, she had.

The closer she got to home, the more appealing the idea of a bath seemed to Paniatowski.

She would surrender completely to the warm, soothing water, she promised herself, and for the first few minutes, she would think about nothing at all. Then, when her body had relaxed a little – when her muscles had started to feel a little less knotted – she would turn her mind to what had happened in the Martinezes' hallway, and see if there was anything she could rescue from the wreckage.

She realized the plan was a non-starter as soon as she opened her front door, and saw Louisa standing there expectantly.

'Was it her, Mum?' Louisa demanded excitedly.

'Yes, it was her,' Paniatowski confirmed.

'Brilliant!' Louisa said.

'It's not brilliant at all,' Paniatowski said severely, as she took off her coat. 'A woman has died, you know.'

'That's true,' Louisa agreed, only slightly subdued. 'It's not brilliant that a woman has died, and it's not brilliant that the dead woman has turned out to be Doña Elena – but you have to admit that it is brilliant that I was right.'

'Don't you feel even a little bit of pity for her?' Paniatowski asked, a little worriedly.

'I only saw her that once, at Tía Pilar's house,' Louisa replied. 'I never even talked to her. Besides, don't you always say that you shouldn't let your emotions get in the way of an investigation – that if you stop being completely objective, then you're not doing your job properly?'

Yes, she did say that, Paniatowski agreed silently. It was a rule she had learned from Charlie Woodend – though neither of them had ever been particularly good at applying it.

'I do feel sorry for Don Roberto, though,' Louisa continued, as they entered the lounge.

'Really?' Paniatowski asked, as they sat down.

133

'I would have thought that the person you should really feel sorry for is Mr Martinez senior, who's just found out that his wife is dead.'

Now what made me say that? she wondered.

Was it because she didn't want Louisa to know how upset Robert had been? Was she protecting him?

'It's true Don Javier's just lost his wife, but Don Roberto's just lost his mother,' Louisa countered. 'That can't have been easy for him, even though he hasn't seen her for all those years. Anyway, Don Roberto's bound to feel it more, because he's very sensitive, whereas his dad's a bit of a cold fish.'

She would have agreed with her daughter's assessment of Javier Martinez earlier in the day, Paniatowski thought, but a lot had happened since then. She had seen him in the mortuary, and she had listened to him tell his tale when he got back home, and now she looked at him in quite a different light.

On the other hand, she had to admit that Louisa was spot on with what she'd said about Robert.

'Do you like Don Roberto, Mum?' Louisa asked.

Christ, can even my daughter read my mind now? Paniatowski wondered.

'He's all right,' she said, non-committally.

'I think when this case of your is over, we should see more of him,' Louisa said.

Had Louisa got a crush on him? Had she actually got a crush on Robert Martinez?

'I think seeing more of him might be rather

difficult,' Paniatowski said. 'In case you've forgotten, Mr Martinez is a member of parliament, so he's a very busy man. And we're both busy, too – especially you. You've got your exams in eight months, and though that might seem a long way away now, it'll be here sooner than you realize.'

'I'm sure Don Roberto gets some free time, even if he is an MP,' Louisa said, 'and if I was too busy with all my school work, you could always see him on your own.'

Not a crush then – an attempt at matchmaking!

'Do you resent the fact that there's not a man around the house?' Paniatowski asked.

'No,' Louisa said.

'Good!'

'But I think that you do.'

'That's ridiculous,' Paniatowski told her daughter.

'How many dates have you been on in the last few years, Mum?' Louisa asked.

'Plenty,' Paniatowski said defensively.

'Hardly any at all,' Louisa said. 'And a woman of your age still has her biological needs, you know.'

'If you don't mind, I'd rather we didn't discuss my "biological needs",' Paniatowski replied.

'Please yourself, but they won't go away, you know,' Louisa told her. 'Or rather, they will go away, which is why you should take full advantage of them while they're still there.' And then suddenly her face changed, and she was little Louisa again. 'I used to hope that you and Uncle Colin would get married eventually,' she

135

continued, 'but now he's decided to play the field as far as girlfriends go, there's not much chance of that.'

'First of all, there was never any chance of me marrying Colin,' Paniatowski said. 'He's my best friend, and I'm very fond of him, but I've never been attracted to him in that way.'

'Sexually,' Louisa said, once more the almost-grown-up.

'Sexually, if you like,' Paniatowski agreed. 'And secondly, there's no law that says you have to have a man, you know.'

'I won't always be here to keep you company,' Louisa said. 'I might not even be living in the same country as you. You'll soon start to feel the need for a companion once I've gone.'

'If I do, then I'll get myself a cat,' Paniatowski snapped.

'You do fancy Don Roberto, Mum,' Louisa said seriously. 'I can tell that by the way your face changes when I mention his name.'

Oh yes, I fancy him, all right, Paniatowski thought.

'You're treading on dangerous ground, Louisa,' she said, smiling to show that her daughter shouldn't be too concerned.

'Am I?' Louisa asked.

'Very dangerous ground – because if you think it's all right to meddle in my love life . . .'

'You haven't got one, Mum. That's the whole point.'

'. . . what's to stop me thinking that I've got the right to meddle in yours, when you finally start going out with boys?'

Louisa looked shocked. 'You wouldn't really do that, would you, Mum?' she asked.

'I might,' Paniatowski replied, 'if only so that you'd know just what it felt like.'

'I promise never to mention Don Roberto again,' Louisa said.

'Very sensible of you,' Paniatowski agreed.

Eleven

The team had arranged to meet in the public bar of the Drum and Monkey at ten o'clock, and it was quarter past ten by the time Paniatowski had reached the end of her briefing.

'So this is the sequence of events,' she said, summing up. 'They've eaten the paella. Everybody at the table is looking at the pictures Louisa took with her to Spain, and when they eventually reach Elena Vargas, she finds herself gazing down at a newspaper photograph of a husband she probably thought was long dead. And not only that, but standing beside her husband is another man who she doesn't recognize – after all, she's not seen him since he was a baby – but who has her son's name. There's no wonder she went into shock, is there?'

'But why did she decide to run the risk of coming to England on a false passport?' Beresford asked. 'Why didn't she just write to them?'

'Travelling on a false passport wasn't much of a risk at all, because, according to Charlie

137

Woodend, the communist party have got pretty adept at forging,' Paniatowski said. 'And if she'd written a letter, there's a good chance that it would never have got through. Franco may be dead but, so far, nothing much seems to have changed, and there's still strict censorship in Spain.'

'And if the censor happened to see that she was writing to a man who is – presumably – still wanted for the murder of an officer and two soldiers, she'd be in deep trouble,' Meadows added.

'But I don't think that was her main consideration,' Paniatowski said. 'In fact, I don't think the decision to come to England was logical at all. She was acting on pure instinct. It's been thirty-six years since she's seen her husband and her son.' She paused. 'Just think about that. None of you had even been born the last time she held her baby.'

'Jesus!' Beresford said.

'Exactly,' Paniatowski agreed. 'And then she suddenly finds out not only that they're both still alive, but where they're actually living. And what's her first thought? That she wants to see them as soon as possible!'

'I think I can see why she didn't write from Spain,' Beresford said. 'What I don't understand is why she didn't call them once she'd arrived in England.'

Kate Meadows gave an audible sigh.

'Am I being particularly thick again, Sergeant Meadows?' Beresford demanded.

'No, sir – not thick, exactly.'

'Then what?'

'Perhaps just a little unimaginative.'

'Then why don't you explain to me where you think my reasoning is going wrong?' Beresford suggested.

'It wasn't just that she thought they were probably dead, they probably thought she was, too,' Meadows said.

'That's true,' Paniatowski agreed. 'Right up until the point that he identified the body, Javier Martinez was insisting that the chances were that she'd been killed a long time ago.'

'So the last thing she wants is to ring him up and baldly announce to her husband that she's alive,' Meadows said. 'What she does want to do is to break it to him as gently as she can, to look into his eyes as she's telling him, and then to hug him to her.'

'But she never made it,' said Crane sombrely.

'Which means that she must have been killed soon after she arrived in Whitebridge, and before she had a chance to pay her husband a call,' Paniatowski said. 'Do we think the killer was local or an outsider?'

'An outsider,' Beresford said firmly. 'My lads have spent all afternoon checking the Spaniards on the list that Robert Martinez gave us. None of them come from the same part of the east coast of Spain as Elena and her family. Besides, as far as we know, nobody in Whitebridge had any idea she was coming.'

'So she was followed here?' Paniatowski asked.

'She must have been.'

'In which case, why didn't the murderer kill her before she ever got to Whitebridge?'

'He may not have had the opportunity.'

'What about motive?'

'I think it might have been political,' Crane said. 'I've been reading the papers to find out exactly what's happening in Spain.'

'That'd be the highbrow papers, would it?' asked Beresford, with just a little inverted snobbery. 'The *Guardian* and *The Times*?'

'That's right,' Crane agreed. 'And also the *Telegraph*, the *Economist* and the *Washington Post*. What they all seem to be saying is that now Franco's dead, a lot of the right-wingers are in a state of near-panic. So maybe they've decided to kill off a few of their enemies, before those enemies have a chance to turn on them.'

'But surely Elena was only small fry,' Paniatowski said.

'Get enough small fry together, and they start to become a significant force,' Crane argued.

'Even so, just killing one old woman's not going to change a lot,' Beresford said.

'How do we know they have only killed one old woman?' Crane asked. 'How do we know there haven't been a string of murders of communist party officials, all over Spain?'

'If there had been, we'd have heard about . . .' Paniatowski began. 'No,' she corrected herself, 'we wouldn't have heard, because of the censorship.'

'I don't think it's about politics at all,' Meadows said. 'I think it's about the gold.'

'There is no gold,' Paniatowski said. 'Javier

140

Martinez told me that himself – and if anybody should know, he should.'

'There doesn't *have to* be any gold,' Meadows said. 'All that matters is that there are people who *think* there is.'

'Let's hear your theory,' Paniatowski said.

'There are certain people in Spain who've heard the story about the gold, and who know that Javier was the man who was supposed to have it,' Meadows said. 'They also know that Elena is his wife, and when they get to hear she's coming to England, they assume it's to join him, and they see that as a good way to track him down.'

'There was no need to track him down,' Beresford said. 'He's been living quite openly, under his real name, for the last thirty-six years, and if they'd bothered to check, they'd soon have found that out for themselves.'

'Yes, but they wouldn't have bothered to check – because if he'd had the gold, as they thought he did, they'd assume he'd have changed his name,' Meadows said.

'If they were that keen to get their hands on the gold, wouldn't they have checked anyway, just to be sure?' Paniatowski wondered.

'I'm not saying they've been obsessing about it for the last thirty-six years,' Meadows said. 'It's more the kind of thing they might have talked about when they'd had a few drinks. One of them might say, "If only we knew what Javier Martinez had done with the gold." And another would reply, "Yes, if we could get our hands on that, we'd be sitting pretty." Then they forget about it until the next time they get drunk. But when they hear that Elena is coming to England, the little game they've been playing suddenly becomes more serious.'

'So they follow her from Spain, because they want to find Javier, and once she's reached Whitebridge, they kill her?' Paniatowski asked. 'Why would they do that?'

'Perhaps she saw them following her,' Meadows suggested. 'Or perhaps they just wanted her out of the way, because they knew they needed time to watch Javier and work out where he might have hidden the gold. Whatever the reason, they didn't want her to be found, because that would have tipped Javier off – which is why they dropped the body in the canal.'

'What you're all overlooking is that it may have nothing to do with politics or money at all – that it's all to do with revenge,' Beresford said. 'We know that Javier killed at least three people . . .'

'He didn't kill the lieutenant,' Paniatowski pointed out.

'No, but the lieutenant wouldn't have died in a burning building if Javier hadn't knocked him out,' Beresford said.

'Fair enough,' Paniatowski agreed.

'We know he killed at least three people, and he probably killed a lot more, and maybe one of their friends or relatives wanted to pay him back.'

'So, essentially, your theory is like Kate's, except that it's revenge, not gold, that's the motive,' Paniatowski said.

'I suppose so,' Beresford agreed.

142

'And they killed Elena in case she warned him?'

'Yes.'

'I'm not saying that any of your theories is definitely right,' Paniatowski said, 'but if there's even a glimmer of truth in even one of them, Javier Martinez's life is in danger. So as soon as we've finished up here, Colin, I want you to get on to HQ and make sure there are regular patrols going past his house.'

'Right,' Beresford said. 'And would you like me to inform Javier Martinez himself?'

'No, I'll do that,' Paniatowski said.

And she found herself thinking, *Why did I say that? Am I just looking for an excuse to talk to Robert Martinez again?*

'So what's our next move?' Beresford asked.

'We need to trace Elena's movements from the second she first set foot in Britain,' Paniatowski said. 'That means, for a start, checking all the seaports and airports.'

'It's a big job,' Beresford said.

'Yes, it is,' Paniatowski agreed, 'but the more accurate a picture we build up of her journey here, the more likely it is that we'll be able to establish if she was being followed – and if she was, who was following her.'

'The problem is, the time she spent in Britain is only the end of the trail,' Meadows said. 'If the motive for the murder has its origins in Spain, then Spain should be the focus of the investigation, and since we can't investigate in Spain . . .'

'We can't,' Paniatowski said, reluctantly giving in to the inevitable, 'but Charlie Woodend can.'

* * *

143

It was nearly a quarter to twelve when Paniatowski finally got home again, and as she stepped into the hallway, she wondered if it was now a little too late to ring Javier Martinez.

No, of course it wouldn't be too late. No man minds being disturbed if it's to be told that his life is in danger. Besides, after the traumatic evening he'd had, he was unlikely to be asleep yet.

She reached for the phone and dialled the number. She could hear it ringing at the other end, but no one was picking it up. A couple of minutes passed with no reply, and she was on the point of hanging up when she heard a voice say, 'Robert Martinez. Who's calling please?'

'It's Monika,' she said, then added quickly, 'I mean, DCI Paniatowski. I'm sorry if I woke you.'

'You didn't wake me – I've only just got in,' Martinez said. And then, as if he considered further explanation necessary, he added, 'I've been out walking. I needed to think about what happened earlier.'

We both needed to think about that, Paniatowski told herself.

But aloud, she said, 'I'm actually calling on official police business, Mr Martinez.'

'Of course,' Martinez mumbled. 'I'm sorry. What can I do for you, Chief Inspector?'

'I'd like to talk to your father,' Paniatowski said. 'Do you think he'll still be awake?'

'I should think so,' Robert Martinez said. 'I tried to get him to take some sleeping pills earlier, but he refused. I asked him if he wanted me to sit with him, and he said he didn't. He said he needed some time to meditate on his life. I left him in his bedroom – staring at the wall – and went out to do a bit of meditating of my own.'

'Does he have a phone in his bedroom?'

'No, he's very old-fashioned in that way. He says one phone in the house is enough.'

For a few seconds, neither of them spoke, then Paniatowski said, 'So perhaps you could go and get him for me?'

'What?' Robert Martinez asked, as if he had been deep in his own thoughts and had absolutely no idea what she was talking about.

'Could you go upstairs and ask your father to come to the phone, please,' Paniatowski said.

'Yes. Of course. That was why you called, wasn't it?' Martinez said.

'It was,' Paniatowski agreed.

'I'll get him right away. Sorry if I sounded stupid just then – I'm a little confused.'

'Don't worry about it,' Paniatowski said. 'It's been a confusing evening for all of us.'

Martinez put down the telephone, and there was the sound of his footsteps as he climbed the stairs.

Why was she such an idiot? Paniatowski asked herself.

Why did she always fall for either the wrong men or – as in this case – the right man at the wrong time?

She heard footsteps again, but this time they were louder and more irregular – as if whoever was responsible for them was coming down the stairs two or three steps at a time.

145

Someone picked up the phone again – and whoever it was, was gasping for breath.

'Is that you, Robert?' Paniatowski asked.

'Yes.'

'What's happened?'

'It's . . . it's my father. He's . . . he's dead!'

'Are you sure of that?'

'Of course I'm bloody sure!' Martinez said hysterically. 'His eyes are bulging and he isn't bloody breathing!'

'Calm down, Robert.'

'Calm down! Did you hear what I said? My father's been murdered!'

'I want you to leave the house immediately, Robert,' Paniatowski said soothingly. 'I want you to open the front door, and step out into the garden. Do you think you can do that for me?'

'I don't know. I'm not sure.'

'You can do it. I know you can. Go into the front garden and stay there until the police arrive. All right?'

'All right,' Martinez agreed.

Paniatowski heard a clatter as Martinez dropped the phone, then a series of dull thuds as it swung to and fro, pendulum-like, and collided with the telephone table. And then – thank God – there was the sound of Robert Martinez's slow, heavy footsteps, as he made his way towards the front door.

She pulled her police radio from her handbag.

'This is DCI Paniatowski,' she said, clicking it on. 'There's been a serious incident, and I want at least two patrol cars and an ambulance sent to seven, Tufton Court immediately.'

146

She suddenly felt a little light-headed, and put her palm against the wall, to steady herself.

'Jesus,' she groaned, 'what a bloody mess!'

Twelve

After the giddiness came the nausea, and Paniatowski was sure that – very soon – she was going to be violently sick. She made it to the bathroom just in time, and spent the next ten minutes kneeling over the toilet, spewing up the contents of her stomach into the bowl.

It must have been something she'd eaten, she told herself, as she continued to dry heave – but she knew it wasn't that at all. Rather, it was a combination of guilt and self-disgust which had forced her into this position.

Finally, when she was sure there was nothing left inside to eject, she stood up. Her legs felt weak, and her head was pounding. Her body was screaming that it needed to go to bed, if only for a little while, but she knew that, with this second murder, rest was not an option.

She took a few cautious steps along the landing, then lit up a cigarette.

She would be all right now, she told herself – she would bloody well have to be!

By the time Paniatowski arrived at Tufton Court, there were already three patrol cars, Beresford's Cortina and an ambulance parked in front of the

Martinez home – and in the houses adjacent and opposite to it, neighbours in dressing gowns stood looking on with ghoulish fascination.

'Where's Robert Martinez?' Paniatowski asked Beresford, who was waiting for her at the front door.

'I put him in one of the patrol cars,' Beresford said. 'I got Jack Crane to ask a neighbour to make him a cup of tea, but I don't know if he's drunk it.'

They stepped into the hallway – the very same hallway, Paniatowski reminded herself, in which she had kissed Robert Martinez, and from which he had been talking to her only a few minutes earlier.

'Several of the rooms – both upstairs and down – have been completely ransacked, but there are others which seem untouched,' Beresford said. 'It's possible that whoever was responsible for it was disturbed in the act.'

'Robert Martinez had been out for a walk, and they probably heard him returning,' Paniatowski said.

And she was thinking, Robert was very lucky to come out of it unscathed, because the murderer had already killed two people, and he'd have had no compunction about making it three.

Or perhaps it wasn't a matter of luck at all. Killing a helpless woman and an old man was comparatively easy, but taking on a big strong feller like Robert Martinez was another matter entirely. Perhaps the murderer hadn't felt up to the task – especially if he was quite elderly himself.

'Would you like to see the body now?' Beresford suggested.

'In a minute,' Paniatowski said. 'First, I'd like you to tell me what you've got so far.'

'We think he came in through the French windows which open on to the back garden, because they were wide open when we got here, and one of the panes was smashed.'

'And how would he have reached the French windows?'

'There are two possible ways. He could have walked along Tufton Court, and then taken the path around the side of the house. Or he could have come along the service road that runs behind the houses – which is what all the garages open on to – and climbed over the back gate.'

'Would he have to have been particularly fit to climb over the back gate?' Paniatowski asked.

'Not really. It's not a lot higher than the one at the front.'

'And what about the burglar alarm? Is there one?'

'Yes, but when I talked to the housekeeper on the phone – she doesn't live in, and goes off duty at six – she said that Javier Martinez only switched on the alarm when he went to bed.'

'I thought that he was in his bedroom when Robert found him,' Paniatowski said.

'Robert?' Beresford repeated quizzically.

'That is his name, isn't it – Robert Martinez?' Paniatowski asked, while silently cursing herself.

'Oh yes, that's his name, all right,' Beresford

agreed. 'I was just surprised to hear you using just his . . .' He caught the look in Paniatowski's eyes, and paused. 'Anyway,' he continued shakily, 'the point is that though he was in his bedroom, he wasn't actually . . .'

'Shall we go and look at the body now?' Paniatowski interrupted him.

'OK,' Beresford said.

It was a relief to both of them.

Javier Martinez's bedroom, which overlooked the street, was at the end of the corridor. As well as the bed and all the other usual bedroom furniture, it contained a big old-fashioned roll-top desk and bookcase which held a couple of dozen leather-bound ledgers. The only sign of a personal touch to the room was in the large-framed pictures on the walls of mountain ranges, castles and long, flat plains – and just looking at them evoked the spirit of Spain.

Martinez himself was sitting in an upright chair, a few feet from the bed. His hands were tied together behind the back of the chair. He was gagged, and there was a cord around his throat, cutting deeply into his flesh.

'Look at him from behind,' Beresford said.

Paniatowski did, and saw that behind Martinez's neck, the two ends of the cord had been wrapped around a short, thick piece of wood.

'What, in God's name, do you call this?' Paniatowski asked.

'It's called garrotting,' replied Jack Crane, who had been babysitting the corpse until his boss arrived. 'You keep twisting the stick, and the cord

150

wraps around it and presses tighter and tighter on the throat. It's one of the two officially approved methods of execution in Spain. The other one is the firing squad.'

'Let me get this clear,' Paniatowski said, horrified. 'You're telling me that this is how the Spanish state still kills people?'

Crane nodded. 'Two men were garrotted only last year. The garrotte they use is not quite as crude as this one, but the principle's the same.'

'Take a look at the victim's hands, boss,' Beresford said.

Paniatowski bobbed down, so that her eyes were level with them. When hands were tied together, it was normally palm-to-palm, she thought, but in this case they were back-to-back. And the reason for that was obvious – the killer had needed the palms exposed so he could burn them with a cigarette.

'He was probably tortured because the killer wanted information on where to find whatever it was he'd come looking for,' Beresford said. 'But it's obvious that Martinez wouldn't talk, because if he had, there would have been no need to ransack the house.'

The gold! Paniatowski thought. It was possible he had been looking for the gold!

And if there wasn't any gold, then there was nothing Javier Martinez could have said to end the torture – however bad it got – and death had probably come as a merciful release.

She had a scenario pretty much worked out in her mind now. The murderer had broken into the house, and surprised Javier Martinez in his

151

bedroom. After torturing and killing Martinez, he had searched some of the upstairs rooms, and then gone downstairs. And it was while he had been searching the lounge that he heard the key turn in the front door.

By this point, he was probably panicking, because if he was an old man – and it seemed increasingly likely, given the whole nature of the case, that he was – the last thing he wanted was for big, strong Robert to discover what had happened before he had a chance to get away.

And then he'd had the most incredible stroke of luck, because – under normal circumstances – Robert would probably have gone into the lounge, or else upstairs to see how his father was getting on. But he hadn't done either of those things. Instead, he'd stopped in the hallway to answer the phone – to speak to her – and that had given the killer his opportunity to escape.

Paniatowski stood up again. 'I want all the neighbours questioned at length,' she said. 'I particularly want to know if they've seen anything suspicious in the last half hour or so.'

'You think we just missed him, do you?' Beresford asked.

'I think we just missed him,' Paniatowski confirmed. 'I also want roadblocks set up on all roads out of town. Nobody gets through them without being thoroughly checked.'

'That's already being done,' Beresford told her.

'And I want the railway station and the bus station checked.'

'That's being done too.'

'Right,' Paniatowski said heavily, 'then I suppose I'd better talk to Robert Martinez.'

'Wouldn't you prefer me to do it, boss?' Beresford asked.

It was tempting, Paniatowski thought – but it was also copping out of her responsibilities.

'You've already got enough on your hands as it is,' she said.

Robert Martinez was sitting in the back of a patrol car. He had a mug of tea clasped tightly in his hands, but he did not appear to have drunk any of it.

'It feels very cold in here,' he said, when Paniatowski slid in beside him. 'Or is that just me?'

'You're in shock,' Paniatowski told him. 'When we've finished talking, I'll get one of my lads to bring you a blanket.' She paused. 'You are up to talking, aren't you, Robert?'

Martinez gave her a weak grin. 'Oh, I can talk,' he said. 'It's what I do for a living.'

'I left you and your father at around six o'clock,' Paniatowski said. 'What did you do after that?'

'As I told you on the phone, I asked my father if he wanted some company, and he said he would prefer to be alone. I tried to deal with some of my constituency correspondence, but I couldn't concentrate, and after a couple of hours I just gave up.'

'And then?'

'And then, I went to see my father again. He was in his bedroom, sitting at his desk as if

153

he was working, but I think he was finding it just as hard to concentrate as I was.'

'So what happened next?'

'I thought I might as well go for a walk – I get too little exercise when I'm in London – and I left the house at about nine o'clock.'

'Did you get the impression when you were leaving that anyone was watching the house?'

'I'd never have gone out if I had. But to be honest, there could have been a whole team of watchers out there, and – the state I was in – I probably wouldn't have noticed them.'

'Where did you go on this walk of yours?'

'I can't tell you the exact route. I remember crossing the Boulevard at one point, and I was certainly down by the river, but my mind was somewhere else entirely, and I wasn't really thinking about where I was going.'

'Did anybody see you on your walk?' Paniatowski said. 'I'm sorry, but I have to ask.'

'Of course you do,' Robert Martinez agreed. 'Two thirds of murders are committed by members of the immediate family, aren't they?'

'Yes, it's around that figure.'

'Somebody may have seen me – I'm the local MP and I've had my picture plastered over half the hoardings in town, so probably most people would recognize me. But it's a chill night, and there weren't many people out and about, so I can't say whether or not I was noticed.' Martinez paused. 'You seem to be growing tenser with every word I say.'

'I'm just concentrating on what you're saying, that's all,' Paniatowski replied unconvincingly.

154

'You don't have to feel guilty about treating me as a suspect, Monika,' Martinez told her. 'Anybody in your position would do that.'

'Yes, you're right, I do have to treat you like a suspect,' Paniatowski said. 'I'd lose the confidence of my team if I didn't – but I know you didn't kill him.'

'Don't box yourself into a corner because of what happened earlier,' Martinez cautioned her. 'For your own sake – for the sake of your career – you need to keep an open mind.'

'Do you seriously imagine that I think you're innocent just because we had a quick kiss in the hallway?' Paniatowski demanded angrily. 'Do you actually see me as that weak a person?'

'No, I don't think you're weak at all,' Martinez said. 'So why are you ruling me out?'

Because we already know who killed your father, Paniatowski thought – *it's just that we don't know his name or what he looks like.*

But she couldn't tell Robert that without revealing details of the investigation to him – and on the scale of sins a police officer could commit, giving a civilian those kinds of details ranked just below bribery.

'Why am I ruling you out?' she asked. 'I'm ruling you out because, though I don't know you well, I know you well enough to be sure that you'd never torture your own father.'

'He . . . he was tortured?' Robert Martinez asked.

Oh God, he wouldn't know about that, Paniatowski thought.

He was only in his father's bedroom for a few

155

seconds, and because Javier's hands were tied behind his back, he wouldn't have seen them.

'There were cigarette burns on his hands,' she said.

'Cigarette burns! On his hands!'

'There were only a few of them. I don't think it can have gone on for long,' Paniatowski lied.

'That's terrible,' Robert said, 'And you're right, I'd never do that to my own father – but I can think of a few people who might.'

'I thought you said you'd never been to Spain.'

'I haven't.'

'But you've met some of the people who your father knew when he lived in Spain, have you?'

'No,' Robert Martinez said, perplexed.

'Then I don't see . . .'

'I'm not thinking clearly, am I?' Robert asked. 'Or is it more the case that I'm trying to think like a detective – which is something that I'm so obviously unqualified to do?'

'You think his killer is a Whitebridge man!' Paniatowski said, with sudden insight.

'And you don't!' Robert replied – clearly shocked by the idea that it could have been anyone else.

She was digging herself into a deeper and deeper hole with every word she spoke, Paniatowski told herself.

'What I think is entirely irrelevant to this conversation,' she said, with a fresh anger directed more at herself than at Robert Martinez. 'I'm the police officer here. It's my job to ask the questions, and your job to answer them.'

'Maybe we should have held this interview in a more formal setting,' Robert Martinez said.

There's no maybe about it, Paniatowski thought. *I've screwed up.*

'Who do you think might have killed your father?' she asked, in an attempt to pull something out of the hat which might perhaps justify her stupidity.

'I'm not going to point the finger at anybody in particular – because I just don't know,' Robert Martinez said firmly.

'But you do think there were some men here in Whitebridge who hated him enough to torture him?'

Robert Martinez sighed. 'When he was in Spain, my father must have experienced life at its harshest,' he said. 'The lesson he learned from that was that you have to be tough to survive, and that compassion is a weakness which will probably bring you down. And even after all his years in Whitebridge, he could never quite bring himself to unlearn that lesson.'

'Meaning that he cheated people – that he stole from them?'

'I wouldn't go that far,' Robert Martinez said. 'But it's more than possible that there are men who think he cheated them – who are obsessed by the idea – and who wanted to make him confess to it before they killed him.' He paused again. 'I know I'm here to answer questions, but could I ask just one?'

'It depends what it is,' Paniatowski replied cautiously.

'When did my mother die?'

There could be no harm in telling him that.

'As far as we know, she was killed sometime last Wednesday – probably in the late afternoon.'

Robert Martinez let out what could only have been a gasp of relief.

'Then I couldn't have saved her,' he said.

'What do you mean by that?' Paniatowski wondered.

'I was in London all last week. We were drafting a bill on political refugees, and we were working round the clock. So I wasn't in Whitebridge – and I couldn't have saved her.'

'Even if you had been here, it probably wouldn't have made any difference,' Paniatowski pointed out. 'You didn't know she was coming – and you wouldn't have recognized her even if you'd seen her on the street.'

'You're right, of course – on a purely logical level,' Robert Martinez agreed. 'But I'm a son who's lost his mother, and logic doesn't really come into it.'

'I have to go,' Paniatowski said. 'Do you think you'll be all right on your own?'

'Not really,' Martinez admitted. 'I don't think I'll ever be quite right again. But I'll find a way to cope with it – because that's what people do.'

Thirteen

Robert Martinez had been going out with Lynn Jones, the deputy headmistress of a local girls' school, for years. It had been a very old-fashioned

– almost traditional – courtship, and everyone who knew them had automatically assumed that they would eventually end up getting married. And, in fact, Robert had proposed to Lynn, just days after having been selected by his constituency party as prospective parliamentary candidate for Whitebridge.

'If you're elected, I'd have to give up my job, and we'd be spending most of our time in London,' Lynn had said. 'And I'm a northern lass to my core, Robbie – I like living in Whitebridge.'

'You could keep your job, and we'd see each other at the weekends and when parliament isn't in session,' Martinez had replied.

'I'd rather have no husband at all than a part-time husband,' Lynn had countered. 'You've already got work – everybody says what a marvellous job you've done since you've taken over Sunshine Holidays – so why would you want to become an MP?'

'I want to do some good.'

'But you're already doing good. Can you tell me the name of any other coach operator in Lancashire who lends his buses out to charities anything like as often as you do?'

'No, but . . .'

'And then there's your work at the battered wife shelter and the animal refuge – there's dozens of organizations that you support in one way or another.'

'It's not enough,' Robert had said. 'This country didn't have to give me a home, but it did, and I feel under an obligation to do the best I can

159

for it in return. Being in Westminster will give me that opportunity. I can help hundreds of battered wives' shelters and hundreds of animal refuges if I'm an MP.'

And since neither of them would budge on the matter, they had parted. But it had been an amiable parting – so amiable that they both realized they had probably never actually been in love.

In fact, other than them not sleeping together any more, it was barely a parting at all. Lynn had worked long and hard on Robert's election campaign, and Robert had continued to take Lynn out for dinner whenever he was in Whitebridge. So it had been only natural that, when the police had informed Robert that he could not go back into his house, since it was now officially a crime scene, he should ring up Lynn and ask her if she could give him a bed for the night.

Now, at a quarter to six the following morning, the two of them found themselves facing each other across Lynn's kitchen table.

'There's not much point in asking you whether you had a good night's sleep, is there?' Lynn asked, sipping at her cup of coffee. 'You can't have been in bed for more than four hours – and I heard you tossing and turning for most of that.'

'I'm sorry,' Robert said. 'I never meant to disturb your sleep.'

'Don't you go worrying about me,' Lynn said sternly, in her best deputy headmistress voice. 'I'm not the one whose life was turned upside down yesterday. But I do think you need more sleep, Robert, so maybe, when I've gone off to work, you could try and snatch another two or three hours.'

Robert Martinez shook his head. 'I've no time for more sleep. I've got to get out and start talking to the Spanish community.'

'Whatever for?'

'They may be able to throw some light on my mother's murder.'

Lynn shook her head wonderingly.

'Now how could they possibly do that?' she asked.

'I've been thinking about it, and it seems to me that if she was in Whitebridge for any length of time – and that length of time could be as little as a few hours – she might have come into contact with one of them,' Martinez explained. 'Someone might, for example, have met her in a shop. Or perhaps sat next to her on a bus, and realized that she was Spanish, too.'

'That would be a very big coincidence,' Lynn said, sceptically.

Yes, it would be a very big coincidence, Martinez thought – but very big coincidences were the only things he had to work with.

'And anyway, won't they have already been questioned by the police?' Lynn asked.

'Yes, they will – but they might be willing to tell me things they wouldn't tell the police.'

'You're wasting your time, you know,' Lynn said.

Robert sighed. 'Yes, I probably am,' he agreed.

* * *

If the police canteen had been open at that god-awful hour, they would never have chosen to meet at the transport café on the A59, but since it wasn't – and the café was – that was where the team assembled at six-fifteen on the morning after Javier Martinez's murder.

Even given the lack of options available, it hadn't been a brilliant choice, Paniatowski thought, looking around her. There were good transport cafés and there were bad ones, and the River View Café – which didn't even have a view of the river – fell squarely into the second category.

It smelled of fried bacon, chip fat, disinfectant and hand-rolled cigarettes; the counter staff stood grim and silent, counting down the minutes until their shifts ended; and the tea urn sighed plaintively, as if it had all but given up hope of being moved to somewhere classier.

'Right, we'd better get started,' she said, trying her best to inject a positive note into what was undoubtedly a negative situation. 'What have you got for us, Inspector?'

'Not a lot,' Beresford admitted. 'Most of the people who live on Tufton Court like to get to bed earlier, and the only one who says he saw anything at all was a Mr Hodgeson, who got up to let the cat in at about eleven forty-five, and noticed a man entering the Martinez house through the front door.'

'That would be Robert Martinez himself,' Paniatowski said. 'What did Mr Hodgeson do then?'

'Once the cat was safely inside, he went straight back to bed.'

'Which is a pity,' Paniatowski mused, 'because if he'd stayed up a few minutes more, he might have seen another man leaving the house and heading up Tufton Court.'

'I think it's unlikely he did leave that way,' Beresford said. 'Why run the risk of exposing yourself on the Court, when you could slip quietly away down the service road?'

'That's true,' Paniatowski agreed. She forced herself to smile. 'That's the trouble with murderers, isn't it? They go out of their way to make things difficult for us.'

'You'd almost think they didn't want us to catch them,' Meadows said – and her smile was forced, too.

'Did we learn anything interesting from the roadblocks?' Paniatowski asked.

'Yes, we learned that there are still some people around who think they can drive a car when they're too pissed to walk,' Beresford said. 'But nobody who was stopped and questioned came even close to fitting the profile of a possible killer. So we're left with only two possibilities – either the murderer had already managed to leave the area, or that he's still in Whitebridge.'

'At least we know now what his motive was,' Meadows said.

'Do we?' Paniatowski asked.

'I think so. If it had only been revenge he wanted, he'd never have ransacked the house, and the same is true of a political assassination. So he has to have been after the gold.'

'If it was political, he might have been searching for papers connected with the Civil War,' said

163

Crane, who was reluctant to abandon his own theory.

'What sort of papers?' Meadows asked.

'Well, I don't know,' Crane admitted.

'You're forgetting Javier Martinez's background,' Meadows said. 'He wasn't an educated man – he was a practical one. He lived in a small village, and if it hadn't been for the Civil War, he'd probably never have left it. He certainly wasn't the kind to go in for "secret" papers. And even if he had had some, he wouldn't have been carrying them on his person when he was taken from the barn to the priest's house.'

'Good point,' Crane said.

'So for your theory to work, we'd have to accept the idea that a man who had just killed three enemy soldiers – and was desperate to escape with his son – would risk going back to his own home to pick up documents,' Meadows concluded.

'You're right, Sergeant,' Crane admitted, 'my entire theory's a non-starter.'

'There might have been papers in his home in Whitebridge if he'd been in contact with anti-government forces in Spain since he came to England,' Paniatowski said. 'But we don't know whether he had or not. In fact, what's becoming glaringly obvious is that we know very little about him.'

It was true, the rest of the team realized. Thanks to the work Woodend and Ruiz had done in Spain, they knew quite a lot about the first victim, but the second victim was virtually a blank page.

'Let's establish, here and now, what we do actually know about him,' Paniatowski suggested.

'We know he was a political refugee, and that he's been living in Whitebridge since around 1937,' Beresford said. 'We know that over the last thirty years he's built up Sunshine Travel into the biggest coach tour operator in Lancashire. We know that he has a son, and that son is our member of parliament.'

'Is there anything that anyone else would care to add to that?' Paniatowski asked, and when nobody had, she added, 'That's not a great deal, is it?'

'I don't see we need to know a lot more about his time in Lancashire,' Beresford said. 'After all, the roots of both his murder and his wife's were planted in Spain, thirty-six years ago.'

'But were they?' Paniatowski asked.

'I'm sorry, boss?' Beresford said.

'Last night, when I arrived at the Martinez house, I automatically assumed that both Javier and Elena had been killed by the same man,' Paniatowski said, 'but the more I turn it over in my mind, the less it seems to me that had to be the only possibility.'

It was something that Robert Martinez said which had set her off on this new line of thinking, she recognized.

He'd never have tortured his own father, he'd told her, as they sat uncomfortably close together in the back of the patrol car – but he could think of a few people in Whitebridge who might have done.

'Let's consider the way the two victims were

murdered,' she suggested to the team. 'Elena was killed with a hammer or some other blunt instrument. Was that a weapon of opportunity, or a weapon of choice?'

'Could have been either,' Beresford said.

'Exactly,' Paniatowski agreed, 'So we don't know if Elena's murder was a well-planned, cold-blooded one, or if it was carried out in the heat of the moment. But whichever it was, she wasn't tortured, and her body was dumped where, if things had gone according to plan, it wouldn't have been found for a long time. Javier, on the other hand, was tortured, his murder definitely was cold-blooded, and his body was left where his son was bound to find it.'

'That's all easily explained away, without even making a dent in our working theory,' Meadows said. 'Elena's body had to be hidden, otherwise Javier would have been tipped off that the killer was in the area – but there was no need to hide Javier's body, so the killer didn't.'

'And doesn't the fact that Javier was garrotted prove the murderer was a Spaniard?' Crane asked.

'No,' Paniatowski said. 'It proves no more than that he knew what a garrotte was.'

She lit up a cigarette. She'd allowed the team to become too fixated on one theory – a big mistake – and now it was going to be difficult to shift them from that even a little, she thought.

'How about this as an alternative theory?' she continued. 'There's someone here in Whitebridge who wants Javier Martinez dead. He has, in fact, been meaning to kill him for some time, but when

166

he learns that Javier's wife, Elena, has been killed, and is in the mortuary . . .'

'How does he find out about that?' Meadows asked.

Paniatowski shrugged. 'Any number of ways – somebody who works in the mortuary tells him, or tells someone else who tells him; either Javier or Robert rings up a friend, and the news spreads like wildfire through their circle; or perhaps he only heard that Javier had been taken to the mortuary in a police car, and put two and two together.'

The other three merely nodded. They knew from their own experience how quickly news got round Whitebridge.

'So he finds out about Elena, and decides he'll never have an opportunity like this one again. He has the chance, you see, not only to kill his enemy, but to muddy the waters. He knows that in the light of Elena's murder, and his use of the garrotte, we're bound to see a Spanish connection, and if we pursue that, our investigation is never likely to get anywhere near him.'

'So are you saying that the two deaths are probably unconnected?' Beresford asked, clearly unconvinced.

'No, I'm not saying that at all,' Paniatowski told him. 'What I am saying is that, with the chief constable breathing down my neck and just waiting for me to make a mistake, we can't afford to overlook even the slightest possibility that they're unconnected.'

'What does that mean in practical terms?' Beresford asked.

'It means we're going to have to split the team into two. Colin, I want you and your lads to find out everything they can about Elena's time in England – how she got here, whether anybody noticed her once she'd arrived. I also want to know if anyone's seen any strangers – particularly foreign-looking strangers – acting in a suspicious manner.'

'That's a bit like looking for a very small needle in a very large haystack, isn't it?' Beresford asked.

'We've come up against longer odds in the past,' Paniatowski said.

'What about me and young Jack, boss?' Meadows asked.

'I want you to look into Javier Martinez's background,' Paniatowski told her. 'Start from the moment he arrived in Whitebridge. He's made enemies in the last thirty-six years, and I want to hear about them.'

'So we'll be looking for business associates who feel they've been cheated, and husbands who think Javier has been having it off with their wives on the quiet?' Meadows asked.

'Essentially,' Paniatowski agreed.

None of them liked the alternative theory, Paniatowski thought – and they were probably right. But she was right in her own way, too, because George Baxter *was* breathing down her neck, and they couldn't afford to exclude any possibility.

'Will you be asking Mr Woodend to continue his investigation in Spain?' Crane asked.

Now that was an interesting question, Paniatowski thought.

168

On the one hand, she was still worried that Charlie might run foul of the authorities, but on the other, he was clearly the only channel she had for getting any information out of Spain.

'Give me the chance to have a stab at one last big investigation, lass,' said a deep voice in her head. 'You know I'm bursting to do it.'

'Yes, I'll be ringing him,' she said. She looked at her watch. 'Right, that's it, let's get moving.'

Meadows and Crane stood up immediately, but Beresford remained firmly in his seat.

'Is there something wrong, Colin?' Paniatowski asked.

'I'd like a word, if you don't mind, boss,' Beresford said.

'All right,' Paniatowski agreed.

Beresford waited until Meadows and Crane had reached the door, then he said, 'We've been here for over half an hour, and you've never once raised the possibility that Robert Martinez might have murdered his father – and that's despite the fact that most murders are domestic, and he has no real alibi.'

'Nobody else raised the possibility, either,' Paniatowski pointed out.

'Nobody else is leading the team,' Beresford countered.

'So do you think he might have done it?'

'God, no! He's got absolutely no motive – and anyway, I'm still convinced we're looking for just one murderer.'

'So what's your point?'

'You should still have raised the possibility.

Even if we'd dismissed it immediately, it should have been put on the table.'

'Now tell me what your real point is.'

'I just want you to be careful, Monika.'

'What's that – some kind of code?' Paniatowski asked.

'The way you acted last night – and the way you reacted just now – makes me think you're getting far too close to Robert Martinez,' Beresford said. 'And that happened on a case once before, if you remember.'

Oh yes, she remembered well enough.

'I'll be careful,' she said.

But Beresford looked far from convinced.

'You build up a wall between yourself and all the men who are interested in you,' he said. 'Now I don't blame you for that . . .'

'That's more than generous of you,' Paniatowski said, sarcastically.

'. . . because any woman who'd been through what you went through as a kid would probably do the same,' Beresford said, ignoring the comment.

Paniatowski shuddered, and for one brief moment she was back in the shabby council house of her childhood, with Arthur Jones, her stepfather, forcing his attentions on her.

'You see the world as divided into two kinds of men,' Beresford continued, 'the ones that are as vile as Arthur Jones, and the ones who have qualities that remind you of your father.'

'And which kind are you?' Paniatowski asked aggressively.

'Please, Monika, don't!' Beresford begged.

'I'm only saying all this because I care about you.'

She felt both touched and ashamed.

'I know you do,' she said.

'And the problem is that when you come across a man who isn't Arthur Jones, the wall comes tumbling down, and you're completely defenceless,' Beresford told her. 'And that's what I think is happening with Robert Martinez – I think he's breaching the walls.'

'I've said I'll be careful – and I will,' Paniatowski said. 'You'll have to trust me on that.'

But she was not entirely sure that she could trust herself.

By eleven o'clock that morning, Robert Martinez had already been to the homes of half a dozen expatriate Spaniards living in Whitebridge. Each visit had been much longer than he had initially hoped it would be, but he had begun to accept that as inevitable, because most of the people he'd visited were at least in late middle age – and therefore very traditional – and that meant there were always certain protocols which had to be observed.

The seventh person on his list was an old woman called Rosa Bautista, who lived in one of the old weavers' cottages.

He knew all about Rosa's history – including the part she had played in the Civil War – from previous chats they'd had.

Rosa had been a nurse in the early stages of the war, working on the front line under heavy enemy bombardment. Then, as the death toll had risen, she had taken up a rifle, and had found herself in the unusual position of both taking lives and saving lives in the same day. She had become – in her own small way – a symbol of the struggle, and when Valencia was about to fall, her comrades had insisted that she should be on the last boat out.

Looking at her now – a small, frail, wizened woman – it would have been hard to believe she had once been so heroic, had it not been for the aura of simple dignity that surrounded her.

It was clear from the pained expression on Doña Rosa's face that she had heard the news.

'Come inside, Don Roberto,' she said. 'You must have a cup of good Spanish coffee.'

'That would be much appreciated,' Martinez replied, though that would make it his seventh cup of the morning, and he was dreading the thought of even more caffeine entering his bloodstream.

She led him into her kitchen – which, with its herbs and spices, smelled of a Spain he had never known himself – and sat him down at the table.

'It will not take a minute to prepare,' she said, filling the coffee machine with water.

'My father was the second Spanish person to be murdered in this town in only a few days,' Martinez said. 'The first one was a woman – a stranger.'

Had he seen her stiffen slightly when he'd said that?

Yes, he thought he had.

'I had heard about this woman – it was in the

newspapers – but I did not know she was Spanish,' Doña Rosa said.

But she did know – he was sure she did!.

'And since she was Spanish, I feel a responsibility to do all I can to see that her murderer is brought to justice,' Martinez continued, following a script he had been gradually refining during the course of the morning.

Doña Rosa turned slowly to face him, but she would not look him directly in the eye.

'Have you not perhaps got enough on your hands with the death of your father?' she wondered.

'And this morning, I found myself wondering if she might have made contact with any member of the Spanish community,' Martinez ploughed on.

'How would she have done that?'

'It could have been a chance meeting. Such things happen.'

'But they are rare,' said Doña Rosa, with a distinct quiver in her cracked old voice.

'And then I began to wonder if this person, who the dead woman might have met, would have told the police about it – and I decided that she probably wouldn't have.'

'The coffee is almost ready,' Doña Rosa said.

'Because, you see, I know that Spaniards of a certain age – and I hope you are not insulted that I call you that, Doña Rosa, because you are a marvel – Spaniards of a certain age, with memories of the old country, do not trust the police. In fact, they do not trust any officials.'

'That's true,' the old woman agreed.

'I imagine that when you came here as a political refugee, there were any number of government officials who tried to make your life difficult for you,' Martinez said.

'They wanted to send me back,' the old woman said, with a sudden anger in her voice. 'I told them I would face the firing squad in Spain, but they didn't believe me. They laughed, and said that that could never happen. The fools! What they meant was, it could never happen in England. They had no idea what things were like in Spain.'

'But you must eventually have found some official who was prepared to believe you.'

'I did – or I would not be here now.'

'So there are good officials?'

'Yes, of course.'

'And there are good police officers, too. I have met one. Her name is Chief Inspector Paniatowski.'

'No doubt she is nice to you – you are an important man,' Doña Rosa countered.

'I truly believe she is nice to everyone – and that if you had something to say, she would be most interested in hearing it.'

'But I do not have anything to say.'

'There's something I haven't told you about the woman who was killed,' Martinez said. 'She was my mother.'

'Oh, you poor boy,' the old woman gasped.

'We are talking about the honour of my family,' Martinez said. 'I must do what I can to avenge her.'

'Of course you must,' Doña Rosa said.

174

'And that is why, if you know something, I am asking you – I am begging you – to inform the police.'

'There was a time when I feared nothing,' Doña Rose said wistfully, 'a time when I would have laughed in the face of death. But as you grow older, Don Roberto, it is not just your body that shrinks, it is your courage, too. I worry when my cat is away for more than an hour. I worry when I feel a draught under the door. Small matters – truly petty matters – grow to become of huge importance. It is a curse, but we must learn to live with it.'

'Do you know something, Doña Rosa?' Martinez asked gently.

The old woman nodded. 'Yes, Don Roberto, I do.'

'And would you be willing – for my sake, and for the sake of my family's honour – to talk to Chief Inspector Paniatowski?'

The old woman hesitated for a moment, then took a deep breath and said, 'I will do it as long as you are by my side.'

'I will be by your side,' Robert Martinez promised.

Fourteen

With a large man like Charlie Woodend as a passenger, Ruiz's little Seat 500 made even harder work of the mountain roads than it had

175

the last time Paco had visited Val de Montaña, but finally it drew to an exhausted halt in the village square, close to Don Ramon's bar.

'It will be harder for me to question the old men if you are there,' Paco said, as they crossed the square.

'I understand that,' Woodend said, 'but if I'm to be of any bloody use at all in this investigation, I need to soak up the atmosphere, and watch the men's faces as they talk.'

Paco grinned. Woodend had been famous for 'soaking up the atmosphere' back in Lancashire, Monika Paniatowski had told him. He'd even had a nickname – Cloggin'-it Charlie – which acknowledged the fact that rather than stay in his office and coordinate the investigation – as many chief inspectors did – Woodend would walk endlessly around the environs of the crime until, as if by magic, he began to gain an understanding of exactly what had gone on.

'Any information we can gather up will be useful,' Woodend said, 'but the vital thing to find out is whether or not this lieutenant – or one of the other two soldiers killed by Javier Martinez – had a close enough friendship with another of the soldiers for *that* soldier to want to seek revenge, even after all this time.'

Paco's grin widened. 'Is that right?' he asked. 'I would not have known that. But then, I have never been a policeman.'

Woodend grinned too – though his grin was somewhat sheepish, rather than amused.

'Sorry,' he said. 'I've been the boss for so long

176

that it's a little hard to get used to having an equal partner.'

The two old men – Don Ramon and Don Pedro – were at the same table they had been sitting at the last time Paco paid a visit.

Don Ramon smiled an almost-toothless greeting at Paco, then looked with suspicion at Woodend.

'This is Carlito, an old friend of mine,' Paco said to Don Ramon, in Spanish. 'If you trust me, then you can trust him.'

The old bar owner was silent for some time, then he said, 'And does this Carlito of yours play dominoes?'

'Yes,' Paco replied.

'Does he take it seriously?'

'He takes it very seriously indeed. In fact, you would almost think he was Spanish himself.'

Don Ramon gave a nod which looked only half-convinced. 'Ask Carlito if he would like to play a few games,' he said.

Paco passed the information on to Woodend.

'It is a kind of audition,' he said. 'They want to see if you are the kind of man they can talk to.'

'Would it put them in a more receptive mood if I lost the game?' Woodend asked.

'It might,' Paco replied, 'but it will depend on how you lose. These men are experts. If you lose badly, they will take you for a fool, and tell you nothing. If you try to throw the game, they will see you as dishonest, and also tell you nothing.'

'So I should play as well as I can?'

'You should play as if your life depended on it.'

Woodend nodded. 'That seriously, hey? Then I'd better take my coat off,' he said, removing his hairy sports jacket and draping it over a chair.

Don Pedro won the first game, and Don Ramon won the next two, but by now Woodend was getting a measure of their playing styles, and won the fourth.

At the end of half an hour's fast and furious playing, when Woodend was one game ahead, Don Ramon pushed the dominoes to one side, and turned to Paco.

'Carlito is an excellent player,' he said, 'but on a good day, I still think I could beat him.'

'I'm sure you could,' Paco said.

Don Ramon grinned. 'That was the right answer,' he said. 'We are ready to answer your questions about Elena now.'

'We have no more questions about Elena,' Paco said. 'Today, we are more interested in those soldiers who came to Val de Montaña just after the Civil War ended.'

'What has this to do with Elena's legacy from her uncle in the United States?' Don Ramon asked.

'Nothing at all,' Paco admitted. 'We are now investigating something quite different, though it is still related to this village.'

'So that is what you are – a shepherd who also keeps pigs,' Don Ramon said.

Paco laughed. 'And you are a bar owner who sells sardines,' he said. 'In both our lines of work, Don Ramon, it is sometimes necessary to have more than one string to your bow.'

178

'That's true,' the other man agreed. 'And what does this second string of yours involve?'

'I am sorry to tell you that Javier Martinez, who has lived in England since the end of the Civil War, has been murdered.'

'It is sad news,' said Don Ramon, nodding gravely, 'though in a way, he was lucky – as we all are – to have lived so long.'

'We think that his murderer was a Spaniard,' Paco said.

'I do not understand why you should think that,' Don Ramon said. 'Are there not many more Englishmen in England than there are Spaniards?'

'Yes.'

'Then wouldn't it perhaps be wiser to consider the possibility that it was one of them who killed Javier?'

'Under most circumstances, what you have just said would undoubtedly be true,' Paco agreed, 'but you see, Javier Martinez was garrotted.'

'Then perhaps you are right, and it was a Spaniard who killed him,' Don Ramon said. 'And do you think that this murderer might have been one of the soldiers who came to this village?'

'It is a possibility – especially since, before he left the village, Javier killed three of their comrades,' Paco said.

'Thirty-six years is a very long time for someone to hold a grudge,' Don Ramon said.

'Are you saying that you yourself do not hold grudges against the enemy any more?' Paco asked. 'Are you suggesting that if one of those soldiers walked into the village today, you would greet him as a brother, clap him on the shoulder and buy him a drink?'

'I might buy him a drink – but only if I had poisoned that drink first,' Don Ramon said.

'So perhaps one of those soldiers felt the same way about Javier.'

'Perhaps he did.'

'We would like to track them down, and if one of them is guilty, we would bring him to justice.'

'Much chance there is of that in Francisco Franco's Spain,' Don Ramon said dismissively.

'But this is not Franco's Spain any more,' Paco pointed out. 'Perhaps things will change. And if they do not, did I say anything about bringing him to justice through the courts?'

'You would kill him?' Don Ramon asked.

Paco laughed. 'Not me. I'm too old for that. But I have two or three young friends who might be willing to oblige me.'

'I cannot remember the fascists' names,' Don Ramon said. 'Perhaps I never knew them – but I do know that most of them – including the lieutenant – came from a small town called Arco de Cañas in Burgos province.'

'And how they boasted about it,' Don Pedro said. '"Arco de Cañas is a grand town,"' he continued in a voice that was not quite his own. '"Arco de Cañas has four shops." "Peasants like you would be completely lost in a town like Arco de Cañas".'

'They treated us all like dogs,' Don Ramon said. 'They locked us in a barn, you know.'

'I thought you told me they didn't lock you

and Don Pedro up, because you were too old to have taken part in the fighting,' Paco said.

'We were there in spirit, if not in body,' Don Ramon said, his dignity clearly offended.

'Of course you were,' Paco agreed hastily.

'They gave us a slop bucket, but when it was full, and we asked if they could empty it, they laughed at us. They said we were almost animals ourselves, and we should be used to living in shit. And when they took one of us to the priest's house to be questioned, they tied his hands so tightly behind his back that they almost cut off the blood.'

All the time the old men had been speaking, Paco had been providing Woodend with a running translation, and Woodend himself had done no more than just listen, but now he said, 'Their hands were tied behind their backs?'

'Yes.'

'Could you make sure that's what Don Ramon said?'

Paco did.

'It's what he said,' he confirmed.

But that just didn't square with what Monika had told him, over the phone, about Javier Martinez's escape, Woodend thought. According to her, Javier had said that he had stunned the lieutenant with a large crucifix.

'Ask him why they didn't tie Javier Martinez's hands behind his back,' he said to Paco.

'They did tie his hands behind his back,' Don Ramon said, when Paco had translated. 'I saw him myself, being marched down the street, and there is no question about where his hands were.'

'Then if that's true,' Woodend said, when Paco had translated, 'it's not Martinez's enemy we should be looking for – it's his thwarted business partner.'

'We have to start with the assumption that the gold isn't just a legend, but that it actually existed,' Woodend said to Ruiz, as they drove back towards Calpe.

'Do we?' Paco said. 'And why is that?'

'Because if the gold existed, then everything that I'm about to say makes sense,' Woodend told him. 'But if it doesn't exist, then absolutely nothing that went on in that village one night in 1939 makes any sense at all.'

'I'm listening,' Paco said.

'With his hands tied behind his back, it would have been impossible for Javier Martinez to escape from the priest's house on his own, so he must have had help,' Woodend said, 'and that help couldn't have come from any of his fellow villagers, because all the young, able-bodied ones were locked up in the barn.'

'So it must have been one of the soldiers who helped him,' Paco said.

'Exactly,' Woodend agreed. 'We know that the lieutenant wanted the gold for himself, and maybe this soldier – let's call him José for the sake of convenience – had the same idea. So José strikes a deal with Martinez. He will help him to escape, in return for a share of the gold.'

'But there are quite a lot of soldiers guarding the barn, so the only time such an escape will be possible is when Martinez is in the priest's house,' Paco said, following his reasoning.

'Of course, the lieutenant and the other two soldiers will be witnesses to that escape, so they will have to die, but José's so hungry for the gold that that thought docsn't bother him. Anyway, the whole thing goes like clockwork – José shoots the three soldiers, and lets Martinez go, taking the gold with him.'

'Why did Javier Martinez tell Monika such a different story about how he managed to get away?' Paco asked.

'Because he couldn't admit he was helped by one of the soldiers without revealing the reason *why* he was helped. And he doesn't want anybody – and I mean anybody – to know about the gold.'

'Perhaps that is what happens,' Paco said, slightly dubiously. 'But won't the other soldiers wonder how Martinez has managed to escape?'

'Yes, they will, but they know the villagers couldn't have helped him, and it never crosses their minds that one of their own comrades – a man they've fought side by side with – would have killed the lieutenant and the other two soldiers. And so they come up with some other explanation. They decide – I don't know – that Martinez tricked the lieutenant into untying him, or that whoever had tied his hands behind his back hadn't made a very good job of it, and he'd managed to get free. None of their explanations will have entirely satisfied them, but then, in a war, so many things are left unexplained.'

Paco nodded. 'That makes sense,' he said. 'I can think of many unexplained occurrences in my war.'

'Once Martinez has gone, José sets fire to the priest's house to create a distraction,' Woodend continued.

'Why doesn't José keep the gold himself?' Paco asked.

'He daren't run the risk. As things stand, there's nothing to tie him to the murders, but if the other soldiers find out he's got the gold, they'll put two and two together immediately. And can you imagine what they'll do to him then? It won't be a quick death, by any means. Besides, Martinez must be a clever talker to have got him to agree to the plan in the first place, and he's somehow managed to convince José that he'll keep to his half of the deal.'

'But he doesn't.'

'No.'

'So why doesn't José track him down? After all, Javier was living in England under his own name.'

'You and I know that he was living in England, but José doesn't. He probably thinks that since Javier is rich enough to live wherever he wants to, he will have settled in a country as much like Spain as possible – because that's just what José himself would have done in the same circumstances.'

'Somewhere in South America?'

'Exactly! And remember, José isn't much more sophisticated than the people of Val de Montaña – he comes from a town which has only four shops – and he has no idea how to set about searching the world for Martinez.'

'But he does have one link with the gold – Elena!' Paco said.

'Spot on! He is sure that Martinez will contact her eventually, and he keeps watch on her for nearly four decades.'

'There is probably no other country in the world where that would happen,' Paco said reflectively. 'But this is Spain, and, like all Spaniards, José has within him all those characteristics which could make him a great man or a fool – and sometimes both. For him, it is no longer about the gold. Martinez has made a dupe of him – has damaged his pride – and he will not rest until he has had his revenge.'

'And finally, his patience is rewarded,' Woodend said. 'Elena books a flight to England, and he follows her. And once she's led him to Whitebridge, she's no longer of any use to him. In fact, she may actually be a danger to his plans, because Martinez will realize that if Elena can find him, José might, too, and that will put him on his guard. So the first opportunity he gets, he kills her. Then he tortures Martinez to make him reveal where the gold is, and once he has it – or even if he doesn't – he garrottes the man who has betrayed him.'

'It is an elaborate theory . . .' Paco began.

'Sir Arthur Conan Doyle once had Sherlock Holmes say, "When you have eliminated the impossible, whatever remains, however improbable, must be the truth,"' Woodend interrupted him.

'I had not finished what I was saying,' Paco replied, a little sharply.

'Sorry, I'm acting like I'm the boss again, aren't I?' Woodend said.

'Or an excited five-year-old,' Paco said wryly.

'Yes, that's more like it,' Woodend admitted. 'So what were you about to say?'

'That it's an elaborate theory, and elaborate theories have a habit of being widely off the mark,' Paco told him, 'but that in this case, Charlie, I am convinced you're right.'

'So where does that leave us?' Woodend asked.

'It leaves us making an excursion to Arco de Cañas,' Paco said.

Martin Cheavers, Her Britannic Majesty's Vice Consul to the Costa Blanca, was holding the telephone in one hand, and scratching vigorously under his left armpit with the other.

'Yes, Charlie,' he said into the phone. 'I see . . . Do you really think that's wise? . . . Well, you be careful. And that goes for Paco, too.'

He hung up and saw, with some annoyance, that his new assistant – who went by the improbable name of Gerwain Harrington Benson – was looking at him questioningly.

Cheavers had become Vice Consul in the 1950s, at which time he'd been running a largely dormant import–export company. It was a post he had more or less drifted into.

'I suspect the only reason the government wanted a consulate at all was to show that Britain was still a world power – which, of course, it

186

self-evidently wasn't,' he'd tell his dinner guests, 'and that the reason it chose to bestow the singular honour on me was because I was the only person in the entire region who was even vaguely suitable.'

In the fifties, his duties had involved little more than signing the odd letter and showing the occasional British VIP around. But the tourist boom in the sixties had ended all that, and soon he seemed to be spending half his time persuading the Spanish police that the drunken Brits they had in their cells were good lads really, and had just got a bit overexcited.

As the tourist industry had grown even more, he had acquired a staff. It had been locally employed at first, but then the Foreign Office had begun sending out bright young men from London on a one-year attachment.

'It'll be a good experience for them, Martin,' an official from Whitehall had explained to him over the phone. 'You can train them up.'

But what he had really meant, Cheavers decided, was that they could keep an eye on him – the maverick whom the FO had employed when it didn't really seem to matter, and whom it now couldn't quite find the right excuse to get rid of.

'So who was that you were just talking to on the phone?' asked his new deputy/handler.

'That,' said Cheavers, 'was Charlie Woodend.'

'Who's Charlie Woodend?'

'How long have you been here?' Cheavers asked.

'A couple of weeks.'

'And you still don't know who Charlie Woodend is? Haven't you read the files?'

'No, I've been . . . er . . . too busy absorbing the culture,' Harrington Benson said.

'Absorb too much culture, and you'll wreck your liver,' Cheavers told him sharply. 'Well, then, for your information, young man, Charlie Woodend is one half of the best Anglo-Spanish old-age pensioner detective agency on the whole of the Costa Blanca.'

'How many Anglo-Spanish old-age pensioner detective agencies are there on the Costa Blanca?' his new deputy asked.

'Given that combination – Anglo-Spanish, old-age pensioner, and detective agency – how many do you think there are likely to be?' Cheavers asked.

'I've absolutely no idea.'

And to think that one day, this idiot – Gerwain Fartington Bumhole, or whatever his bloody name was – would probably be one of Her Majesty's ambassadors, Cheavers thought with a sigh.

'There's only one,' he said.

'Then it's bound to be the best,' said his assistant, looking puzzled. 'And the worst, too.'

'Do you know, I'd never thought of it like that,' Cheavers said. 'What a sharp, analytical brain you do have, my boy.'

'Thank you,' his assistant said. 'And what was it, exactly, that this Charlie Woodend wanted?'

'Oh, he was just warning me that he could have a spot of trouble, and might need my help to sort it out,' Cheavers said vaguely.

'Trouble?' his deputy repeated. 'Difficulties with his residence permit? Something like that?'

'Yes, something like that,' Cheavers agreed.

Fifteen

Kate Meadows was in a bad mood, and it showed in the way she was driving, Jack Crane thought, as, for the third time since they'd set out, the sergeant only avoided a collision by wrenching violently on the steering wheel.

'Steady on, Sarge,' he said.

'Don't be such a baby, Jack,' Meadows replied, accelerating her way out of yet another potential accident.

'What's your problem?' Crane asked.

'My problem is that, as far as this case goes, good old Colin Beresford's been thrown a real chunk of meat to get his teeth into, and all we've been slipped is a nut cutlet.'

'You think what we're doing is a waste of time?'

'I know it's a waste of time.'

'The boss has to pursue this line of inquiry, if only to cover her back in case anything goes wrong,' Crane pointed out. 'And surely, as part of her team, we should be happy to help her to do that?'

'You're probably right,' Meadows agreed, slowing down to a speed which was only slightly dangerous. 'In fact, you're definitely right. We'll

189

go through the motions because that's what we need to do for the boss – but there's no reason why we can't have a bit of fun along the way, is there?'

Have a bit of fun?

Oh dear, Crane thought. He didn't like the sound of that at all.

Sunshine Holidays' main depot was outside the Whitebridge boundary, just on the edge of the moors. It had been built in a slight dip, and was invisible from half a mile away, so it was only when Meadows' car reached the crest of a small hill that it was suddenly – and dramatically – spread out in front of them.

'Behold – the Martinez Empire!' Crane said, with a flourish.

He had a point, thought Meadows. Covering an area larger than some of the nearby villages, it certainly did have an imperial feel about it.

The depot was surrounded by a large, electrified fence of reinforced wire netting, and the only entrance was the main double gate, next to the security officer's booth.

Meadows pulled up by the booth, and showed her warrant card to the guard, who was an oldish man with a grumpy expression.

'I'm so sorry to disturb you, when you're all so obviously in mourning,' she said.

'In what?' the guard asked.

'In mourning!' Meadows repeated. 'For your boss!'

The guard sniffed. 'I suppose there's some that might mourn him,' he conceded.

Once through the gate, they could see the

complex in all its commercial grandeur. Two large garages – almost as big as aircraft hangars – ran along the east and south sides of it. Next to the south wall garage, there was a car wash, and just beyond the east wall garage were a series of petrol pumps. The north side of the compound was used as a workers' car park, and along the west side there was a row of one-storey buildings where the offices, toilets and canteen were housed.

'It's a big business,' Meadows said.

'It's forty per cent larger than its nearest northern rival,' replied Crane, who had an annoying habit of always doing his homework.

For much of the first couple of hours of their journey northwards, they had the Mediterranean Sea to their right, and orange groves to their left, and given the almost agonizingly slow speed at which they were travelling, Woodend had ample opportunity to enjoy both these sights.

He should have insisted on hiring a bigger car – one that wasn't going to be overtaken by almost every other vehicle on the road – he thought.

But he knew, deep down, that that would have been a mistake. Paco was now too old to legally drive a hire car, and while the two of them might be equal partners in the business, this was still his country, and it would have hurt his pride to have been chauffeured around it.

Where he should have put his foot down, Woodend decided, was over their route. It was clear from the map that the quickest way to get to Arco de Cañas would have been to go through Madrid.

Yet Paco had been adamant on this point, too.

'You can't just go by the maps,' he'd said. 'You must take the road conditions into account, too.'

'But going to Madrid, and from there to Burgos, we'd be travelling on much wider roads than the ones on the route you propose,' Woodend had argued.

'It will be quicker to go north, and then cut across country,' Paco had said firmly.

And Woodend had been forced to accept it, even though he was sure that if they'd gone by the other route, they would have been much closer to their destination by now.

The orange groves began to peter out, and soon they were passing stretches of water which could have been taken for inland lakes, had it not been for the fact they were rectangular, and clearly man-made.

'Those are rice fields,' Paco explained. 'If you look at the military map of Spain in the early stages of the Civil War, you will see that most of the areas held by the Republic grew rice, and most of the areas held by the fascists grew wheat. And the reason for that is obvious, isn't it?'

'Not to me.'

'The wheat areas were controlled by the big, powerful landlords, whose interest was in keeping the common man down, and who forced the workers to join the fascist army. The rice fields were controlled by cooperatives – people working together in the interests of the community.'

'That's interesting,' Woodend said.

And normally, he would have found it interesting. But there was only one thing occupying his mind at that moment, and that was the investigation.

It would be, he was sure, his last big case – and he was eager to get stuck into it.

'When do you think we will reach Arco de Cañas?' he asked.

Paco shrugged – and even that slight gesture seemed to shake the little car.

'Not for a while,' he said.

'Six o'clock?' Woodend suggested. 'Seven o'clock?'

'Not quite so soon,' Paco said evasively.

'Eight o'clock? Nine o'clock?' Woodend asked.

'It will be some time tomorrow,' Paco replied.

'Until he was elected to parliament, Mr Robert was in charge of the day-to-day running of the business,' said Lewis Mitchell, who, according to the brass plate on his desk, was the managing director of Sunshine Holidays. 'And since I've only been in this job for a few months, I'm not sure how much of a help I can be to you.'

She'd got his number, Meadows thought. He was one of those bland men who never want to commit themselves to anything, and who believe that if they can just manage to go through life wearing their amiability on their sleeves, no one will ever have the heart to challenge them.

'Well, I suppose you could start by telling us everything you know about the stiff,' she suggested.

'The . . . er . . . stiff,' Mitchell repeated, uneasily.

'Javier Martinez,' Meadows said. 'He's the stiff that I was referring to – unless you can think of any others.'

'No . . . er . . . as far as I know, there's only Mr Javier,' Mitchell replied.

'So what was he like?'

'I didn't really have much to do with him. He was mainly concerned with accounts and purchasing, and he did most of that from his home. He left the actual business of running the coaches to me. If anybody checked up on how things were going on this side of the operation, it was Mr Robert.'

'But you must have seen Mr Javier from time to time, didn't you?' Meadows persisted.

'Yes, I suppose I must.'

'So what did you think of him?'

'He . . . er . . . wasn't an easy man to get to know.'

'So you didn't like him,' Meadows said. 'And is your view shared by the majority of the people who worked for him?'

'I never said I didn't like him,' Mitchell replied, flustered, 'and if you want to know what other people thought about him, I suggest you ask them.'

'My, my, my, you *really* didn't like him,' Meadows said, grinning.

Despite his concern that Meadows might decide to have a little too much fun, Crane couldn't help smiling inwardly. This direct approach, which he had privately named the 'Jab the Subject with a

Pointy Stick and See How Much He Squeals', was not unique to Sergeant Kate Meadows – but she certainly used it more than most other officers did.

'You really didn't like him, but I don't think you disliked him enough to kill him,' Meadows continued.

'I strongly resent that!' Mitchell told her.

'Oh,' Meadows said, sounding surprised. 'Have I got it wrong?'

'You most certainly have.'

'So you did dislike him enough to kill him?'

'No, I . . . what I meant was . . .'

'Look, Mr Mitchell, all we want is for you to be honest with us,' Meadows said, switching to a soft, persuasive tone. 'I can assure you that anything you tell us will never leave this office.'

Mitchell took out his handkerchief, and mopped his brow.

'I didn't warm to Mr Javier,' he confessed. 'But that's mainly due to his reputation, because, as I said, I've had little personal experience.'

'And what is his reputation?' Meadows wondered.

'They say he was a socialist when he lived in Spain – that he really cared for other people – but having this business seemed to have changed him. In his last few years running the company, he could have given General Franco lessons in authoritarianism.'

'Really?' Meadows said.

'Really,' Mitchell confirmed. 'There were no second chances with him. If you were late for work a couple of times, you were gone, and never mind the fact that the reason you were late was because you'd been visiting your sick wife in hospital or attending your mother's funeral. Of course, things changed when Mr Robert took over. Everybody liked him – and he seemed to like everybody.'

'Which of the staff has worked for Sunshine Holidays the longest?' Meadows asked.

'That would be Fred Sidebotham,' Mitchell said. 'I believe he's been here right from the time the company started.'

'Then given Javier's general attitude, he must have been an exemplary employee to have survived so long.'

'I wouldn't put it quite like that.'

'You're being overcautious again,' Meadows said, with a gentle hint of warning in her voice.

'By all accounts, Fred used to be a very good worker, but some years ago, he started to develop a weakness for the drink,' Mitchell explained.

'And Javier didn't sack him?'

'From what I've heard, he did want to get rid of him, but Mr Robert wouldn't have it. They had a blazing row about it – the only one anyone can remember them having. Mr Javier said that Fred was useless, and had to go. And Mr Robert said that he'd served the company loyally for a good many years, and if that meant the company had to carry him until he retired, then that was exactly what the company would bloody well do.'

'Where can I find this Fred Sidebotham?' Meadows asked.

'He'll probably be behind the south side

196

garage, sitting on an oil drum and reading the newspaper. Chances are, he'll have a bottle of brown ale hidden behind the drum, but if I were you, I'd pretend not to notice it. I always do.'

Meadows stood up and held out her hand. 'Thank you, Mr Mitchell, you've been very helpful,' she said.

It was early afternoon when Paniatowski and Robert Martinez paid their call on Doña Rosa. Martinez had been expecting the interview to take place in the cosy atmosphere of the kitchen, but the old woman had other ideas, and ushered her guests into the formality of her small front parlour. Once inside, Doña Rosa gestured that they should sit on the sofa, while she herself took the straight-backed chair which she had placed facing it.

'Wouldn't you be more comfortable on a padded chair, Doña Rosa?' Martinez asked solicitously.

'My grandmother never sat on a padded chair in her life – and she lived to be ninety-four,' the old woman replied.

'Yes, of course,' Martinez said, giving into the inevitable. 'You know why we're here, don't you, Doña Rosa?' he continued, in a soothing tone. 'Detective Chief Inspector Paniatowski would like you to tell her what you told me this morning, and she's given me her word that you won't get into any trouble for it.'

The old woman nodded.

'I will trust you because Don Roberto trusts you,' she told Paniatowski. 'He is a good man.'

197

'Yes, I know he is,' Paniatowski agreed.

'And the Hispanic Circle – which he, and he alone, created – is a wonderful thing,' the old woman continued. 'It has brought Spain back to those of us who missed it so much that it was breaking our hearts. It has given us a reason to carry on living.' She sighed. 'Of course, it is not quite the same now that he has deserted us.' Then she smiled, to take the edge off her words. 'But I cannot blame him for that – he is still a young man, and he has more important things to do with his time than spend it with people like us, who already have one foot in the grave.'

Robert Martinez laughed awkwardly, then said, 'Tell Monika how you met Elena, Doña Rosa.'

'I was walking past the bus station on last Tuesday evening when I saw a woman sitting on a bench,' she said. 'She was shivering with the cold, and she was singing to herself to keep her spirits up.' She looked Paniatowski straight in the eye. 'People like us know a lot about singing to keep our spirits up.'

'I can understand that,' Paniatowski said sympathetically. 'Are you sure it was on Tuesday that you saw her?'

'Yes,' Doña Rosa said firmly. 'Tuesday is my day for visiting Doña Antonia, a poor old soul who is bedridden. Once, when I had a bad cold, I did not visit her until Wednesday, and she was most upset.' She shrugged. 'The old have strange notions of how they want things to run – and I should know, because I am old myself – but it is not for anyone else to question those notions, and so I have visited her every Tuesday for nearly ten years.'

The porter at the railway station had said in his statement that Elena had arrived on Wednesday, Paniatowski thought, and Dr Shastri was almost certain that it had been on Wednesday evening when her body had been dumped into the canal. Yet here was Doña Rosa claiming that it was definitely Tuesday when she had seen the woman.

'Please go on,' she said.

'To my eternal shame, I think I would have walked right past her if I hadn't heard the words of the song she was singing,' Doña Rosa said. 'But I did hear the words. The song was "*Ay Carmela*".'

'What's that?' Paniatowski asked.

Instead of answering, the old woman began to sing in a voice that was thin and cracked, and yet held great emotion.

'El Ejército del Ebro
Rumba la rumba la rumba la
El Ejército del Ebro
Rumba la rumba la rumba la
una noche en el río paso

Ay Carmela! Ay Carmela!
Rumba la rumba la rumba la
Ay Carmela! Ay Carmela!
Rumba la rumba la rumba la'

'It was one of the most popular songs of the Republican forces,' Robert Martinez explained.

'I asked her who she was, and said her name

was Elena, and that she had arrived here that same day,' the old woman continued. 'I asked her what she was doing in Whitebridge, and she said she was on unfinished business.'

'Did you ask her what that unfinished business was?'

'No, if she had wanted to tell me, she would have done, but she did not, and so it was none of my concern.' Doña Rosa paused. 'Those last few years I spent in Spain, I learned it was safer for everyone not to ask questions – because the less you knew, the less you could betray.'

'What happened next?'

'I said I would walk with her to her lodgings, but she said that she did not have any, because she couldn't afford them. I asked her where she would spend the night, and she told me she would sleep on the bench, as she had often had to do in the old days. That was when I invited her back to my home.'

If Elena really had arrived a day earlier than the porter had said – and it was looking increasingly likely that she had – then why hadn't she gone straight to her husband's house? Why had she, instead, decided to spend the night outdoors, in the freezing cold?

'It was very kind of you to invite her into your home, Doña Rosa,' Paniatowski said.

'Kindness had nothing to do with it!' the old woman said fiercely. 'I was showing solidarity with a comrade!'

'What happened when you came back here?'

'I made her some food – though she seemed too nervous to eat much – and then we talked.'

'What did you talk about?'

'About a world that that *hijo de puta* Francisco Franco has crushed beneath his heavy jackboot – a world of innocence, where the mountain air was always fresh, and people respected themselves and each other.'

'She didn't talk about Javier Martinez?'

'No.'

'And you didn't mention him, either?'

'Why should I have?' Doña Rosa asked, sounding puzzled. 'I didn't know the man. I have never even spoken to him.'

'Not even at meetings of the Hispanic Circle?' Paniatowski asked.

'He never went to a meeting of the Circle,' Doña Rosa replied.

'I thought I'd told you that my father had embraced the British way of life wholeheartedly,' Robert said to Paniatowski. 'He wanted nothing to do with Spain, or with the Spanish community in Whitebridge.'

'But what about the picture in the newspaper?' Paniatowski asked. 'The one in which he's standing with you and Louisa?'

'He's not standing with us, he's standing behind us,' Robert Martinez said. 'It was a mistake.'

'A mistake?'

'Louisa and I were in my office, planning a Hispanic Circle excursion, when the newspaper photographer arrived. He was only intending to take a picture of me, but I said it would be nice if Louisa was in it, too. The photographer was new to the job, and wanted to make sure he'd get it right, so he took rather a lot of

201

shots. My father wandered in halfway through – as he does. He knew that the photographer was taking pictures for the article, but he did not know that he would be caught in one of them. He was furious when he saw it printed in the paper.'

'Why was that?' Paniatowski asked.

'He didn't say, but I assume it was because he didn't want anyone thinking that he was a member of the Hispanic Circle.'

So Javier Martinez really had turned his back on Spain and all things Spanish, Paniatowski thought.

Then why had he had all those pictures of his native country on his bedroom wall?

The Manchester police force had over eight thousand officers on its rolls, while Mid-Lancs had a little over a third that number. The Manchester police had a helicopter. It had crime labs that were state-of-the-art. And though, since the moment he had walked through the door of its headquarters, Beresford had kept reminding himself that he was a good bobby, who had played a part in any number of successful investigations, he still could not help feeling like a bit of a hayseed.

The officer who'd been assigned to look after him while he was in Manchester was called DI Henry James.

'Like the feller who wrote all those books, you know.'

Beresford didn't know, though he had no doubt that Crane would.

'*The Wings of a Dove, Portrait of a Lady, Washington Square*?' James said helpfully.

'I'm afraid that none of them ring any bells for me,' Beresford said apologetically.

'I'm not surprised,' James told him. 'I read one of them once – what with us sharing the same name and everything – and it was so bloody boring and fussy that I never got past the first few pages.'

Beresford grinned, and decided he quite liked Inspector James.

'We showed the sketch you sent us around Ringway Airport, and one of the officers at passport control says he definitely remembers her arriving on a flight from Alicante last Tuesday,' James said. 'But he's almost certain that she wasn't using the name you gave us.'

The name was no problem, Beresford thought – Charlie Woodend had already informed them that Elena had been travelling under a false passport – but the day definitely was.

'Are you sure it was Tuesday?' he asked. 'It couldn't have been Wednesday, could it?'

DI James looked down at his notes. 'There was no flight on Wednesday,' he said. 'The next flight after the Tuesday one is on Thursday morning.'

And Thursday would have been too late – since the canal was frozen over by then – so the porter on Whitebridge station must have got it wrong.

'One of the airport bus drivers remembers taking her to Victoria railway station. He described her as "a little old lady dressed all in black".'

'She was a little old lady, all right, but she wasn't dressed like that when we found her,' Beresford said.

'No, she wouldn't have been,' James agreed. 'When we showed the sketch around Victoria Station, nobody remembered seeing her – despite the fact that dressed as she was, she should have stuck out like a sore thumb. So I started to think that maybe the reason we lost the trail there was because she didn't stick out any longer, and that's when I got some of my lads to canvass all the clothing stores in the immediate vicinity.'

'And did they come up with anything?'

'They had no luck at all with the shops selling new clothes, but we struck pay dirt with the owner of a second-hand shop.' James paused and smiled as if he were remembering a private joke. 'But even though she wasn't dressed in black any more, it's strange that nobody on Victoria Station recognized her from the sketch, don't you think?'

'Yes,' Beresford agreed, 'it is.'

But no stranger than the fact that – with the exception of the porter at Whitebridge railway station – nobody in Whitebridge recalled seeing her, either, he added mentally.

'Well, I think I can explain how that might have happened,' James said, and there was now definitely an amused twinkle in his eye.

'You can?' Beresford asked.

'Yes. You see, she didn't just get her skirt, blouse, cardigan and overcoat from the second-hand store – she also bought her disguise there!'

'Her disguise!' Beresford exclaimed – just as he was supposed to.

'That's right,' James said. 'And now, I imagine you'd like to talk to the owner of the second-hand store yourself.'

'Too bloody right, I would,' Beresford agreed.

'Did you see all the pictures on the wall of that office?' Crane said, as he and Meadows walked towards the south side garage.

'No, I didn't,' Meadows replied.

'The whole history of the company's up there,' Crane said, 'starting from a few old rickety buses in 1945 and going up to the shiny fleet they run now. And while you might not like Javier Martinez's methods very much, you have to admire him for his achievement, don't you?'

'Do I?' Meadows asked, non-committally.

They turned the corner, and found Fred Sidebotham sitting on the oil drum, just as Mitchell had predicted he would be.

He was a small man. He had a greasy cap on his head, and though his overalls were heavily stained with oil, none of those stains looked recent.

'We're from the police, Mr Sidebotham,' Meadows said, producing her warrant card. 'Would you mind if we asked you a few questions?'

Sidebotham blinked. 'This would be about Chavier Martinez's murder, would it?'

'That's right,' Meadows agreed.

'Well, it wasn't me who topped him, though I'd certainly like to shake the hand of the man who did,' Sidebotham said.

'You went back a long way together, didn't you?' Meadows asked.

'We did,' Sidebotham agreed. 'Right back to 1946, in fact. I'd just come out of the army, and was looking for work. And Chavier, who'd spent the war working in the aircraft factory, had built up a little nest egg from his overtime payments, and decided he wanted to start up his own business. He bought these three old buses – they were only held together by sealing wax and string – and started running trips to the local markets.'

'So he was in the right place at the right time,' Meadows suggested.

'Wrong, lass,' Fred said. 'It might have been the right place, but it definitely wasn't the right time. There was still petrol rationing, you see, and sometimes he couldn't run the buses because he didn't have the fuel.' He chuckled. 'He had to sack one of his drivers after a few months. He'd have liked to sack me, too, but he couldn't afford to.'

'Why not?'

'Because I was the only feller who could keep them buses on the road. I went all over Lancashire, searching scrap yards for spare parts, and no sooner had I got one of the buses running than another of the buggers would break down. Anyway, it got to the point where he couldn't afford to keep me and he couldn't afford to let me go – and that's when he offered me a partnership. He said he'd give me twenty per cent of the company if I'd work for half the pay I was getting at that time, and because I'd grown quite fond of those old buses, I agreed.'

'You're not a partner now, are you?' Meadows asked.

'No, I'm bloody well not,' Fred agreed. 'One day in 1951, Chavier came up and said he couldn't see the business ever making much of a profit, and that he was feeling guilty about the fact I'd been on half-pay for the last five years. So he offered to buy my stake in the company for the amount of money I'd missed out on in wages. Well, I thought that was more than generous, and I accepted.'

'And the day after you'd signed on the dotted line, some new coaches turned up,' Meadows guessed.

'It was a couple of months later, and the coaches were good second-hand, rather than new – but you're close enough,' Fred said. 'It didn't bother me at first. Two and a half years' pay was a handy sum of cash. I bought a brand-new stair carpet for the wife, and a whippet for myself. But over time, it slowly started to sink in that when Chavier said he didn't think the business would ever make much of a profit, he'd been lying – that it must have already been making a profit, or he'd never have had the money to buy more coaches. For five years, I'd been scraping by – doing a second and third job when I'd finished work here – just to keep them bloody buses on the road. And then he lied to me. And it was the lying – rather than losing my share – that really got to me.'

'Why didn't you leave?' Crane asked.

Fred shook his head at the younger man's obvious naivety.

'It was in the fifties that this area really began to decline,' he said. 'The mills were starting to close down, and there were more folk looking for jobs than there were jobs to be had. So if you did already have a job, you bloody clung on to it.' He reached down and took a swig from his bottle of brown ale, not caring whether they noticed or not. 'Besides,' he continued, 'I always thought the sting would go away in time – that in a few years, I'd be able to look back at it, and laugh about what a mug I'd been. But it never went away – it just got worse and worse. And that's why I'd like to shake the hand of the man who choked the life out of Chavier Martinez.'

Sixteen

Paniatowski sat at a copper-topped table in the saloon bar of the Hanging Gate, waiting for Robert Martinez to return with the drinks, and examining, without much interest, the horse brasses and pewter mugs hanging on the walls. It was not the kind of pub she would normally have chosen to spend any time in, she thought, but it was close to Doña Rosa's house, and besides, she was unlikely to run into any of her colleagues there.

But why should it bother her if she did run into any of her colleagues? she wondered.

After all – and whatever Colin Beresford might

think – Robert Martinez had just given her considerable help with her investigation, so what could be more natural than that she should go for a drink with him?

Martinez arrived, bearing a pint for himself and a glass of vodka for Paniatowski.

For perhaps a minute, they sat in an uncomfortable silence, as if neither of them was quite sure, now that they were finally alone, what to use as a conversation opener.

Then Paniatowski said, 'I'm very grateful to you for finding Doña Rosa for me, Robert. Really I am.'

'Then could I ask for a favour in return?' Robert Martinez said.

Paniatowski's body tensed.

If he was going to ask her to keep him abreast of the investigation, that clearly couldn't happen.

And if he was just looking for an opportunity to get her into his bed, that shouldn't happen – at least, until the investigation was concluded.

'What kind of favour?' she asked cautiously.

'In Spain, there's a tradition that the dead are buried as soon as practicable – often only twenty-four hours after they have passed away – and for that reason, I wish to hold my mother's funeral as soon as Dr Shastri has released the body,' Robert Martinez said.

'And you want me to do all that I can to speed up the process?' Paniatowski said.

Martinez looked shocked at the very idea.

'Oh no! Certainly not!' he said. 'I wouldn't want you to think I was using you as an *enchufe*.'

'As a what?'

Martinez smiled. 'Forgive me, I didn't mean to confuse you. *Enchufe* is the Spanish word for socket, and what it really means, in this context, is having friends in high places.'

'So what *do* you want me to do?' Paniatowski asked, mystified.

'I want my mother to have someone else – as well as me – standing at the graveside as she is buried,' Martinez said.

'And you'd like that someone to be me?'

'Yes.'

'But why?'

'Because I like you, and I think she would have liked you if she'd lived long enough to get to know you – and because you seem a very caring person, who can feel sorrow even over the death of a stranger.'

The passion and sincerity in his words made her tingle.

God, but I really, really, want to sleep with this man, she thought.

'I'd be honoured to attend your mother's funeral,' she said. 'I'll come to your father's too, if you'd like me to.'

Martinez shook his head. 'That's very kind – but not necessary,' he said. 'My father had enough friends – or at least close acquaintances – to more than fill the chapel in the crematorium.'

'You're having him cremated!' Paniatowski gasped.

'I'm sorry, does that offend you as a Roman Catholic?' Martinez asked. 'It shouldn't, you know. The pope has given cremation his full approval.'

210

'No, it's nothing to do with religion,' Paniatowski said. 'I stopped being a believer years ago.'

'But something's clearly upset you,' Martinez persisted.

'A couple of years ago, I had my father's bones brought from Poland,' Paniatowski explained. 'I had them buried next to my mother. I thought it was a beautiful thing, and I'm a little shocked, I suppose, that you'd consider doing anything else.'

'It wasn't my decision to take,' Robert said. 'My father always expressed a strong wish to be cremated. Perhaps, after seeing my mother in the mortuary, he might eventually have decided that if they could not be united in life, they could at least have been united in death. But we can't know for certain that he would have changed his mind, and since his last instruction to me was that he should be cremated, I must respect that wish.' He smiled awkwardly. 'I have always done my best to be a dutiful son.'

'I'm sure you have,' Paniatowski said.

And the urge to sleep with him was stronger than ever.

The shop was located on Hanover Street. The sign above it said, 'Hope's Fashions', and below it, a second sign said – a little more accurately – 'Quality Second-Hand Clothing at Affordable Prices.'

The owner, Mr Hope, was a middle-aged man with a pot belly. He had lost most of the hair on the top of his head, and had compensated for

211

the fact by growing what looked like small haystacks over his ears.

He seemed willing enough to talk – in fact, the only problem they were ever likely to have with him as a witness was shutting him up, Beresford thought.

'You ask me how I can remember an individual customer a week after she came into the shop,' Hope said – although Beresford had not, in fact, got round to asking that at all. 'Well, I'll tell you. It's not very often an old woman dressed entirely in black comes through that door, and besides,' he added slightly gloomily, 'I've not exactly been rushed off my feet recently, so the customers I do get tend to stick in my mind.'

'What did she . . .?' Beresford began.

'You probably want to know what she bought,' Hope interrupted him. 'She wanted a full outfit – head to toe. "I'm starting a new life," she told me, "and I want new clothes to go with it."'

She was starting a new life, Beresford repeated silently – a life based around two people she thought she had lost nearly forty years earlier. And she deserved a new life, if anybody did. Yet less than twenty-four hours later, she would be dead.

'Did she buy her underwear from you?' he asked.

'I don't sell second-hand underwear,' Hope said. 'I tried it once, but people just wouldn't go for it. I even had this sign up, "All our underwear has been double-bleached," but you could see the customers thinking about where

212

it might have been before it was double bleached, and . . .'

'Do you happen to know where she did buy her underwear from?' Beresford interrupted.

'I sent her to my cousin Hymie's shop, which is just down the road. I told her to show him my card, so he'd give her a discount.'

'So you sold her what, exactly?'

Hope gave a perfect description of the clothes Elena had been wearing when she'd been fished out of the canal.

'Did she have a suitcase with her?' Beresford asked.

Hope closed his eyes, as if he thought that would help him remember.

'No,' he said, 'she had a small carrying bag – no more than a big handbag, really, and certainly not large enough to hold a change of clothes.'

'So what happened next?'

'What do you think happened? We made a deal – she didn't even bother to haggle – she handed over the money, and then she asked me where the changing rooms were.'

'Is there a changing room?' Beresford asked.

'Well, no, as you can see for yourself, this isn't the type of business that has one, but she looked so dropped on when I told her that, so I said she could go into the back room, which is where I make my brew. And that's just what she did. She looked quite a different woman when she came out again. I mean, she still wouldn't have had builders wolf-whistling after her as she walked down the street, but she at least looked as if she belonged in the twentieth century.'

'You've forgotten the hat,' Inspector James said.

'So I have,' Hope admitted. 'I'll be forgetting my own head next.' He turned to Beresford. 'She said she wanted a hat – and that it had to be a big one.'

'A big one?' Beresford repeated. 'What do you mean by that?'

'I mean that she didn't want one that sat on the top of her head, a bit like a cherry on a cake. What she said she needed was one with a wide brim.'

'Her disguise,' Inspector James mouthed.

Beresford nodded.

'Did you find her a hat?' he asked the shopkeeper.

'I did,' Hope replied, 'but hats for women aren't really fashionable any more, and I had to rummage through the whole of the storeroom to find it. It didn't really suit her, to be honest – she looked like a very tiny John Wayne – but she seemed more than happy with it.'

'What happened to the clothes she was wearing when she came in?' Beresford asked.

'She left them here,' Hope told him. 'She said if I could sell them, I could keep the money.'

'That was nice of her.'

'Yes, it was,' Hope agreed. 'She was a nice woman – though to be honest, it would have been easier to sell Buckingham Palace to the Queen than it would have been to shift that stuff.'

'So what did you do with it?'

'Put it in the bin outside,' Hope said, and before

Beresford could ask the inevitable question, he added: 'It was collected on Wednesday.'

It was less than eighteen hours since Javier Martinez's body had been discovered, and the two Scenes of Crime Officers (SOCOs for short), were still hard at work in the house that Javier Martinez had shared with his son.

That the two men had surnames was beyond doubt, but almost no one on the Whitebridge police force used them. Indeed, it was doubtful if most of the officers knew what their surnames were. Instead, they were always referred to as Eddie-n-Bill – as distinct from Eddie and Bill – which reflected the fact that it was virtually impossible to think about one of them without also thinking of the other.

It was Eddie, the short, round one, who responded to the knock on the door, to find Meadows and Crane standing there.

'Good evening, Sergeant Meadows,' he said, the delight evident in his voice. 'And what can we do for you on this cold, dark winter's evening?'

And he was thinking, *If I was a few years younger, quite a bit taller, a lot better looking, and about three times more sophisticated than I am now, I might just have a chance with you, darling.*

'There's a couple of things I'd like to check on inside, if that's all right with you,' Meadows said.

'Anything your little heart desires would be more than all right with me,' Eddie said.

Bill, who was tall and thin, appeared in the doorway behind his partner.

'Actually, that's not strictly true, Sarge,' he said hastily. 'We're not supposed to let anyone in until we've finished the job, and this is a big house, so we're nowhere near done yet.'

'Have you finished in the victim's bedroom?' Meadows asked.

'Well, yes,' Bill admitted. 'It being the actual scene of the crime, it was the first room we examined.'

'That's the only room I want to look at,' Meadows told him. 'In fact, I don't even want to look at the room – I just want to skim through the accountancy ledgers that Javier Martinez kept in there.'

'There couldn't be any harm in that, could there?' Eddie asked his partner.

'No, I suppose not,' Bill agreed.

'And if you want somebody to turn the pages over for you, Sergeant, you've only to ask,' Eddie said.

Meadows grinned at him. 'I'd love to have you turn over my pages, Eddie,' she said, running her tongue along the edge of her lips suggestively. 'I'd even let you carry my briefcase home for me, but if I did, my friend here,' she pointed at Crane, 'would start getting jealous.'

'Fair enough,' Eddie said philosophically.

'Eddie fancies you, you know,' Crane whispered to Meadows, as they walked up the stairs.

'You don't say,' Meadows replied. 'You know, Jack, with a keen eye like yours, you ought to be a detective.'

They entered the bedroom, and Meadows

walked straight over to the bookcase containing the row of leather-bound ledgers.

'What does the fact that Javier Martinez kept the ledgers here tell you about the man himself, Jack?' Meadows asked, as she pondered on which of the ledgers to select.

'I'm not sure,' Crane admitted. 'What does it tell you?'

'It tells me that the closest thing in the world to his heart was money.'

Meadows selected the ledger that had 1957 stamped on it, and took it across to the roll-top desk.

'I didn't know that you'd had any formal training in accountancy, Sarge,' Crane said.

'I haven't,' Meadows replied, flipping the ledger open at random. 'But I used to employ a whole team of accountants, and I picked up a few tricks from them.' She paused. 'By the way, that particular piece of information is not for general dissemination.'

'Of course not,' agreed Crane, who had made a sort of hobby out of attempting to piece together Kate Meadows' past history from the occasional hints she let slip – though so far, he had to admit, it was a hobby in which he had made very little progress.

Ten minutes passed, then fifteen and Meadows was still poring over the ledger.

Crane wandered up and down the room, stopping occasionally to examine one of the framed photographs hanging on the wall. The mountains were impressive, he thought, and even the plains had a kind of bleak grandeur about them. The only thing that was missing was any pictures of the sea, and he wondered why that was.

Another fifteen minutes slipped by, and Crane was starting to get both bored and hungry.

'There's one thing I don't understand, Sarge,' he said.

'There are many things that you don't understand, young Jack – in fact, I could fill a book with them,' replied Meadows, who was obviously annoyed at being disturbed. 'What particular thing are you fretting about now?'

'When we were driving out to the Sunshine Holidays' depot, you said this line of investigation was a complete waste of time, didn't you?'

'Yes, I do seem to remember saying something along those lines,' Meadows agreed.

'And yet here we are, long after we could – in all conscience – have called it a day, still pursuing that line.'

'So clearly, I must have changed my mind about it being a waste of time,' Meadows said.

'And what's made you do that?'

'There's something that's not quite right about Sunshine Holidays,' Meadows told him. 'I can sense it, I can smell it – but I haven't quite been able to put my finger on it yet.'

'I can't say I've noticed anything,' Crane said.

'That's because you're an admirably straightforward young man,' Meadows said. 'I, in stark contrast, am neither particularly admirable nor particularly straightforward. Now why don't you stick your hand in your trousers and play

218

pocket billiards with yourself, while I finish the job?'

It was another half an hour before Meadows finally closed the ledger with a frustrated slam.

'I'm out of my depth,' she announced. 'I'm going to have to get some help on this job.'

'You mean a forensic accountant?' Crane asked.

'No, I was thinking that I might ask a bricklayer or a national hunt jockey to give me a hand,' Meadows said, somewhat tartly. 'Of course I mean a forensic accountant, Jack!'

'Well, good luck with the mountain of request forms you'll have to fill in first,' Crane said.

Meadows smiled. 'You seem to be under the impression I'll be getting my forensic accountant through the good offices of the Whitebridge police force.'

'And won't you?'

'Absolutely not. I don't want someone who's prepared to work for the pittance that this town will pay him – I want the best.'

'And, of course, you know exactly where to get your hands on the best, don't you?' Crane asked.

'Naturally,' Meadows agreed.

Seventeen

Once they had crossed the provincial border and entered Cataluña, they turned away from the sea and headed towards the mountains. The roads soon became steep, narrow and twisty. Several times, it seemed as if the little Seat was about to give up the ghost, but then, in response to its driver's urgings, it found the strength to make another effort.

As night was falling, they arrived at a mountain inn, which was built of huge blocks of stone and had a sharply sloping roof. Inside, the beams were exposed, and the only illumination came from the flickering oil lamps and the blazing log fire.

They were the only overnight guests, but they were not the only customers. Several shepherds – hard mountain men of an indeterminate age – stood drinking at the bar, and though they nodded to the new arrivals in an accepting manner, they made no attempt to start a conversation.

The meal the two ex-policemen were served consisted of mountain ham as a starter, followed by a thick, rich peasant stew, all of which was washed down with rough red wine.

It was as the plates were being cleared away that Paco said, 'I have a confession to make.'

'Go on then,' Woodend said. .

'When I told you that this was the quickest route to Arco de Cañas, I was lying,' Paco told him. 'I should not have done that.'

'It doesn't matter,' Woodend assured him.

'It does matter,' Paco insisted. 'You are my friend, Charlie. I should never have lied to you, and my only excuse – which really is no excuse at all – is that I was ashamed.'

'Ashamed of what?'

'Ashamed that I was not quite brave enough to go back to Madrid. May I explain?'

'Yes, of course.'

'I was a country boy when I first went there – an orphan – but it is a city with a big heart, and it soon adopted me. I loved it, Charlie – I still love it. And I could not bear the thought of seeing how it has changed – how the whole place has become a monument to that fascist butcher Franco.'

'I should have understood that right from the start,' Woodend said sympathetically. 'I should have appreciated how hard it would be – and if anyone should apologize, it should be me.'

'I have added perhaps half a day to our journey,' Paco said.

'It's not important,' Woodend told him. 'The roots of the crime we're investigating are nearly forty years old. Getting to them a few hours later isn't going to make much difference.'

Paco smiled – perhaps a little sadly.

'Not important?' he repeated. 'It's almost killing you that we're taking so long to reach Arco de Cañas. Why is that, Charlie? Why does this case matter so much to you?'

'It's a major investigation,' Woodend said, 'and it seems a long time since I was involved in a major investigation.'

'But that's not the whole story, is it?' Paco asked.

'No,' Woodend admitted, 'it isn't – but it's as much as I'm prepared to say for now.'

Paco nodded. 'We have a long drive tomorrow, and I think I will go to bed now,' he said.

'I'll be up in a few minutes myself,' Woodend said, reaching for the wine flagon.

Ben Higgins, the railway porter, was far from pleased to see Beresford standing on his front doorstep again, but then he caught the look in the policeman's eyes and decided it probably wouldn't be very wise to complain too much about it.

'You told me the woman you identified arrived in Whitebridge on Wednesday,' Beresford said, without preamble.

'That's right, I did,' the porter agreed.

'And you're sure it was Wednesday, are you?'

'Yes,' Higgins said. 'I'd stake my wife's life on it.'

'Well, that is strange,' Beresford said, 'because you see, she was spotted in Manchester, getting on the train for Whitebridge, on Tuesday afternoon, and while I know some of the services between Manchester and Whitebridge are slow, I've never heard of one taking twenty-four hours before!'

'It may have been Tuesday that I saw her,' Higgins admitted.

'It may have been Tuesday,' Beresford repeated in disgust. 'And what about the bloody hat?'

'The hat?'

'The hat that, according to the man who sold it to her, was nearly as big as a bloody Stetson! Why didn't you think to mention that?'

'You asked me what she was wearing,' the porter said, sounding as if he felt he was being unfairly persecuted.

'Yes, I most certainly did,' Beresford agreed.

'Well, there you are then – she wasn't wearing the hat, she was carrying it in her hand.'

Once Paco had gone to bed, Woodend closed his eyes, and thought about what would probably be happening at that moment back in Whitebridge.

The team would already have gathered around their usual table in the Drum and Monkey, and perhaps by now they would have finished briefing each other on what they had discovered during the day, and begun hammering out theories that fitted with the facts.

He found himself wishing he could be there in the Drum himself – just for half an hour.

Not at the corner table, of course. That table was Monika's now. She had earned the right to preside over it.

No, he wished that he could be a fly on the wall, proudly watching his protégée at work.

Eyes open again, he looked into the warm glow of the fire and turned his mind to what might happen the next day, when they finally reached Arco de Cañas.

'You will take care, Charlie, won't you?' Joan had asked, before he and Paco had left Calpe.

And he had replied, 'Of course we'll take care – not that there's likely to be anything we'll need to take care about.'

He'd meant the words when he'd said them, but now, up there in the mountains – up there in a world so different from his cosy seaside existence that he might almost be on another planet – he was not quite so confident.

223

The Civil War was far from dead and buried –
the recent events in Whitebridge proved that
– so there might well be trouble waiting for them
in Arco de Cañas, and a wise man, it seemed to
him, would turn back now.

'But then you've never been particularly wise,
have you, Charlie?' he asked himself.

'The most important thing we seem to have
learned about Elena is that she didn't arrive on
Wednesday, as we previously thought, but on
Tuesday,' Paniatowski told the team, across the
corner table in the Drum and Monkey.

'And we know that for a fact, not just because
Doña Rosa said it, but because it's been confirmed
by the Manchester police,' Beresford added.

'So the really interesting question is why she
didn't go straight to Martinez's house,'
Paniatowski continued. 'We know she hadn't got
a change of clothes with her. We know she hadn't
got any money. And we know she'd come all
this way to see her husband and son. So why
didn't she go to the bloody house?'

'Maybe she did,' Jack Crane suggested. 'Maybe
she went to the house, but not into it.'

'What makes you say that?' Paniatowski
wondered.

'The hat she bought from the man in the second-
hand clothing shop,' Crane replied. 'We all agree
she wanted that as a disguise, don't we?'

'Yes, we do,' Paniatowski said.

'But the question is why she should think she'd
need a disguise at all,' Crane continued. 'And I
think the reason was that she didn't want her

husband to know she'd arrived here until the time was right.'

'And when would the time be right?'

'When Robert Martinez returned from London.'

'Go on.'

'Elena knew that the only reason the soldiers had been able to identify Javier as a captain in the militia was because of what she'd said to the lieutenant. She'd never meant to give her husband away – but that's exactly what she did do.'

'True,' Paniatowski said.

'Now, we know that Javier had forgiven her for it long ago. He told you himself, didn't he, boss?'

'He did.'

'But Elena didn't know that. And I think what she wanted was for their son to mediate between them. So she was watching the house on Tuesday, waiting for Robert to turn up, and when he didn't, she went to the bench outside the bus station, which is where Doña Rosa met her and took her home.'

'And what happens the next day?'

'What happens the next day is a direct result of what happens that night,' Crane said. 'The killer has been watching her. Her disguise doesn't fool him, because he's followed her all the way from Spain, and he's watched her acquire it in Hope's Fashions. And when he sees Doña Rosa take her home, that panics him, because he's no idea what the two women might say to one another.'

'Elena never mentioned either her son or her husband to Doña Rosa,' Paniatowski pointed out.

'But the killer doesn't know that – he can't know that. He decides it's just too dangerous to leave her walking around, and the next morning, he lures her somewhere quiet, and kills her.'

'And dumps her body in the canal, because he doesn't want Javier to know she's been murdered?' Paniatowski asked.

'Exactly. And it's no surprise he chooses the canal. He's had all night to scout around for somewhere to hide the body, and he's decided that's his best bet.'

'Your theory is based on the fact that the killer is after the gold, is it?' Beresford asked.

'Yes,' Crane replied.

'So why, once he's seen Elena go off with Doña Rosa, doesn't he do, that night what he eventually did several nights later – which is to break into the house and torture Javier Martinez?'

'He has to nerve himself up for that. Javier Martinez is still a relatively fit man, and the killer knows it won't be as easy to deal with him as it will be to deal with Elena.'

'And he continues to nerve himself up for another four days?' Beresford asked sceptically.

'Yes – and it might have taken him even longer than that if circumstances hadn't changed. But they did change, and once Javier had identified Elena's body, the killer knew he had no choice but to act quickly, so he went to the house that same night.'

'Have I got this wrong, or do we seem to have completely abandoned the theory that there could have been two distinct killers?' Meadows asked, somewhat waspishly.

226

'No, we haven't abandoned it,' Paniatowski said. 'We're still pursuing the two lines of investigation, because we daren't ignore either of them.'

'Although the single killer proposition is looking stronger and stronger all the time,' Beresford said.

'Maybe it is,' Meadows conceded. 'But after what I've found out today, the opposite proposition is looking rather stronger, too. There seems to have been any number of people in Whitebridge who had a grudge against Javier Martinez, and would have liked to have seen him dead.'

'Do you agree with that, Jack?' Paniatowski asked Crane.

Crane shifted awkwardly in his chair.

'I agree with the sergeant that any number of people might have been glad to see him dead – but I'm not sure we've come across anybody yet who hated him enough to actually kill him,' he said cautiously.

Meadows gave him a look which said, 'Thank you so much for your support, Jack.'

Then she turned her attention back on Paniatowski. 'Martinez's account books just don't smell right to me,' she said. 'I'd like to have them put through a forensic audit.'

'All right. I'll see what I can do about getting you the funding,' Paniatowski said.

'I don't need funding,' Meadows told her. 'I've found an accountant who's willing to do it for free.'

Paniatowski frowned. 'That's unusual,' she said.

'Yes, it is,' Meadows admitted. 'But he owes me a favour.'

And knowing Meadows, Paniatowski thought, it was probably wise not to inquire too closely about the nature of the favour she'd done him.

'And is this accountant of yours Lancashire Constabulary Approved, Kate?' she asked.

'Yes, he is,' Meadows said confidently – and her eyes flashed a warning to Jack Crane that if he knew what was good for him, he'd keep his mouth very firmly shut.

'In that case, go ahead,' Paniatowski said. 'Right, that's it for tonight. Tomorrow morning, I want your lads out on the streets again, Colin. But this time, they'll be showing round a sketch of Elena wearing the kind of hat she got in Manchester, and maybe with that we'll have better luck pinning down her movements than we've had so far.'

'Got it,' Beresford said.

'Kate will be busy with her forensic accountant,' Paniatowski continued, 'and you, Jack . . . you can come to Elena's funeral.'

'OK, boss,' Crane said, without much enthusiasm.

'Wrong attitude, Jack,' Paniatowski said, a little sharply. 'You can learn a lot from funerals, especially if you can spot people who have no reason to be there. And for a job like that, two pairs of eyes are always better than one.'

'Right, boss,' Crane said again, more positively this time.

And there was another advantage to having Crane at the funeral, Paniatowski thought. His presence would serve to prevent her – or Robert

228

Martinez, or both of them – from doing anything foolish.

Eighteen

It was eight-fifteen on a cold and frosty morning, and Meadows was standing outside the office at the small private aerodrome close to Manchester, looking up at the grey winter sky.

In her right hand, she was holding a bulky suitcase which contained all the financial ledgers relating to Sunshine Holidays.

In her left, she held a zipped bag containing a backless leather corset, a set of handcuffs, a mask, a wig and a collection of small whips – which was really all she needed to shuck off the identity of Detective Sergeant Kate Meadows and assume the role of Zelda, Daughter of the Night.

She could still not see the Cessna approaching, but she could hear its twin engines, buzzing away in the distance, like angry mosquitoes.

Jonathan Sowerby would be piloting the plane himself, she thought – because Jonathan Sowerby always liked to be in charge.

The Cessna emerged from behind the clouds, and as it came in to land, she thought about the last time that she and Sowerby had met, and the phone calls that he – but not she – had made following that meeting.

The plane landed perfectly, and taxied over to

the hangar. And a few moments later, Sowerby was walking across the tarmac towards her.

He was a tall man, with a confident stride which hinted at a privileged background – and given that Sowerby had attended Eton College, studied at Cambridge and served as an officer in the Guards, the stride did not lie.

He drew level with her, and came to a halt.

They did not kiss, because kissing had never played any part in their relationship.

They did not hug, because when they did get to the stage of making physical contact, there was nothing warm or friendly about it.

And so they stood there for a few seconds, each carefully – and almost clinically – examining the other.

'You're looking wonderful, Katherine,' Sowerby pronounced finally, with an easy drawl.

'It's Kate now,' Meadows said firmly. 'And you're not looking too bad yourself, Jonathan.'

'When was the last time we saw each other?' Sowerby asked. 'Was it in Martinique?'

Oh God, yes, it was in wonderful Martinique, all right, Meadows agreed silently.

But aloud, all she said was, 'Yes, thinking about it, I believe it might have been there.'

'And what a good old time we had together, didn't we?'

'It was good,' Meadows agreed, because if she'd denied it, she'd have been lying – and Sowerby would have known she'd been lying, which would have put her at a definite disadvantage.

'And yet, when I called you up to arrange a

rematch, you didn't seem interested,' Sowerby said, sounding both a little hurt and a little mystified. 'Why was that?'

Because it was too good a time, Meadows thought – *because I was in danger of losing my independence.*

She shrugged. 'I suppose it was because we'd done what we wanted to do, and I'd moved on,' she said. 'That's what I do.'

'Are you really as unemotional about sex as you seem to be – or is it all a pretence?' Sowerby wondered.

'I'm not unemotional about sex at all,' Meadows countered.

'No?'

'No. I get very emotional about sex. What I think you're doing, Jonathan, is confusing emotion and affection – and I much prefer to save my affection for my friends.'

'I didn't know you had any friends,' Sowerby said, with a hint of maliciousness in his voice.

'I didn't used to have any – not when you knew me – but I do now,' Meadows said.

And what an unusual collection of friends they were, she thought – a Polish chief inspector who was sometimes plagued with doubts over her own ability; a detective inspector who could sometimes act like a throwback and with whom she had once had gentle – and therefore disastrous – sex; and a sweet young detective constable who could have been a poet.

'So when you do have sex, you're just using your partner, are you?' Sowerby asked accusingly.

'Yes, and my partner's just using me,' Meadows

231

replied. 'I find that works out nicely for everyone concerned.'

'That could be very hurtful for someone who has real feelings for you.'

Meadows smiled. 'And do you have feelings for me, Jonathan?'

'Well, yes, as a matter of fact, I do.'

'Honestly?' Meadows challenged, looking into his eyes.

'Well, no,' Sowerby admitted. 'If the truth be told, I'm not sure I even like you.'

'But you do want to have sex with me?'

'Desperately.'

Of course he did. That was why, when she'd rung him, he had dropped whatever high-level financial negotiations he was conducting in Frankfurt, and had flown straight to Lancashire.

'I've booked a hotel room,' Meadows said. 'You can go over the books there.'

'I don't suppose we could have a little session before we get down to work, could we?' Sowerby asked hopefully.

'A sort of payment in advance?'

'If that's the way you want to look at it.'

'No,' Meadows said, 'we couldn't.'

'Oh come on, Katherine, you know that you want it as much as I do,' Sowerby cajoled.

'It's Kate,' Meadows reminded him. 'And yes, I do want it as much as you do – but I'm strong enough to put business before pleasure.'

As they approached the sign which said that Arco de Cañas was only three kilometres away, Paco pulled into the side of the road.

'It is time for me and my little car to don our disguises, Charlie,' he told Woodend.

From his small travelling suitcase in the boot, he produced a portrait of General Franco, and a Fuerza Nueva key ring. He tacked the portrait to the back window, and hung the key ring from his rear-view mirror.

'Do you think those little changes will be enough to fool them?' Woodend asked.

'I don't see why not,' Paco replied. 'Fascists are greedy, and fascists are ruthless – but no one ever accused them of being intelligent.'

Arco de Cañas was bigger than Val de Montaña, just as the soldiers had claimed so long ago, but it was still no more than a small, dreary town in the middle of a large, empty plain, which had no more interest in the modern world than the modern world had in it.

Paco parked in the town square, and looked around. There were three bars under the arcade, but only one of them – the Bar del Pueblo – had the sound of martial music blearing from it.

'I assume that's the place we'll be going into,' Woodend said.

'No,' Paco replied. 'First we go to one of the other bars, to give the men in Bar del Pueblo time to do what they need to do.'

The bar Paco chose was called Pedro's, and they were the only customers. They ordered a glass of wine each, and then Paco positioned himself at the window. He did not have to wait long before four old men emerged from the Bar del Pueblo, crossed the square, and stood looking at his little car.

233

'Fascists are so predictable,' he said, with some disgust. 'If they had not had help from Hitler and Mussolini, we would have beaten them hollow.'

The four old men had finished their inspection of the Seat 500, and walked slowly back to the Bar del Pueblo.

'And now we join them?' Woodend asked.

'Now *I* join them,' Paco replied. 'If this is going to work, you must content yourself with the role of observer.'

Javier Martinez's neighbours on Tufton Court were not pleased to see Detective Constable Andrew Bailey.

They had already told the police – more than once – that they had never seen the woman in the sketch, they said, and if he thought that drawing a hat on her head would make them admit that they had seen her, he was very much mistaken.

Bailey was neither surprised nor disappointed. If he had been watching the Martinez house – which was, apparently, DCI Paniatowski's latest theory on what the dead woman had done – he wouldn't have chosen to do it from the cul-de-sac, because there was nowhere to hide, and someone would have been bound to spot him.

So where would he have positioned himself? he wondered.

He walked to the point at which the cul-de-sac met Ashton Avenue. The houses on this road were not as large as the ones in Tufton Court, but they were still substantial dwellings with double frontages – family homes – and anyone hanging around in front of them would have been very conspicuous.

He shifted his gaze. Fifty yards down the road was a copse of trees for which the council – in the interest of creating a balanced environment, and much to the annoyance of the owner – had refused to grant planning permission.

It's certainly a possibility, he thought.

He walked across to the copse and stood between two of the trees. From there, he had a clear view of the entrance to Tufton Court. At that distance, it wasn't a perfect view, of course, but it was close enough for him to see that the man just turning into the court was probably middle-aged. And choosing that particular location had another advantage, which was that while he was not exactly invisible, he probably wouldn't be noticed by anyone who wasn't specifically looking at the copse.

It was unfortunate that the ground was hard – and had been the previous week – because there would be no footprints. But if the woman in the hat had been there, she might have left some other evidence.

He looked around, and his eyes fell on a small red object. He picked it up and found that it was a piece of meat, and though it was too frozen for him to smell, he was almost certain that it was something called *chorizo*, which he had once tried when on holiday in Spain, and hadn't liked very much.

He took an envelope out of his pocket, and slipped the meat into it. It was a good morning's work, he told himself, and it would earn him brownie points with Shagger Beresford, who was the inspector in charge of the team.

It was when he turned around again that he noticed the curtain move in the house across the road from the copse.

Could he be that lucky, he wondered?

It appeared that he could.

He crossed the road and knocked on the front door. It was some time before his knock was answered, the reason for which was quickly explained by the fact that the old woman who opened the door was using a Zimmer frame.

'I'm from the Whitebridge police,' Bailey explained. 'Have you talked to us before?'

'Talked to you before?' the old woman repeated. 'Well, I used to talk to the constable on the beat, but it's all cars these days, isn't it?'

Bailey smiled indulgently. 'I meant, has any policeman talked to you about this woman?' he said, holding up the artist's sketch.

'Oh, her!' the old woman said. 'No, nobody's talked to me about her.'

'But you have seen her?'

'Yes, of course I have. I couldn't miss her.'

Bailey felt his heart skip a beat.

'It's a bit cold for both of us, standing on the doorstep,' he said. 'Would it be all right if I came in?'

'I suppose so,' the old woman said.

The old woman's name was Mrs Potts, and she suffered from an arthritis the like of which no woman in human history had ever had to suffer before.

'So I don't get around much,' she told Bailey, once they were in the living room which overlooked the copse. 'That's why I spend so much time looking out of the window. It's nice to watch the world go by.'

'If you saw the woman, why didn't you contact us before now?' Bailey asked, in an effort to establish whether she was any more than a lonely old lady who would say anything to get a bit of company.

'I didn't know you were looking for her,' Mrs Potts replied.

'But surely you must have seen the picture in all the newspapers,' Bailey prodded.

'Don't read them,' Mrs Potts said.

'Or seen it on the news?'

'Don't watch the news. It's too depressing.'

'So tell me about this woman,' Bailey suggested.

'The first time I noticed her was last Tuesday afternoon.'

'You're sure it was Tuesday?'

'Yes, I'd just been watching my favourite programme on the television when I saw her. It only comes on once a week, and it's always on a Tuesday.'

'So what was she doing?'

'Nothing. Just standing there.'

'For how long?'

'I don't know. Once it gets dark, you can't really see across the road, so she could have been there, and I wouldn't have known it.'

She wouldn't have been there after dark,

237

because she wouldn't have been able to see the turning into Tufton Court, either, Bailey thought.

'When did you see her again?' he asked.

'She was back there the next morning.'

'Didn't that worry you?'

'Why would it? It wasn't as if she was a young thug or something. She was an old woman, just like me, though you could tell from the way she moved that she didn't suffer like I do.'

'How long did she stay there on Wednesday?'

'All day. She must have been cold. I'd have offered her a cup of tea, but there was no way I could have crossed that road – with my legs – to ask her.'

'And you don't know when she left?' Bailey asked.

'As a matter of fact, I do know,' Mrs Potts said.

'So when was it?'

'She left just as dusk was falling.'

Many, many brownie points, Bailey thought happily.

The Bar del Pueblo was bigger than the one that Woodend and Ruiz had just left. It had a long zinc counter, and behind the counter there was a large picture of General Franco and two crossed Spanish flags. The loud military music they'd heard earlier had, it seemed, been coming from the radio, but now it had ended, and there was only a man's voice explaining how the general's tragic death had been an almost incalculable loss to Spain.

'Sit down over there,' Paco said to Woodend,

pointing to a table which was as far as it could be from the table at which the only other customers – the four old men who had inspected his car – were sitting.

Paco walked over to the bar. In the mirror behind it, he could see that one of the old men had stood up and was walking towards him, and as he ordered the drinks, he felt a tap on his shoulder.

He turned. The other man was in his late sixties, he guessed. He had a low forehead, and eyes which showed cunning, rather than intelligence.

'How did you like Pedro's bar?' he asked.

'How do you know I have been to Pedro's bar?' Paco countered.

'I saw you go in.'

'I was not aware I was being watched.'

'In Spain, you are always being watched,' the other man said.

'That's true,' Paco agreed. 'And in answer to your question, Pedro's bar was fine, as far as it went, but it was not quite patriotic enough for me.'

'So you're a patriot?' the other man said. 'Then why didn't you come into this bar in the first place?'

'My friend, who is English, does not like loud music,' Paco said, jabbing a thumb in Woodend's direction. 'He only eventually came in here because I insisted on it.'

'And why would you wish to have a friend who is English?' the other man asked.

'I'm not sure I like all these questions, especially from a man who – for all I know – may have been on the other side in the war.'

239

'Would I be in this bar if I had been on the other side?' the other man demanded.

'I don't know,' Paco said. 'You could be here just to camouflage your true colours. You'd be surprised how many communists and anarchists claimed to have spent the war fighting for God and country once it was becoming plain that the Generalissimo would triumph.'

'I was there at the Battle of the Ebro,' the other man said, almost losing his temper.

'So you say. So many people say, now that it's over and we have won. What rank were you?'

'I was a private. Why do you ask?'

'Because I was there at the Ebro myself, and the only man that I met from Arco de Cañas was a lieutenant.'

'Are you talking about Luis Suarez?' the other man asked.

'How many lieutenants who fought at the Ebro came from Arco de Cañas?' Paco asked.

'He was the only one.'

'Then it should be obvious, even to you, that Suarez is the one I am talking about,' Paco said. He held up his glass. 'Here's to Luis Suarez, a good man and good soldier, who once saved my life.'

'I fought side by side with Luis Suarez for over two years,' the other man said.

'Then I would like to shake your hand, because if you were good enough for him, then you are good enough for me.' Paco held out his hand. 'I'm Paco Ruiz.'

'Antonio Crespo,' said the other man, taking

240

it. He turned to his friends in the corner. 'This man knew Luis Suarez.'

'I did not say that I knew him . . .' Paco began.

'You met him – and that's enough,' Crespo said. 'Why don't you and your friend . . .?' He paused. 'I was going to say, "Why don't you and your friend come over to our table?" but I am still troubled by the fact that he is an Englishman.'

'Then worry no more,' Paco said. 'Carlito used to belong to the British Union of Fascists. The British government put him in gaol for his views.'

'Ah, if only Hitler had won,' Crespo said.

'True,' Paco agreed.

'So will you join us?'

'I will join you, but there would be little point in Carlito coming, since he does not speak Spanish,' Paco said. 'Take a bottle of wine to my friend's table, and when he has finished it, take him another,' he told the barman. 'Carlito will be quite happy on his own,' he continued, turning to Crespo again. 'As long as he has a drink, he does not need any other company.'

Crespo led Paco across to his table, and introduced him to the other old men, whose names were Iñigo, Adolpho and Jaime. All three of them, it seemed to Paco, were already quite drunk.

'So how did Luis save your life?' Crespo asked.

'It is a long and complicated story, and I am sure that Lieutenant Suarez will be able to tell it better than I could,' Paco replied.

The table fell silent for a few moments, then Crespo said, 'I am sorry to tell you that Luis is dead.'

Paco sighed philosophically. 'Well, we must

all go sometime, and I trust he had a long and happy life.'

'He was killed shortly after the war ended, by a dirty, slimy dog of a communist.'

'And no doubt that communist met a slow and painful death as his reward for such treachery.'

Crespo shook his head. 'No, like the coward he was, he escaped.'

'And took the gold with him,' Iñigo said.

'There was no gold,' Crespo said dismissively. 'That was just a story.'

'Luis Suarez believed in it,' Iñigo said.

'So he did,' Crespo replied. 'But that doesn't make it any the more true.' He reached into his wallet. 'Would you like to see a photograph of Luis, Paco?'

'I would be honoured to see it,' Paco said.

Crespo took out a sepia photograph and laid it on the table. It showed a group of young soldiers, grinning at the camera.

'How young we all were,' Crespo said wistfully. He pointed to a man in the centre of the photograph. 'Look, that's Luis.'

'That's just how I remember him,' Paco said.

'And can you identify any of the others?' Crespo asked, with a slightly roguish air.

'That's you, standing next to Suarez – and, I have to say, you don't look a day older.'

Crespo slapped him on the back. 'You have a silver tongue for an old soldier,' he said.

'If I cannot talk to Suarez himself, then it is good to talk to his friends,' Paco said, 'and you were all, I assume, his friends.'

There was a chorus of affirmation around the

242

table, and more sepia photographs appeared from other wallets.

Paco reached into his pocket, took out a packet of Celtas cigarettes, and offered them round.

'Did you never try to track down the man who had killed Luis Suarez?' he asked, when all the cigarettes had been lit.

The old men looked suddenly guilty.

'It would have been a very difficult task, if not a completely impossible one,' Jaime said.

'But surely, if he had a wife and children, you could have watched them, and waited for him to contact them,' Paco said.

'He had a wife,' said Adolpho, and the others laughed.

'Oh yes, he had a wife,' Crespo agreed. 'Luis screwed her every way possible – on the table, on her hands and knees, in a chair. She said she didn't like it, but the truth is that she was probably grateful, after being married to a limp-dicked Commie, to be with a real man at last.'

'Luis was always a great one for the ladies,' Iñigo said. 'There was Colonel Hierro's daughter, for example. He . . .'

'We do not talk about what happened to Colonel Hierro's daughter,' Crespo said sharply.

'No, of course we don't,' Iñigo agreed, bowing his head. 'I had forgotten that.'

'The point I was making was that surely it wouldn't have been difficult to keep this woman under observation,' Paco persisted.

'How could we have done it?' Adolpho asked. 'She lives in Alicante Province, and we live here in Burgos.'

'Pepe Durante lives on the coast,' Jaime said.

'Yes, but that's only because he married a girl from Denia, and she wouldn't move away,' Crespo told him.

'Calpe,' Adolpho said. 'She wasn't from Dénia, she was from Calpe.'

'You're right,' Crespo agreed. 'She was from Calpe.'

'And does Pepe Durante still live there?' Paco wondered.

'Who knows?' Crespo said. 'We have lost touch.'

'Which one is Durante?' Paco asked.

Crespo pointed to a man standing at the edge of one of the photographs. 'That's him.'

'And he's the only one of you who didn't return to this town after the war ended, is he?'

'No, not the only one, but we have heard that all the others are dead. Pepe himself may well be dead, for all we know.'

But I'd be willing to bet he isn't, Paco thought.

'I will buy another round of drinks,' he said, taking out his wallet. Then he frowned. 'I had a hundred peseta note in this wallet before I came into the bar, and now it's gone,' he continued. 'No, wait a minute. I remember now, I took it out of my wallet, and put it in my jacket pocket.' He reached into the pocket, and his frown deepened. 'It isn't there. I must have pulled it out with my cigarettes, and it will be on the floor.'

The other four, moving very quickly for men their age, were soon down on their knees, searching the floor beneath the table. Then they stood up again, shaking their heads.

'It isn't there,' Iñigo said.

'You must have been mistaken when you thought you put it in your pocket,' Jaime added.

'I am not a man who can easily afford to lose a hundred pesetas,' Paco said, standing up. 'I must go and search my car.' He walked towards the door. 'Come outside with me,' he called in English to Woodend. 'We must search for some money I have lost.'

'You didn't lose the money, did you?' Woodend asked, when they were outside. 'You dropped it under the table deliberately.'

'Yes, I did,' Paco admitted.

'And when they said they couldn't find it, they were lying, because I saw one of them pick it up and slip it in his pocket – and the others saw him do it.'

'Well, there you are,' Paco replied. 'They say there is no honour among thieves, and it appears, as I always suspected, that there is no honour among fascists either, because even though they thought I was one of their own, they still stole from me.'

Woodend grinned. 'That seems a pretty expensive way to confirm your prejudices,' he said.

'But it seems a fairly cheap way to acquire a picture of Pepe Durante, who may well turn out to be our murderer,' said Paco, showing Woodend the sepia photograph that he had in his pocket.

Nineteen

They had been more successful than he'd ever dared hope, Woodend thought, as he and Paco reached Ruiz's little car. They had the photograph which could well turn out to be the vital piece of evidence in Monika's investigation, and in a couple of minutes, they would be back on the road, heading for home.

It was the church bell that changed everything. It began to ring just as Paco was reaching into his pocket for his car keys – and the sound of it made him freeze.

'Is something the matter?' Woodend asked.

Paco turned slowly in the direction of the church, which lay just beyond the square.

'I want to show you something,' he said.

And then he strode quickly and furiously across the square, and down an alley which led to the church, with Woodend following in his wake.

When they reached the front of the church, Paco came to a halt.

'Look at that!' he said angrily, pointing to a large stone tablet which was set in the front wall of the church.

Across the top of the tablet, carved in large letters, were the words *'¡José Antonio Presente!'* and below that there was a list of names.

'I told you about José Antonio, didn't I?' Paco

said. 'He was the leader of the fascist movement, who was executed in Valencia.'

'Yes, I remember,' Woodend replied, 'but I don't quite see why . . .'

'The rest of the names on this tablet are of men from this town who died in the Civil War,' Paco continued, and the anger was rising in his voice. 'And they are all Franco's men. If anyone from Arco de Cañas had died fighting on the Republican side, he could have whistled for his memorial!'

'Why are you telling me all this now?' Woodend wondered. 'What's got into you, Paco?'

The words seemed to break the spell – to bring Paco out of what had almost been a semi-trance.

'I don't know why I'm telling you now,' he admitted. He reached into his pocket with a hand trembling with rage, and produced his packet of cigarettes. 'Perhaps it is because I have just been talking to those pigs in the Bar del Pueblo,' he continued. 'If they had died, their names would have been on this tablet – they would have been honoured forever – but the brave men who fought and lost their lives beside me got nothing.' He ran his eyes up and down the list as he lit his cigarette. 'Why is there not a tablet somewhere with the names of Enrique Diaz, Tomas Arroyo and Joachim Morales on it? They were good men – they were brave men who sacrificed everything for the real Spain – and now it is as if they'd never lived.'

'Best to leave it now,' Woodend said softly.

'You are right,' Paco agreed. He took a deep drag on his cigarette, and turned away. Then, almost immediately, he wheeled around again. 'Where is Lieutenant Suarez's name?' he demanded.

'*Whose* name?'

'Lieutenant Suarez's. He was from this town. He died in action. Why isn't his name on the list?'

Woodend examined the tablet more closely. All the names were equally spaced except for two, which had a much larger gap between them. He wet the end of his finger, rubbed it across the gap, and inspected the fingertip.

'There was another name there, but it's been chipped away, and the space filled with plaster,' he said.

'And why would anybody have wanted to do that?' Paco asked.

'I don't know.'

'Neither do I – but I want to find out.'

There were only two 'official' mourners at Elena Vargas's funeral mass, and as the priest intoned the Offices of the Dead, Paniatowski found her thoughts dwelling on Robert Martinez's words as they entered the church.

'John Donne wrote that any other man's death also diminishes him,' Robert Martinez had said. 'I believe that, too, and if other people wish to attend the mass, they have my respect – and perhaps even my gratitude. But I didn't want to invite anyone else, Monika. I was unfairly cut out of my mother's life – so is it so wrong to want her to myself in death?'

'No, it's not wrong at all,' Paniatowski had replied.

And she meant it, she thought. She had felt exactly the same at her father's funeral mass, after which the bones of the gallant colonel had finally been laid to rest next to the body of her long-dead mother.

While the priest continued to talk directly to a God whom she no longer believed in, Paniatowski allowed her mind to wander free.

She thought about the part of her life that had already gone, and the part that lay ahead.

She wondered if she would ever find the right man for her – and then she wondered if she had already found him.

'Monika,' she half-heard a voice say close to her ear.

Why hadn't she got to know Robert before the murders? she thought. Would that have been too much to ask for?

So maybe she was wrong, and there was a God, she decided – but if he did exist, he was a particularly malicious god, who took his pleasure from twisting her feelings into knots.

'Monika!' the voice said again, still in a whisper, but rather more sharply this time.

She looked up and saw the coffin was leaving the church.

'It's time to go,' Robert said.

She found it a relief to get out of the church – away from the cloying smell of incense – and to be able to breathe in fresh air again.

Looking around, she saw Jack Crane standing near the lychgate. She shot him an inquiring look, and he shook his head as if to say that if there had been anyone hanging around the church whose presence needed to be questioned, then he certainly hadn't seen them.

She and Robert followed the coffin – carried by hired pall-bearers – to the grave, and stood on the edge as it was slowly lowered in.

As the priest said a final short prayer, Paniatowski felt Robert's hand reaching for hers, and she did not resist.

The priest sprinkled the holy water on the grave, and the funeral was all over and done with, but when Paniatowski tried to pull her hand free, Robert Martinez kept a tight grip.

'Do you think that we can go somewhere quiet?' he asked hopefully. 'Just to talk?'

There was one simple answer to that, and the answer was 'no', because the mass was over now, and she still had two murders – his mother's and his father's – to investigate.

'Can we?' Robert pleaded.

'I'm sorry, but I have to go,' she said, and then she added, 'You will be all right on your own, won't you?'

'I don't know,' he admitted. 'Perhaps things will start to get a bit easier after the cremation.' He turned away from the grave. 'I never knew either of my parents – and that's a terrible weight to bear.'

'You didn't know your father?' she said, before she could stop herself.

Robert gave a slight jump, as if he had detected an unkind and unfair criticism of him in her words.

'I'm sorry,' she said quickly, 'I didn't mean to suggest . . .'

250

'I didn't really know him,' Martinez said. 'We lived in the same house. We ate at the same table. We talked about the weather and how the business was going, but it was like two strangers, who were just using the words to fill the space between them. I tried, over the years, to make some kind of real contact with him – God alone knows how hard I tried – but it did no good.' There were tears forming in his eyes. 'I think my father was simply a hard-hearted man.' He paused. 'Is it wrong to say that, so soon after his death?'

Not if all the stories I've been hearing about him are true, Paniatowski thought.

'People don't suddenly become better people – nicer people – just because they're dead,' she said. 'If that's what he was, that's what he was.'

'Thank you for that,' Robert Martinez said, and released her hand.

'Look, Robert, I can probably spare you half an hour or so,' she said, relenting.

'No, you were right before – you have to go,' Martinez said. 'Perhaps when all this is over . . .'

'Yes,' she agreed. 'Perhaps when all this is over.'

When Pablo Ortega had first opened his bar on the square in Arco de Cañas, he had wanted to deck it out with Nationalist symbols, just like those in the Bar del Pueblo, which was a few doors up from his new business, but the secret policeman who paid him a small monthly salary had told him that was not a good idea.

251

'If you proclaim yourself a patriot too loudly, only patriots will drink in your bar,' he had pointed out. 'And it is the enemies of the state – not the patriots – who I am interested in.'

'But I will get more customers by showing my loyalty to the Generalissimo,' Pablo had protested.

The secret policeman had seen his point, and had nodded.

'Perhaps we can compensate for that by increasing your monthly payments a little,' he suggested.

And Pablo, who much preferred informing on others to actually working for a living, had readily agreed.

He had already phoned through one piece of information that day – the number plate of the Seat 500 driven by the man with an English friend – but he'd thought he was done with them, and was surprised to see them walk into the bar for a second time.

'Two more glasses of wine?' he asked.

'No, all we want this time is information,' Paco said, laying a five-peseta note on the table.

'What kind of information?' Pablo asked suspiciously.

'Nothing much. I just want to know if the man who carved the war memorial on the church is still around.'

'He retired long ago.'

'But he is still around?'

'Yes, he lives at number twenty-seven Calle de Jesús.'

'Thank you very much,' Paco said, turning

from the counter, but leaving the five-peseta note still on it.

Pablo waited until the two men had gone, then swept up the note and reached for the phone.

The old man was bald, and almost blind. A hand-rolled cigarette dangled from the corner of his thin lips, and his hands twitched convulsively as they rested on his bony knees.

'I have lived here with my daughter since my dear wife died,' he said, in a cracked voice. 'Most of my old friends are dead, too, and I get very few visitors these days.'

'The reason we have come is that we wanted to ask you about the war memorial on the church,' Paco said.

'The war memorial,' the old man said, with some disdain. 'That is the sort of work you do to pay the bills – to put food on the table. But there is nothing wrong with it,' he added quickly, as if Paco might get the wrong impression. 'No one else could have made a better job of it than I did.'

'I'm sure they couldn't,' Paco agreed.

'But that kind of work gave me no opportunity to show my real skill,' the old man continued. 'Now there is an angel in the church which took me months to carve. I would like you to go and see it before you leave the town.'

'We will,' Paco promised.

'You will not regret it,' the old carver told him. 'You will see with your own eyes what a real artist I once was.'

'To get back to the war memorial,' Paco said,

'once you had completed it, you chipped out one of the names and filled it with plaster, didn't you?'

'Yes, I did.'

'Why did you do that?'

'I had just finished the tablet when I was visited by a young army officer. He said that I should remove the name of Lieutenant Luis Suarez. I did not want to – it would unbalance the whole memorial – so I asked him why. Was Lieutenant Suarez alive, after all? I said. No, the officer told me, there was no question that he was dead – he had been killed by a communist in Alicante. Then there seems to be no sense in removing his name, I said. Here is the sense, he replied – and his voice was suddenly very cold – it is to be removed because Colonel Hierro wants it removed.'

That was the second time that Colonel Hierro's name had come up in an hour, Paco thought.

'Hierro has been in his grave for many years, now,' the old carver said, 'but back then, he was a very important man in this town – a man you did not argue with – so I chipped out the name and filled it with plaster.'

'And that was all that the officer said?' Paco asked. 'It should be removed because Colonel Hierro wanted it removed?'

'That was all he said.'

There was the sound of screeching tyres outside, and looking through the window, Woodend saw that two army jeeps, containing armed soldiers, had pulled up outside.

'We're in trouble,' he said to Paco.

And in a way, he'd always known they would be.

The morning had slowly drifted into the afternoon, the afternoon became the evening, and still Jonathan Sowerby sat at the desk, his calculator in one hand, studying the ledgers which purported to tell Sunshine Holidays' financial history.

Finally, at seven-thirty, he slammed the last ledger closed and smiled triumphantly.

'There are perhaps only six people in the whole world capable of doing what I've just done,' he told Meadows. 'And even then, they'd have needed a large back-up staff, a full office, and direct access to a computer, whereas I've achieved it all alone, working in a drab little hotel room.'

Meadows looked around her. The room contained a huge television set, a luxury three-piece suite, and the big desk at which Sowerby had been working. And beyond it lay the bedroom – with a king-sized bed – and the bathroom.

She smiled to herself, and thought that only Jonathan Sowerby could describe the best suite that the Hilton had to offer as a 'drab little hotel room'.

'What have you uncovered?' she asked.

Sowerby glanced longingly at the Zelda bag, which was sitting on the sofa.

'Couldn't we talk about that later?' he asked.

'Now,' Meadows said firmly.

Sowerby sighed. 'All right then – if you insist. Sunshine Holidays has grown in a number of steps. The first step was in 1951, when it bought three second-hand – but comparatively new – coaches. Two years later, it took the next step, which was to buy three absolutely new coaches. Move on another two years . . .'

'I could have worked all that out for myself,' Meadows snapped. 'Cut to the chase.'

'There are only two ways that a company can finance its expansion – either by using the profits it has generated itself, or by getting a loan from some financial institution. And that is what – from a superficial study of the ledgers – Sunshine Holidays seems to have done.'

'But when you go deeper . . .?'

'When you go deeper, you find that it's been counting things as assets when it's useful to do so, and writing those same things off as a loss when there's some advantage to that. And that creates a void right in the middle of the accounts, into which it has been possible to pump money from another source – an unexplained source.'

'Wouldn't it have been easy for anyone who knew what he was doing to spot that?'

'If it had been done as crudely as I've explained it, yes, it would. But as you go deeper, you find yourself in a positive labyrinth. You follow a trail down what seems to be the obvious tunnel and find yourself at a dead end. So you try to retrace your steps, and find you can't. After that's happened a few times, you get frustrated, and tell yourself that you must be having a bad day. And because you can't face going through it all again, you convince yourself that the books are probably all right.' Sowerby paused. 'When I say you, of course, I'm not talking about me, I'm referring to one of those pathetic little HM Inspectors of Taxes whom I wouldn't even employ as an office boy.'

'So whoever cooked the books was good at it?'

'Whoever cooked the books was almost as clever as I am. In fact – and this is in the nature of a confession here – maybe even I wouldn't have spotted it, had it not been for the Middle Eastern crisis.'

'Could you explain that?' Meadows asked.

'I'd be delighted to. In 1967, Syria, Egypt and Jordan attack Israel, and because the West is seen as being too much on the side of the Israelis, the Arabs, in a fit of pique, raise the price of oil massively. Everybody in the West feels the effect, but for a company like Sunshine Holidays, which (on paper) is so heavily indebted that there's no room for manoeuvre, it should have been disastrous. That's when this accountant – this Leonardo da Vinci amongst bookkeepers – is forced to start taking risks. That's when his handiwork really becomes apparent, and when he leaves a marker which can be traced backwards to the start of the company and forwards to the present day.'

'Was unexplained cash coming into the business right from the beginning?' Meadows asked.

'No. At the start, it was far too simple a business for there to be any really creative accounting.'

The gold was real, Meadows thought. It had to be real. Javier Martinez had brought it with

257

him from Spain, and converted some of it – or perhaps even all of it – into cash.

But his problem was that he couldn't use the money without explaining where it came from.

And what would have happened if he'd done that?

Britain had recognized General Franco's government as the legitimate government in Spain back in 1939, and that government might, with some justification, have claimed the gold was its property, and that Martinez had stolen it.

But that was by no means the worst thing that might have happened.

He could have lost his political asylum status. And since the war had been officially over when the priest's house was burned down, he could have been sent back to Spain and put on trial for the murder of the lieutenant and the two other soldiers.

The risk was too great, so he had simply sat on his wealth – because he had no choice in the matter.

That was why he had offered Fred Sidebotham the deal in 1946 – he had the money, but he didn't dare use it. But in 1951, when the business was becoming more complex, he could launder a little of it – just enough to buy Fred Sidebotham out. Then, as Sunshine Holidays continued to grow and grow, he found himself able to launder more and more.

'I've done all you asked me to, haven't I?' Jonathan Sowerby asked, with a hint of anxiety in his voice.

'Yes, you have,' Meadows agreed.

'So I was wondering if we could now get down to what we both know we're really here for.'

'Absolutely,' Meadows said, walking across to the sofa and unzipping her Zelda bag.

The cell was located in the centre of the punishment block of an army camp, a few miles from Burgos. It was four metres square, and had whitewashed walls into which messages of hope and desperation had been scratched by its previous residents. Its only furniture was a narrow bed, on which, at that moment, Paco Ruiz was sitting with his head in his hands.

'I'm sorry, Charlie,' he said.

'There's nothing to apologize for,' Woodend told him.

'If we had only left Arco de Cañas straight after we came out of the Bar del Pueblo, we would have got away.'

'I wouldn't be so sure about that,' Woodend said. 'It's my belief that the army were probably alerted the moment we arrived in the bloody town, and even if we'd left, they'd have caught up with us before we'd gone more than a few miles.'

'It was still a stupid thing to do,' Paco insisted. 'What did it matter that Lieutenant Suarez's name had been chipped off the war memorial? I should never have pursued it any further.'

'Then why did you?'

'Because I had a policeman's gut feeling that it was somehow connected with the case.'

'Well, there you are, then,' Woodend said. 'If I learned one thing as a bobby, it was that you should always follow your gut instincts. Half the time, they take you up a blind alley. But doesn't it feel grand when they work out?'

'It feels wonderful,' Paco agreed. 'It is one of the finest feelings in the whole world.'

'Anyway, the information that the stone cutter gave us might not be much help with the murder case, but we can certainly use it in our present situation,' Woodend said.

'Use it?' Paco repeated, mystified. 'Use it to do what?'

'To create confusion,' Woodend told him.

Twenty

Major Ernesto Trujillo had started his career in the Spanish army with several distinct disadvantages. He did not have the dashing looks that many of his contemporaries at the Military Academy in Zaragoza had been blessed with, for example. He did not have a particularly good seat when on a horse, either, and was – at best – a fairly average shot.

All these failings could have been compensated for if he had had one of those personalities which automatically drew the other officers in the mess around him like moths around a candle, but unfortunately, he was deficient in that area, too, and so his time in the academy had been far from happy.

His fortunes had changed for the better once

he had decided to join the military police. He liked the uniform, he liked the pay, and he liked the fear he inspired in others. But most of all, he liked the fact that he could use what he considered to be his obviously superior intellect to play games with the minds of lesser mortals – games which, he was convinced, the handsome, athletic arseholes who'd laughed at him at the academy would have no idea how to play.

It was because of his love of games that he never used violence to get the answers he wanted, leading some of his colleagues in the military police to think – quite wrongly – that he was too soft.

Anyone can beat a confession out of a prisoner, he always told himself, but it took real skill – the kind of skill that few people had – to get the suspect to confess voluntarily. And these two suspects who had just been brought in – the Englishman and the communist – would make a real change from the dull conscript soldiers he was usually given to play with.

He had, at first, considered interrogating them separately, but they were both old men – and no doubt both terrified – and he decided that it might be more fun to let each one hear the other betray him.

When he entered the interrogation room, he could see that, unlike in his imaginings, neither of them looked the least bit terrified, but then, he told himself, the process had not yet begun.

Trujillo sat down at the opposite side of the table from the two suspects and lit up an American cigarette.

261

'My name is Major Ernesto Trujillo, and you are Charles Woodend and Francisco Ruiz,' he said, practising his English.

The big Englishman in the hairy jacket turned to his companion. 'Which of us is which?' he asked.

'I think you are Woodend, and I am Ruiz,' the other man replied.

'Well, that's all right then,' Woodend said.

'You were arrested in the town of Arco de Cañas, for asking questions about army officers,' Trujillo said.

'Dead army officers,' Woodend pointed out.

'It is irrelevant whether they are dead or alive,' Trujillo told him. 'Its honour is very important to the army – it is the foundation stone on which we stand – and if you insult any officer who has ever served, you are insulting us all.'

'And we wouldn't want to do that,' Woodend said.

'No,' Trujillo agreed, 'you would not.' He turned to Paco. 'You, Ruiz, claimed to be a devoted admirer of the Generalissimo when you were in the Bar del Pueblo, although we know from your record that you are a communist and fought on the side of the rebels.'

'I was never a communist, and since you were against the elected government, you were the rebels,' Ruiz replied.

Many interrogators in his position would have slapped the old man across the face for making a remark like that, Trujillo thought, but then they did not have his subtlety.

'You also talked to an old stone carver, and

262

asked him why he had removed a certain Lieutenant Suarez's name from the war memorial,' the major continued. 'And what did the stone carver tell you?'

'You know what he told us,' Paco said.

Trujillo sighed theatrically. 'This is how an interrogation works,' he said. 'I ask the questions, and you answer them. What did he tell you?'

'He told us that Colonel Hierro ordered Lieutenant Suarez's name to be removed,' Paco said.

'That's probably because Suarez was Colonel Hierro's daughter's boyfriend,' Woodend said.

'That is not true!' Trujillo said vehemently. 'You can get into trouble for telling lies like that.'

'I thought we were in trouble anyway,' Woodend said. 'What was the problem with Lieutenant Suarez anyway? Was he too low-class for her? Or did he get her pregnant?'

'Shut your foul mouth!' Trujillo bellowed.

'Pregnant,' Woodend said to Ruiz.

'Pregnant,' Paco agreed.

This was not going as well as it was supposed to have done, Trujillo thought. Maybe it had been a mistake to interrogate them both together after all.

'You will be taken back to the cells – and this time you will be in separate cells – and I will talk to you again tomorrow,' he said.

'I'd like to make a phone call to my consul,' Woodend said.

'That will not be possible,' replied Trujillo, who had been anticipating just such a request.

He had been expecting one of two responses to his refusal. The first was that Woodend would plead with him – which would be very gratifying indeed. The second was that the man would lose his temper – and it was always a good thing when a suspect lost control.

He got neither of those responses.

Instead, Woodend turned to Ruiz, and smiled.

'I told you that you were backing the wrong horse, Paco,' he said. 'Well, we all have to pay for our mistakes, and that's five cigarettes you owe me.'

'I never imagined that a Spanish army officer – a major – would display so little courage,' Paco replied.

'Courage?' Trujillo repeated. 'What are you talking about?'

'You're too scared to meet my consul, aren't you?' Woodend said cheerfully. 'Oh, you're happy enough interrogating two old men – though even there, I have to say, you're not doing a particularly good job of it – but just the thought of being face-to-face with a British diplomat is enough to make you shit your pants.'

'I am ashamed of my countrymen sometimes,' Paco said. 'Spain produced El Cid and Hernán Cortés. Even Franco, I am told, was a brave man when he was fighting the Moors in North Africa. But our golden days are gone, and all we have now is men like Major Trujillo.'

'I choose not to let you speak to your consul,' Trujillo said hotly.

'Of course you do, lad,' Woodend said sympathetically. 'You keep on saying that often enough,

264

and you might just about be able to look at yourself in your shaving mirror tomorrow morning.'

'I will offer you a deal,' Trujillo said, looking for a way to save face. 'I will allow you to speak to your consul, and the next time we talk, you will tell me everything you know.'

'Of course,' Woodend said.

'We have nothing to hide,' Paco Ruiz added.

Crane, Beresford and Paniatowski were already at their table in the Drum and Monkey when Meadows entered.

'You seem a little stiff, Kate,' Paniatowski said, as she walked across the room.

'I think I've overdone it on the exercise front, boss,' Meadows said, lowering herself gently into her chair.

'I'm surprised you found the time to exercise,' Paniatowski said. 'How was your meeting with the forensic accountant? Did he manage to come up with anything useful?'

Meadows nodded, and outlined what she had learned from Sowerby about the creative bookkeeping.

'The gold has to be real,' she said, as she drew to a conclusion, 'because a huge amount of money has been going into that firm, and there's no other way that Javier Martinez could possibly have got his hands on it. And it's not so much a case of him using the gold to build up the business, as it is of using the *business* to launder the *money*.'

'Whatever happened to his ideals?' Crane

wondered. 'Whatever changed him from an ideal-istic communist into a crook who was willing to trample on anyone who got in his way?'

'That'd be the gold, again,' Meadows said. 'He wouldn't be the first person who's been turned by thoughts of wealth. Bob Dylan said, "When you've got nothin', you've got nothin' to lose," but when you've got something, you suddenly start to want much more. And I should know.'

'What does that mean?' Beresford asked.

'Nothing,' Meadows said, flushing slightly. 'It's just the kind of stupid thing you say at the end of a long and tiring day.'

It wasn't the sort of thing he'd say at the end of a long, tiring day, Beresford thought, but from the look on Meadows' face it was obvious she wanted him to let the matter drop, and – with uncharacteristic diplomacy – he did.

'But he had the gold when he returned to his village after the war,' Crane said, unconvinced. 'If he was so rich, why did he even bother to go back?'

'Because he was still hoping to return to his old life,' Meadows said. 'And it was only after he realized that could never happen – after he had killed the three soldiers – that the gold started to be important.'

Life was full of ironies, Paniatowski thought. It would have been much easier for Javier Martinez to have escaped from Val de Montaña on his own, but he had chosen instead to increase his own personal risk immeasurably, by taking his young son with him.

266

What an act of love that had been.

And yet once they were in England, he had seemed totally incapable of expressing that love.

Poor Robert.

But perhaps, as loath as she was to think it, poor Javier, too.

'Now that you're convinced the gold exists, are you happy if we drop the theory that Javier was killed by someone local, who had a grievance against him, Sergeant Meadows?' Beresford asked.

'Yes,' Meadows said. 'That would be just too much of a coincidence. From the very start, this whole thing has been about the gold.'

'Does everybody accept that?' Paniatowski asked, and when Crane and Beresford nodded, she continued, 'So we're back to one killer and one motive,' and there were more nods.

'There's still one thing that's puzzling me,' Crane said.

'And what's that?' Paniatowski asked.

'Elena had been watching the house on Tufton Court for nearly a day and a half . . .'

'A day and a half, did you say?' Meadows interrupted. 'I don't know anything about this.'

'One of my bright young lads has uncovered the fact that Elena was standing in a copse of trees on Ashton Avenue, watching the entrance to Tufton Court on Tuesday afternoon – which is when she got off the train – and all day Wednesday, which as far as we know, is the day she died,' Beresford said.

'DC Crane's still not explained what was puzzling him,' Paniatowski pointed out. 'Go ahead, Jack.'

'The killer has been following her all the way, so he'll certainly have followed her to the copse of trees,' Crane said. 'Right?'

'Right,' the others agreed.

'Now according to our theory, the point at which he really decided he had to kill her was when he saw her go home with Rosa. Is that right, too?'

'Yes, it is.'

'So we get to Wednesday morning. Elena is back in the copse. She's being watched from across the road by Mrs Potts, but she probably doesn't know that, and neither does the killer. And the other thing the killer doesn't know is whether or not Elena will get tired of standing there, and set off for Martinez's house – which, from his point of view, would be a disaster.'

'We're with you so far,' Paniatowski said.

'Now, it would be easy enough for him to kill her in the copse,' Jack Crane continued, 'but once she steps out on to the road, where there are people walking about, and cars constantly driving past, he'd be bound to be spotted. So here's what's bothering me – why did he wait until Wednesday night – after she'd left the copse – to kill her? Why didn't he do it on Wednesday morning?'

And from the blank faces around the table, it was clear that no one knew the answer to that.

It was eight in the evening – the hour at which the consul habitually took cocktails with the latest deputy that London had foisted on him – when the phone rang in Martin Cheavers' office.

'I'd better take this,' said Cheavers, who had

268

started his own personal cocktail hour some considerable time earlier.

The phone call took a little over three minutes, during which time, his deputy counted, he used the word 'Charlie' seven times.

'That was Charlie Woodend,' Cheavers said, when he put down the phone. 'It seems that he and Paco Ruiz have got themselves into a bit of trouble in Burgos Province. Apparently, they've both been accused of spying, and got banged up at some army base.'

'And will you be making representations to the government about it?' Harrington Benson asked.

'No, I'll be flying up to the arsehole of nowhere first thing in the morning, and demanding that the soldiers stop playing silly buggers and release our chap immediately,' Cheavers said.

Harrington Benson smiled uncertainly. 'You're joking, aren't you, sir?' he asked.

'I most certainly am not,' Cheavers said emphatically.

His assistant's tentative smile turned to a worried frown.

'London won't like that,' he said. 'We've been instructed that, in this current climate of uncertainty, we should keep our profiles very low – and that certainly doesn't include taking on the army.'

'I don't recall seeing any cable to that effect,' Cheavers said.

Harrington Benson looked slightly embarrassed. 'Er . . . no,' he agreed. 'It will be arriving tomorrow.'

The little shit probably had an uncle in the FO, Cheavers thought. That explained a lot.

'No doubt we will be getting such a cable, but that doesn't matter one way or the other,' he said. 'We owe a debt to Charlie and Paco, and I intend to see that debt discharged.'

'How are we in debt to them?' Harrington Benson wondered.

Cheavers hesitated for a second, before deciding that if his assistant did have a direct line to the Foreign Office, then using him as a conduit would be much pleasanter than talking to the stuffed shirts in Whitehall himself.

'A few months ago, we had a visit from a member of a European royal family,' he said.

'It was Prince Juan Carlos,' Harrington Benson said. 'Now that is something I've read in the files.'

It was typical of the snobbish young turd to know that, but not to have taken the trouble to find out about Charlie Woodend, Cheavers thought.

'It could have been Prince Juan Carlos – or King Juan Carlos as he is now – but it could just as easily have been some other royal, from some other country, who asked me not to keep a record of his visit,' Cheavers said, knowing he didn't really sound convincing – and not giving a damn. 'At any rate, this visiting royal struck up a brief friendship with one of the more attractive girls in our typing pool.'

'A brief friendship? You mean . . .'

'I mean what I say – a brief friendship. I'm sure it was all perfectly innocent. However, some unscrupulous photographer with a criminal

270

bent managed to take some pictures of them together.'

'They weren't actually . . .?' Harrington Benson began.

'No, they weren't, though it has to be admitted that the pictures were open to misinterpretation. At any rate, had those photographs been published, they could have caused considerable embarrassment, both for us and for the Span . . . for the government of the country from which the young prince hailed. The blackmailers knew that, and the price they put on the photographs was so substantial that even though it was imperative we got our hands on them as soon as possible, the Foreign Office went into a dither about where the money was to come from. And it was while they were dithering – and thus giving the photographer time to explore other markets – that I hired Charlie and Paco.'

'And what happened?'

'Charlie Woodend brought me the photographs – and the negatives – two days later.'

'Had they paid any ransom?'

'They said not. The only thing they asked for was their fee – which was a very modest one.'

'So how did they do it?'

'They didn't say, and I didn't ask. But given that Charlie is in his sixties and Paco is in his seventies, it seems unlikely that they used strong-arm tactics. My guess would be that they relied on their brains and their cunning,' Cheavers looked Harrington Benson straight in the eyes, 'which is something we should all – and some more than others – learn from. And that, young

Benson, is why I don't give a toss what the Foreign Office says, and why I will do my damnedest to get Charlie out of the pokey.'

Twenty-One

It was eight o'clock on a cold Castilian morning, and the empty plain around the army camp was still covered with a skein of frost.

Inside the camp, Major Trujillo leaned back in his chair and studied the man sitting across the desk from him.

Martin Cheavers' hair spilled over his collar, which made it too long for a man of any age, and looked particularly ridiculous for a man in his late fifties. His bloodshot eyes lacked seriousness, his teeth were too neat and regular, and his chin was weak. He was a typically decadent northern European – probably a homosexual – and after his debacle with Woodend and Ruiz the day before, Trujillo was determined to show this man who was boss.

'You are the British vice consul for the Costa Blanca. Is that correct?' he asked.

'It's correct,' Martin Cheavers agreed.

'But this is not the Costa Blanca,' the major said. 'You are aware of that, are you not?'

'Too bloody right I'm aware of it,' Cheavers said. 'And if you'd caught your first plane at five-thirty this morning, and changed flights twice since then, you'd be aware of it, too.'

'What I mean is, you are not accredited here,' Major Trujillo said.

'Strictly speaking, you're right, but Charlie Woodend lives on the Costa Blanca, and hence is my responsibility. Besides, I've grown very fond of Spain and the Spanish Army – which I think has done a marvellous job – and I wouldn't like to see anyone get into trouble.'

'Are you threatening me?' Trujillo asked, in the sort of growl which would have the conscripts whom he normally had to deal with shaking in their cheap army boots.

But Cheavers did not look frightened – merely shocked. 'Threatening you?' he said. 'Of course not. I'm merely here to give you some advice.'

'I do not need your advice,' Trujillo countered. 'This Woodend came to Arco de Cañas with another man, a known troublemaker and former rebel. They were asking questions about the backgrounds of army officers. We consider that to be spying.'

It would help if he knew exactly what Charlie had *really* been doing in the town, Cheavers thought. But he didn't know – and so he was just going to have to bluff his way through.

'He's a private detective, so perhaps he wasn't so much spying as working on a case,' he suggested.

Was that the best this Englishman could do? Trujillo wondered. If so, it was pathetic.

'Are you suggesting that he was working for the wife of an army officer, collecting evidence of adultery – which is how most private

273

detectives outside Spain seem to earn their living?' he asked with a sneer.

'Well, it's a possibility, isn't it?' Cheavers asked weakly.

'No, it is not. There is no adultery in Spain, and even if there were, there is no divorce. A man may get an annulment of his marriage if he can prove that he did not understand his vows at the time he had made them, but a woman . . . well, even if her husband was having an affair, she would gain nothing but humiliation from learning about it.'

'Oh,' Cheavers said, looking crestfallen.

'If you have nothing more to say on the matter, this interview is over,' Trujillo told him.

'I do have one more question,' Cheavers said. 'Are you a gambler, Major Trujillo?'

'Why do you ask that?'

'Because you are gambling at the moment. It's possible that in a few days, or a few weeks, the army will be in control of this country – and a damn good thing if it is, in my opinion.'

'Yes, Spain has always put its faith in its brave soldiers,' Trujillo said complacently.

'But we don't always get what we wish for, unfortunately, and I have access to sources at the centre of your government which say that there is little chance of the army taking the reins.'

The meeting was suddenly turning out much better than he could ever have hoped, Trujillo thought. This popinjay in suede boots who was sitting opposite him had all but admitted that he was employing spies, and if he could just be persuaded to reveal a few of their names, then the promotion of a certain major in the military police was assured.

'Tell me about these sources,' he said casually.

'They are men who want the best for their country but also the best for themselves – and who see being friendly with the British government as the best way of achieving both ends,' Cheavers said.

'I'm not sure I know quite what you mean,' Trujillo said cunningly. 'Could you perhaps give me a few examples?'

'All right,' Cheavers agreed. 'There are important men in this country who wish to see their sons enrolled in one of the finer English schools, like Eton or Harrow. There are men with pregnant mistresses, who have taken the British Embassy's advice on which abortion clinics they should use, and have asked us to make the necessary arrangements. There are men who have business interests in England, and are concerned that . . .'

'Enough!' Trujillo said.

These men were not spies, Trujillo thought, they were merely seeking a little *enchufe*, which was the Spanish way. And besides, they were already sounding too powerful for a mere major to ever think of accusing them of anything.

'What we have learned from these men is that your young king has plans to turn this country into a liberal democracy,' Cheavers said.

'It will never happen,' Trujillo said.

But yet, if that was what these important men thought . . .

'And one of the first things a liberal democracy inevitably does to prove its credentials is to turn the spotlight on past abuses, like, for example, the illegal detention of foreign nationals.'

Trujillo relaxed. This was – it was clear to him now – nothing more than a bluff.

'No one will make much of a fuss over this Woodend,' Trujillo sneered. 'He is nothing but a retired policeman.'

'Now that's where I think you're misreading the situation,' Cheavers said. 'The British government thinks very highly of Sir Charles . . .'

Warning lights were beginning to flash in Trujillo's head.

'Sir Charles!' he repeated.

'Oh dear, I should never have said that,' Cheavers said, putting his hand to his mouth. 'His knighthood is not due to be announced until the New Year's Honours List.'

Trujillo decided to ignore the warning lights.

'They would never give a knighthood – or any other honour – to someone like Charlie Woodend,' he said. 'The man wears an old tweed jacket which my dog would reject as a bed.'

'One of Woodend's last cases as a policeman was the investigation of a child prostitute ring,' Cheavers said. 'Several of the clients of that ring were politicians. Woodend arrested the men running the ring, and also some of their clients – but he kept the politicians' names out of it.'

Trujillo nodded. Of course that was what he had done – that was what any policeman anywhere would have done in his situation.

'The politicians are very grateful to him for

that, but also – since he still holds evidence which could send them to gaol – a little frightened of him. So the knighthood is both by nature of a reward and a bribe. Now if you put him on trial for spying in Spain, he will find some way to reveal those names, because he is a spiteful man who, if he is going down, wishes to drag everyone else with him.'

'Why should I be concerned about that?' Trujillo wondered.

'You should be concerned because the politicians who are consequently disgraced will want their revenge too – and they will extract it from the man who brought about their downfall. In other words, Major Trujillo, they will extract it from you!'

'I am an officer in the Spanish army – foreign politicians could do nothing to me,' Trujillo said.

Yet his own words did not convince him, because he knew that was not the way it worked.

The ruling classes, bound together by their mutual interest in maintaining the status quo, knew no national boundaries, he told himself, and while the British politicians themselves could not get to him, they would know men in Spain who could.

'Perhaps the best solution all round might be for you to kill him,' Cheavers suggested, out of the blue.

'What!' Trujillo exclaimed.

'It would be easy for him to fall down the stairs and break his neck,' Cheavers said. 'Or

277

perhaps you could hang him, and make it look like a suicide. The British government would not look into his death too closely, because, as I said, he still poses a threat to some very influential men.'

'You're . . . you're giving me permission to kill him?' Trujillo asked, astounded.

'Not my permission, exactly,' Cheavers replied, hedging. 'I don't think I could go quite that far. But let's just say, shall we, that a nod is as good as a wink to a blind horse?'

'I need to think,' said Trujillo, starting to sweat.

'Wait a minute – while it might be a jolly good idea on paper, it would never work in practice,' Cheavers said, disappointedly. 'A clever man like Woodend has probably arranged that, in the event of his death, certain incriminating evidence will be released.'

'So what am I to do?' Trujillo asked.

'I don't know,' Cheavers confessed. 'You can't put him on trial, and you certainly can't kill him, so what *are* you to do?'

The two men sat there in silence for perhaps two minutes.

Then Trujillo, with an edge of desperation in his voice, said, 'I could always let him go.'

'No, that wouldn't work either,' Cheavers said.

'Why wouldn't it work?' Trujillo pleaded. 'What's to stop me just handing him over to you?'

'The paperwork,' Cheavers said. 'Once the paperwork's filled in, you're snookered. I mean

278

to say, how would you explain to your superiors that you'd released a man you'd only recently arrested for spying?'

'But there isn't any paperwork!' Major Trujillo said, with a gasp of relief. 'Woodend was only arrested late yesterday afternoon, and I have not yet had time to file a report on him.'

Or more likely, in order to avoid your superiors getting any of the credit, you were not going to file any report until you had the whole case neatly tied up, Cheavers thought.

'Well, that is good news,' he said aloud. 'If there's no report, then I think your solution is probably the best one we're likely to come up with.' He frowned. 'But there is still one small difficulty we will have to overcome.'

'Yes?' Trujillo said worriedly.

'You may not have realized this, Major, but Paco Ruiz is Charlie Woodend's lover.'

'That's disgusting!' Trujillo said.

'Yes, it is rather unsavoury,' Cheavers agreed. 'But the fact is that if you don't release Ruiz, too, Woodend will use the evidence he has to put pressure on the politicians in London, who will put pressure on the politicians in Spain . . . And we all know whose head will end up on a silver platter, don't we?'

'I will release Ruiz, too,' Trujillo said, defeated.

'Yes, that would certainly resolve all the problems,' Cheavers agreed.

'How the hell did you manage that?' Woodend asked admiringly, as the car left the army camp and sped across the flat plain.

279

'I lied through my teeth,' Cheavers replied. 'I even told Trujillo that you were screwing Paco.'

'But that is not true!' Paco said.

'I know,' Cheavers said, apologetically. 'And I also know that by even making such a suggestion, I will have offended a macho man like you – but I'm afraid that it had to be done.'

Paco grinned. 'I am the man in our relationship,' he said. 'It is me who is screwing Charlie.'

'That's quite true,' Woodend agreed. 'We tried it the other way, and it didn't work.'

Cheavers laughed, then reached into his pocket, produced an envelope, and handed it to Woodend.

'What's this?' Woodend asked.

'Plane tickets,' Cheavers said. 'One from San Sebastian to Bordeaux, and another from Bordeaux to Manchester.'

'And why are you handing them to me?'

'Because I've not yet worked out what lies I'll tell the Foreign Office to cover the lies I told Major Trujillo,' Cheavers replied. 'And while all this lying is going on, I'd much prefer it if you were out of the country.'

The funeral mass for Javier Martinez was a large affair, and was attended by everybody who was anybody in Whitebridge's Catholic community, but there was one person who was notably absent – his son, Robert Martinez.

'There's a rumour going round that he's had a nervous breakdown,' Meadows told Beresford and Crane, as they stood in the churchyard.

'I can't say I'm entirely surprised about that,' Crane said. 'He looked on the point of collapse yesterday.'

'It's probably because of the guilt,' Beresford said sombrely. 'He'll have been telling himself that he should have done more for his father while he was still alive, and that if had done more, he could somehow have prevented the death. It's not logical – but it's what will be going through his mind.'

Meadows and Crane exchanged glances. They both knew that Beresford's mother had had Alzheimer's disease, that he had sacrificed virtually his entire twenties to caring for her, and that though he might be talking about Robert Martinez, he was really thinking about himself.

'Anyway, we're not here to speculate on Robert Martinez's state of mind – we're here to see if we can catch ourselves a killer,' Beresford continued, in a much more upbeat voice.

And that was indeed why they were there. Killers – for any number of twisted psychological reasons – often did attend the funerals of their victims, and that had been the downfall of any number of them. But the respectful – if not exactly broken-hearted – congregation that was inside the church at that moment showed absolutely no sign of homicidal tendencies.

The big oak doors of the church swung open, and the corpse and congregation appeared. The coffin was carried solemnly to the hearse, which was waiting outside in the street, and then a convoy of cars set off in slow procession towards the crematorium.

'Are we going to the crematorium ourselves, sir?' Crane asked.

What would be the point of that? Beresford wondered.

The killer wouldn't be there to watch the coffin make its slow journey on the conveyor belt towards the fiery furnace. He was long gone – had probably already been long gone by the time the roadblocks went up on the night Javier Martinez was murdered – by now he would be sunning himself on some South American beach, and looking forward to a comfortable old age paid for by his bars of Spanish gold.

'Sir?' Crane said.

'You two can put in an appearance at the crematorium,' Beresford told him. 'I have to get back to headquarters.'

Though since the case seemed to have stalled, what he would actually do when he got to headquarters was something he hadn't yet worked out.

It had only been a short flight from San Sebastian to Bordeaux, and Woodend had barely got off one plane before he was boarding another. Now he was crossing the Bay of Biscay, and in a little more than an hour's time, he would be landing at Manchester's Ringway Airport.

He would go straight to Whitebridge, he'd decided, because he needed to talk to Monika's team as soon as possible.

He hoped that she wouldn't think he was interfering by turning up – literally out of the blue – because that was not his intention at all.

No, he would simply hand over the evidence that would close the case for them, and be on his way.

They would probably never catch the killer, of course – but at least they would have the satisfaction of knowing who had done it.

He took the sepia photograph that Paco had purloined out of his pocket, and studied the rank of smiling young men. They looked so innocent – almost childlike. But they had been far from that. Several – if not all – had been responsible for executions in the village of Val de Montaña. One of them – Lieutenant Suarez – had repeatedly raped Elena. And another man, who had married a woman from Calpe and settled on the coast, had killed again, very recently.

'We're on your trail, Pepe Durante,' he said softly to himself.

There were a number of men having a smoke on the steps of the crematorium, and one of them – who had made no effort to dress up appropriately for such a solemn occasion, and frankly seemed quite drunk – was Fred Sidebotham.

'I'm surprised to see you here, given how you felt about Javier Martinez,' Meadows said.

Sidebotham looked at her through bleary eyes.

'You're that bobby,' he said.

'That's right,' Meadows agreed.

Sidebotham blinked.

'What was the question again?' he asked.

It had been a statement rather than a question,

283

but there wasn't much point in explaining that to a man in his condition.

'Why did you come to the cremation?' she asked, putting it as simply as she could.

'I wanted to make quite sure the old bugger didn't escape this time,' Sidebotham said. He took a long drag on his cigarette. 'My only regret is that they're burning him up, instead of burying him.'

'Why's that?'

'Because if they'd buried him, I could have danced on his grave.' A puzzled expression came to Sidebotham's face. 'Why *didn't* they bury him? Do you know the answer to that?'

'As I understand it, from what his son told my boss, Javier had expressed a wish to be cremated.'

'Funny, that,' Sidebotham said.

'In what way?'

'Well, when him and me were still mates – though, as it turned out, we never really were mates, at least as far as he was concerned – he always used to say that he hated the thought of cremation.'

'He hated the thought?'

'Yes, he was one of them old-fashioned Catholics, you see – the sort that believes that if God's going to resurrect you on Judgement Day, he needs a body to work on, and that he can do bugger all with a handful of ashes. I wonder what made him change his mind.'

'So do I,' Meadows said thoughtfully.

Twenty-Two

The phone in the corridor of the Drum and Monkey was not the ideal one from which to make a sensitive and personal phone call, but Monika Paniatowski knew there was simply no way that she could wait until she was back in her office to make it.

'I've just been told by one of my team that you didn't attend your father's funeral,' she said, to the man on the other end of the line.

'You're right, I didn't,' Robert Martinez replied. 'I know it was wrong of me, but . . .'

'Oh, for God's sake, Robert, I don't care about the bloody funeral,' Paniatowski interrupted him exasperatedly. 'It's you that I'm worried about. How are you feeling?'

'When I woke up this morning, I was shaking, and I haven't been able to stop since,' Martinez said.

'Have you seen the doctor?'

'I've got an appointment.'

'And is your ex-girlfriend there with you?'

'No, she's in Harrogate, at a conference.'

'So you're all alone?'

'Yes.'

'That's not a good idea.' Paniatowski hesitated before speaking again. 'You're not thinking of harming yourself, are you?'

Robert Martinez laughed, but there was no trace of humour in it.

'No, don't worry about that,' he said. 'I might wish I was dead – but I'm a Catholic, and I'm certainly not going to top myself.'

She should go to him, she thought. He needed her. But her team needed her, too, because the investigation was going nowhere fast, and without her to lead them, there was no chance of ever catching the killer.

'I'll come round to see you as soon as I can,' she said, 'but it might not be until the evening.'

'I understand,' he replied. 'I'll be waiting for you.'

'I . . .' Paniatowski said, then she stopped herself.

'What?' Robert asked.

'I'll . . . I'll get there as soon as I possibly can,' Paniatowski said, and quickly hung up.

But that hadn't been what she'd been about to say at all.

What she'd been about to say was, 'I love you.'

As she walked down the corridor, she was feeling light-headed – almost as if she were a different person – but by the time she had crossed the bar and sat down at the team's usual table, she had got a grip on herself, and DCI Paniatowski was back in charge.

'Where were we?' she asked the team.

'Before you went to make your phone call, I'd just told you that Robert Martinez wasn't at his father's funeral,' Meadows said.

'Right, that's dealt with,' Paniatowski said, over-crisply. 'What have you got to report, Colin?'

'I've had my lads out all morning trying to trace Elena's movements after she left the copse – and they've got nowhere,' Beresford said.

'The logical place for her to have gone would have been Tufton Court,' Crane said.

'Why should she have gone there then, when she hadn't gone before?' Meadows asked.

'She might have thought that she saw Robert Martinez walking along the road and turning into the Court.'

'He was in London, working on the draft of an important bill,' Paniatowski said, then she added, aggressively, 'And before any of you ask, Inspector Beresford, I have checked on that.'

'The inspector wasn't going to ask, boss,' Meadows said softly. 'Nobody was.'

'I wasn't saying that she did see Robert Martinez,' Crane continued, as if he hadn't noticed the sudden tension in the atmosphere. 'I was only suggesting that she might have thought she'd seen him. It was getting dark by then, remember, and it would have been easy for her to make a mistake – especially since she was cold and desperate to talk to Robert.'

You shouldn't have snapped at Colin like that, Paniatowski told herself. *You might be upset about Robert, but that's no excuse for falling to pieces – especially in front of the people who you're supposed to be leading.*

'I'm sorry if I was a little abrupt with you just now, Inspector Beresford,' she said.

'That's all right, boss,' Beresford said generously. 'We're all feeling a bit under pressure.'

'Too bloody right, we are,' Paniatowski agreed.

'Let's get back to Jack's idea that Elena entered the Court because she thought she'd seen Robert Martinez. If she'd done that, surely one of the neighbours would have seen her.'

'Not necessarily,' Beresford told her. 'Everybody would have drawn their curtains for the night by then. And there wasn't even much chance of anybody driving down the Court, because, as you know, all the houses have their garages at the back, next to the service road.'

'So the murderer sees where Elena is going, follows her, and kills her,' Paniatowski said. 'He will have needed a car to take the body away. Check with the car rental firms, see if they rented a car out to someone with a Spanish driving licence on either Tuesday or Wednesday, Colin. And also check up on the cars that were stolen on those days.'

'I've already done that, boss,' Beresford said.

'Then do it again!' Paniatowski told him.

But it would do no good, she thought. Nothing they tried seemed to be doing any good.

'There was one small point I was about to bring up before you made your phone call, boss,' Meadows said.

'And what was that?'

'I was talking to an old man called Fred Sidebotham at the crematorium. He's known Javier Martinez for a long time, and he said that – for religious reasons – Martinez absolutely hated the idea of being cremated. Of course, he was very drunk, so he may have been talking rubbish, but I thought I should mention it.'

'He was talking rubbish,' Paniatowski said vehemently. 'Robert Martinez would never have done anything that was against his father's wishes.'

If anyone had asked the young Charlie Woodend where he thought he would be living in his mid-sixties, he would have answered, without a moment's hesitation, that it would be in Whitebridge.

Because that was the way it had been in those days, Woodend thought. You were born in the town, and you would die in the town. It was simply one of the laws of nature.

And yet there he was, fresh from sunny Spain, walking up the old cobbled street which led to the Drum and Monkey, and thinking how strange and alien it all seemed.

Life rarely worked out as you thought it would, he told himself. It was sometimes better, and sometimes worse, but it was never quite what you'd imagined it would be.

He saw the front door of the Drum and Monkey ahead of him, and felt a familiar surge of excitement.

He opened the door, and saw Monika and Beresford sitting at their usual table, with a younger man and woman, who, from Monika's descriptions of them, he knew had to be DS Meadows and DC Crane.

Then they saw him, too.

Beresford sprang to his feet and held out his hand.

'Well, just look what the cat's dragged in,' he

289

said. 'It's really good to see you, sir. Would you fancy a pint?'

'Too bloody right I would,' Woodend told him.

Paniatowski, who was still in her seat – and seemed to have been having difficulty processing the fact that Woodend was actually there – looked up at him and said, 'Hello, Charlie.'

'Hello, Monika,' Woodend replied. 'Would it be all right if I sat down?'

'Of course it would,' Paniatowski said. 'Get him a chair, Jack.'

Crane got the chair, everyone budged up a little, and by the time Woodend's pint arrived, there were five of them sitting round the table.

Woodend took a sip of his pint. He had been looking forward to it, but he found it strangely disappointing.

Perhaps all that Spanish lager he'd been drinking had spoiled his palate, he thought.

'The first thing I want to make clear is that I'm not here to try and take over the investigation, Chief Inspector Paniatowski,' he said.

'No, you'd better not be,' Paniatowski replied – though there was a part of her that wished he could do just that.

'The reason I've come is to personally hand over a piece of evidence which might be vital to your case,' Woodend continued. 'Now you know my theory – Javier Martinez was taken to the priest's house to be questioned about the gold, but what the men inside didn't know was that Martinez had already gone into partnership with another of the soldiers, who killed all three of them, and then helped him to escape.'

'You're spinning it out a bit, Charlie,' Paniatowski said, with just a hint of impatience in her voice.

'I'm well aware of that,' Woodend replied, 'but after spending a night in a military prison cell, I think I'm entitled to.'

'Spending a night in a *what?*' Paniatowski asked.

'I'll come on to that later, but now – if you don't mind – I'll continue with my carefully crafted exposition,' Woodend said, smiling.

Paniatowski grinned back at him. 'Go right ahead,' she said.

'Up till now, we've had no idea who Javier's partner might be,' Woodend told her, 'but I think that Paco and me – at great inconvenience, and not a little danger, to ourselves – have whittled it down to just one man.' He took the sepia photograph out of his pocket, and handed it to Paniatowski. 'That's him – the man on the end of the second row. His name is Pepe Durante and he used to live in Calpe, like me, though I'm doubtful if you'll find him there now.'

He had been expecting the photograph to cause something of a sensation, but nothing like the sensation it actually did cause.

Monika Paniatowski grew wide-eyed with shock and amazement, and when she handed the photograph on to the rest of the team, their reaction was equally dramatic.

'We never knew!' Kate Meadows gasped. 'It never even crossed our minds for a second!'

'I want the Martinez house searched from top

to bottom,' Paniatowski said to Beresford. 'I want it torn apart if necessary.'

And the whole team stood up.

'Am I missing something here?' Woodend asked, looking up at them.

'There's no time to explain the whole thing now,' said Paniatowski, who was already taking her coat off the back of the chair, 'so you'll have to settle for a quick summary.'

'Fair enough,' Woodend agreed.

'You were dead wrong about Pepe Durante being the killer, Charlie,' Paniatowski told him, pulling her coat on, 'but when you told us that you'd brought us a vital piece of evidence, you were right on the money.'

The team of four officers had spent over an hour searching the lounge in the Martinez house.

They had been through all the drawers and cupboards. They had lifted the carpet, and checked that none of the floorboards was loose, or looked like it had been tampered with. They had undone the stitching on the three-piece suite, and peered inside. They had examined the pelmets over the curtains, and unscrewed all the electrical sockets to make sure that nothing was hidden behind them. And so far, neither they, nor any of the officers pulling the rest of the house apart, had come up with anything.

The problem was that the evidence they were searching for might not even be there any longer, Paniatowski thought, as she watched the officers at work. It could, instead, be lying at the bottom of the canal, or even buried out on the moors. And if that was the case, then even though she knew *who* had killed Doña Elena – and *why* he had killed her – she would never be able to prove it.

A constable appeared in the lounge doorway.

'DI Beresford wondered if you could come down to the basement, ma'am,' he said.

'Has he found something?' Paniatowski asked.

'He thinks he might have done,' the constable replied.

The basement had been used as a dumping ground for objects that Robert Martinez and his father had discarded, but could not quite bring themselves to throw out. There was chipped furniture, an old bicycle, and rolled-up carpets. There were cardboard boxes which had held crockery and knick-knacks, and now had their contents spread all over the floor.

But none of these things seemed to be of any interest to Beresford. All his attention was focused on a small section of wall close to the floor.

'Do you notice anything about this bit of brick-work, boss?' he asked Paniatowski.

Paniatowski squatted down, and shone her torch on it.

'The mortar between the bricks is dirty,' she said, 'much dirtier than the mortar on the rest of the wall.'

'That's because somebody's made an attempt to disguise the fact that this mortar is new, though all he's actually succeeded in doing is drawing attention to it,' Beresford said.

'You think there's something behind it?' Paniatowski asked.

'I'm bloody sure there is.' Beresford tapped it with the hammer he had been holding in his hand. 'It's hollow.'

'Then let's take a look,' Paniatowski suggested.

They could have simply smashed the wall in, but since they were still not entirely sure what lay behind it, they decided to approach the task with caution, chipping away at the mortar until they had loosened a brick, and then pulling that brick free, and moving on to the next one.

It was five minutes before there was a hole big enough for Beresford to put his arm through and reach inside, and when he finally could, he groped around for a couple of seconds before saying, 'There are two things in here.'

'Then bring them out one at a time,' Paniatowski said.

The first object he removed was rectangular, and encased in oilskin. When Beresford unwrapped the covering, they found they were looking at a small bar of gold, which had the words Banco de España stamped on it.

There must have been more bars at one time – perhaps as many as three or four – but they had been sold off, and the money they had raised had been laundered through Sunshine Holidays.

It was strange to think that only a couple of hours earlier, the whole team had believed that this gold had been the motive for two murders, Paniatowski mused.

But the murders had never been about the gold – the gold had nothing to do with it all.

'Bring the other thing out now,' she said. 'And let's hope it's what we think it is.'

The second object, which was also wrapped in oilskin, was a ball-peen hammer, and Paniatowski nodded her head with satisfaction.

'What do you think the lab boys will find when they examine that?' she asked Beresford.

'I think they'll find that it was probably the blunt instrument that was used to kill Doña Elena.'

Paniatowski nodded again. She knew now why Elena had come to England, and why she had watched this house from the copse of trees, instead of going straight to the front door and ringing the bell. She knew why the woman had had to die, and why her killer had attempted to hide her body.

There was much more she knew, too – and though she couldn't prove it, she didn't think she'd need to.

Since he had no official status on this investigation, Charlie Woodend had not come into the house, and Paniatowski found him in the garden, walking up and down to keep warm.

'It's a bloody horrible climate you have in this country,' he said when he saw her. 'I don't know how you stand it.'

'You can get used to anything in time,' Paniatowski said. 'Listen, Charlie, I have to talk to someone off the record, and I'd be grateful if you could be there with me.'

'That someone would be Robert Martinez, would it?' Woodend asked.

295

'Yes, it's Robert, and the reason I want you to be there is that . . .' Paniatowski began.

'You don't have to tell me if you don't want to, lass,' Woodend interrupted her.

'But I do want to tell you,' Paniatowski said. 'The reason I want you to be there is that I've become rather emotionally attached to him.'

'Aye,' Woodend said. 'I'd rather gathered that.'

Twenty-Three

Standing in the doorway of his ex-girlfriend's flat, Robert Martinez looked better than he had sounded on the phone – but not much.

'We need to talk, Robert,' Paniatowski said.

Martinez nodded. 'I know that.'

'This is an old friend of mine, Charlie Woodend,' Paniatowski said.

'Chief Inspector Woodend,' Martinez said, holding out his hand.

'Ex-Chief Inspector,' Woodend replied, shaking it.

'I'd like Charlie to sit in on our talk, if you wouldn't mind, Robert,' Paniatowski said.

'Would it make it easier for you?' Martinez asked.

'Yes, I think it would.'

'Then why would I mind? I care for you, Monika – I really do – and I hate it that you're in this situation because of me.'

'It's not your fault,' Paniatowski said. 'It just happened.'

Martinez nodded again, though Paniatowski was unsure whether that meant he was in agreement with her or not.

'You'd better come in, then,' he said.

He led them into the lounge, and they all sat down.

'Would you like to start, Charlie?' Paniatowski asked.

'Why not?' Woodend replied. 'The story really begins with a young Spanish Nationalist army officer called Luis Suarez. Suarez was a bit of a ladies' man, and one of the ladies he was particularly friendly with was the daughter of a Colonel Hierro. In fact, he was a bit too friendly, and she got pregnant. Now Suarez knew that when the colonel found out – and he was bound to find out, by the very nature of things, in a few months – he himself was as good as dead. So he decided to make a run for it, but before he could run, he needed to get some money – and that's when he took his unit to Val de Montaña, looking for the gold that he'd heard one of the communist militiamen had.' He paused. 'It doesn't seem as if any of this is news to you, Mr Martinez.'

'It isn't,' Martinez said.

'He has the man who's supposed to have the gold – Javier Martinez – brought to the priest's house, and tells him that if he doesn't hand it over, he'll kill him and his entire family. And Martinez – who, by all accounts, was a very decent man – does give him the gold. It's

297

probably at this point – though it may have been even earlier – that Suarez realizes that Martinez can not only provide him with the gold, but also with a new identity. And he needs a new identity, you see, because if he keeps using his real name, Hierro will find him wherever he's gone, and have him taken back to Spain. Now, what he does next shows just what a ruthless bastard he really is. He kills Martinez and two soldiers who know he's got the gold, and he sets the priest's house on fire. But he doesn't kill the baby Roberto – he takes him with him. Do you know why that was, Mr Martinez?'

'I imagine he thought it would make it easier for him to be granted political asylum if he had a small child with him,' Robert Martinez said.

'We seem to be thinking along the same lines,' Woodend agreed. 'So he leaves the village with you and the gold. Everybody will think Luis Suarez has died in the fire, and he's got papers identifying him as Javier Martinez, so he's in the clear.' Woodend paused to light a cigarette. 'I think we can forget the heroic story he fed Monika, about living off roots and berries as he made his way through Spain. My guess would be that he travelled by train, wearing his army uniform, and that it was only when he got to the Pyrenees that he ditched it.'

'I agree,' Martinez said.

'Once he's in France, he has to work out what to do next,' Woodend said. 'He probably thinks about going to South America, and looking at it from the cultural and linguistic viewpoint, that would be his logical choice. But there's a lot of moving around in the Spanish-speaking world, in much the same way as there is in the English-speaking world.'

'So there's always a chance that if he does go to South America, he'll eventually run into somebody who knew either Luis Suarez or Javier Martinez,' Paniatowski said.

'Exactly,' Woodend agreed. 'So what he decides to do instead is to make a complete break with the past. He comes to England – to Whitebridge – and, after a while, starts up his coach business.' He took a drag on his cigarette. 'Monika tells me he wasn't very mechanically minded,' he said to Robert Martinez.

'No, he wasn't,' Robert agreed. 'In the first few years, he was entirely dependent on Fred Sidebotham to keep his buses running.'

'Whereas the real Javier Martinez was an absolute wizard with engines,' Woodend said. 'People used to come from miles around to have him look at their engines. But that's very much by the by. Where was I?'

'He comes to Whitebridge,' Paniatowski prompted.

'Oh aye, he comes to Whitebridge, and even here, he's very careful. There are not many Spaniards living in this town, but he still makes sure he keeps well clear of them.'

'He was against me starting the Whitebridge Hispanic Circle from the start,' Robert said. 'He tried his best to talk me out of it. But I went ahead anyway – I think it was my first real act of defiance.'

'You told me he'd turned his back on

everything Spanish,' Paniatowski said, 'and so he had – except that his bedroom was full of pictures of Spain. That was the one place where he could really be himself.'

And even there, there'd been no pictures of the sea, she thought, because Luis Suarez had been brought up on the Castilian Plain. He probably hadn't even seen the sea until he'd joined the army in the Civil War – and it simply wasn't the real Spain to him.

'Now we fast-forward thirty-six years, to a lunchtime paella party in Calpe,' Woodend said. 'My god-daughter Louisa is there, and so is Martinez's wife, Elena. Louisa shows her a picture of you and your father in the *Whitebridge Evening Telegraph*. But it's not her husband she sees – it's her rapist. So she buys a plane ticket to England. Her plan – as far as we can reconstruct it – is to tell you who this man claiming to be your father actually is. But you're not in Whitebridge. You're in London. She waits for two days – watching Tufton Court from a copse of trees – for your return. And maybe she does see someone she thinks might be you turning into Tufton Court. Or maybe she's just so cold and frustrated that she decides to confront Luis Suarez on her own. And that's a fatal mistake, because he's just as ruthless a bastard as he ever was, and he kills her.'

'I think it's time that you said something now, Robert,' Paniatowski said quietly.

Martinez nodded. 'While my mother was in Whitebridge, she wrote me a letter, explaining

300

everything. But she didn't send it to my home – maybe she was afraid the man I thought was my father would intercept it – she addressed it to the House of Commons, and it arrived when I wasn't there.'

'And when that happens, the mail is couriered to Whitebridge,' Paniatowski said.

'Yes, it is.'

Paniatowski puts her hands on Robert's shoulders to console him, and suddenly they are kissing.

This is insane, she tells herself – yet she does not want to let go.

The kiss continues, and it feels wonderful and natural – as if it has always been meant to be.

Someone outside rings the doorbell, and as the chimes reverberate down the hall, she forces herself to break away from him.

'I'm sorry,' she says.

'It's as much my fault as it is yours,' Robert Martinez says.

The doorbell rings again, more insistently this time.

'It won't happen again,' Monika tells Martinez. 'I promise it will never happen again.'

'But I want it to happen again,' Robert says. 'I so desperately want it to happen again.'

'For God's sake, you're part of my investigation,' Paniatowski tells him.

'But once the investigation's over . . .' he says hopefully.

The doorbell rings for a third time.

'Who is it?' Robert Martinez calls out.

301

'Courier service,' says a voice from the other side of the door.

And what the courier had been delivering, Paniatowski now realized, was a death sentence.

Robert took a cheap envelope out of his pocket and extracted a photograph from it.

'She sent me this, too,' he said.

There were three people in the photograph. One of them was clearly Elena, and the second – a man – was proudly holding up a small baby.

'That's your real father,' Paniatowski said.

'Yes,' Robert agreed. 'That's Javier Martinez.'

'When you'd read the letter, you went up to his room, tied him up, and tortured him with a cigarette end,' Woodend said.

'That's right,' Robert agreed. 'I wanted to know all the details. I wanted to know just how big a *hijo de puta* he'd been.'

'Robert would never torture his own father,' Paniatowski had assured the team.

And she'd been right – he hadn't.

'So, from the very start, you believed everything in the letter, Mr Martinez?' Woodend said.

'The letter had the ring of truth about it,' Robert told him. 'I'd always known something was wrong between me and the man I thought was my father – but now I knew why. And he confirmed it all. It didn't take much to make him talk. The man was a coward through and through.'

'And when you'd finished torturing him, you killed him,' Woodend said.

'And when I'd finished questioning him, and he'd confessed to all crimes, I executed him in

302

the approved judicial manner,' Robert Martinez corrected him.

'You didn't want him buried with your mother, for obvious reasons,' Woodend said. 'But why did you have him cremated?'

Robert Martinez smiled. 'He cremated my father, didn't he? It seemed only fair that I should return the compliment.'

'You're not ashamed of killing him, are you?' Paniatowski asked.

'No,' Robert replied. 'I'm proud of it. It was a matter of honour.'

'Then why didn't you confess right away?' Paniatowski demanded, with a catch in her throat. 'Why did you choose instead to . . . to . . .'

Woodend stood up. 'I think my part in these proceedings is about finished,' he said. 'I'll be outside when you want me.'

He walked over to the door, and stepped out into the corridor.

'Why did you choose, instead of confessing right away, to put me on the rack?' Paniatowski asked. 'Why did you let me fall in love with you?'

'I did it for my mother – because I was a dutiful son,' Robert Martinez said, sadly.

'I don't understand.'

'What would have happened if I'd confessed to you the moment you arrived at the house?'

'You'd have been arrested.'

'And what would you have said when I told you that Luis Suarez had killed my mother?'

'I'd have said that I believed you!'

'But would anyone else have believed me?'

303

'Of course they would,' Paniatowski said.

And then she thought, *But would they?*

'What proof did I have that anything I'd have told you was true?' Robert Martinez asked. 'A letter from a dead woman? An old photograph? That's really no proof at all.'

'If you'd been straight with us from the start, we'd have found the proof for you,' Paniatowski said.

'You *did* find the proof for me, but only because I *wasn't* straight with you,' Robert countered.

'Are you suggesting that if you'd confessed, we'd never have investigated your claims?' Paniatowski asked angrily.

'No, I'm suggesting that if you already had one killer locked up, and thought – even though you couldn't prove it – that the other one was already dead, you wouldn't have investigated it half as thoroughly as you did,' Robert said.

It was true, Paniatowski thought. The chief constable would never have allowed a full-scale investigation if Robert had already been in jail. And if she'd already known who'd killed Elena, she herself would have hesitated before asking Charlie Woodend to stick his neck out in Spain.

'Without the proof, would people have believed that Suarez had killed my mother and I'd killed him – or would they have believed Suarez was my father, and that I'd murdered them both?' Robert Martinez asked.

'You had an alibi for the time of Elena's death,' Paniatowski said weakly.

'Please, Monika, answer the question,' Robert said.

'It would have been completely illogical, but there would have been a lot of people who believed that you'd murdered them both,' Paniatowski admitted.

'And in their eyes, Luis Suarez would have been an innocent victim – rather than the monster that he really was,' Robert said. 'My mother deserved better than that – and that's why I did what I did. It was the only thing I could still give her.'

'Did you . . . did you ever feel anything for me?' Paniatowski asked.

'Yes, in that at least, I've been honest with you,' Robert said. 'I love you, Monika – but it's a doomed love, isn't it?'

'It doesn't have to be doomed,' Paniatowski said. 'You'll go to prison, of course, but . . .'

'How long will I go to prison for?' Robert interrupted her.

'I don't know.'

'I tortured an old man, and then I killed him.'

'There were mitigating circumstances, and . . .'

'I'll get a long sentence, won't I?' Robert asked.

'Yes,' Paniatowski admitted, 'you'll get a long sentence.'

'And I don't want you to throw away your life waiting for me, because prison changes people, and by the time I'm released, I won't be the man you know now.'

'No, you won't,' Paniatowski agreed.

She cleared her throat. 'Officially, this meeting

has never taken place,' she said. 'What I'd like you to do now is to go down to the police headquarters, and make a full confession.'

'Of course,' Robert Martinez agreed. 'Can I ask one more favour?'

'What is it?'

'I don't want you to be the one who questions me – I don't think it would be good for either of us.'

Paniatowski stood up. 'It'll all be fairly straightforward,' she said. 'Colin Beresford can handle it.'

She walked over to the door, then turned around again.

'Goodbye, Robert,' she said.

'Goodbye, Monika,' Martinez answered.

Epilogue

They had arrived at Ringway Airport with plenty of time to spare, but somehow all that time had melted away, and they found themselves standing ten yards from the passport barrier, with only a few minutes left together.

'How are you feeling, lass?' Woodend asked.

'I'm sorry to see you go, obviously,' Paniatowski said.

'Don't be so bloody thick, lass, you know that's not what I meant,' Woodend told her.

'It hurts when I think about Robert,' Paniatowski admitted. 'I expect it will hurt for quite a while.'

'Yes, I expect it will,' agreed Woodend, who had never been one for sugar-coating the pill.

'Flight two-six-four for Alicante is now boarding,' said a tinny voice over the public address system.

'And how are *you* feeling, Charlie?' Paniatowski asked.

'To tell you the truth, I'm feeling a little embarrassed,' Woodend said. 'I don't think my deductive reasoning's ever been stronger than it was on this case. I don't think I've ever been better at getting inside other people's heads. And what was the result? I got the whole thing completely wrong.'

'We all did,' Paniatowski said. 'But sometimes you have to be wrong before you can be right.

If you'd never gone to Arco de Cañas for the *wrong* reasons, you'd never have got your hands on the photograph, and if you'd never got your hands on the photograph . . .'

'So it turns out I was brilliant after all?' Woodend asked.

'Yes, Charlie, it does.'

'Well, anyway, I really appreciate you giving me the opportunity to play a part in one last case.'

The airport suddenly felt much colder, and Paniatowski shivered.

'Do you know, I don't like the way you said that,' she told him.

'What?'

'One last case.'

'I only meant that the chances of being involved in another murder are pretty minimal.'

'No, you didn't.'

'No, I didn't,' Woodend agreed. 'I've got cancer, lass.'

Paniatowski gasped. 'Is it serious?'

'Well, it's not a laugh a bloody minute, if that's what you're asking.'

'You know what I mean.'

'The doctor said I had a fifty-fifty chance of survival, but while he was talking, I was looking at his nurse, and from the expression on her face, I reckon he'd told her it was closer to thirty-seventy – and I don't mean in my favour.'

'You'll beat the odds, Charlie – it's what you do,' Paniatowski said.

'Maybe,' Woodend replied, non-committally.

'Does Joan know?'

'Not yet. I didn't see the point in bothering her with it until I absolutely had to.'

'She's got a right to know,' Paniatowski said.

'Maybe she has,' Woodend agreed. 'On the other hand, there's a lot to be said for remaining in a fool's paradise for as long as you can.' He lit up a cigarette, and immediately starting coughing. 'It's a funny thing,' he continued. 'We're living in death's shadow from the moment we're born, yet it always comes as a surprise when that shadow starts to get darker.'

'Last call for flight two-six-four to Alicante,' said the public address system.

Woodend stubbed his cigarette in the nearest bin. He seemed almost glad to have an excuse to get rid of it.

'I'd better go,' he said.

They hugged each other.

'I love you, Charlie,' Paniatowski said.

'I love you, too,' Woodend said – and sniffed.

She watched him walk over to the passport desk – a big man in a hairy sports coat which would never wear out – and thought about all the years they had worked together, and all the cases they had solved.

The customs official had stamped Woodend's passport, and he was moving beyond the desk. In a few moments, he would turn the corner and she would lose sight of him.

She rushed across to the desk, and shouted out, 'I don't want you to die, Charlie!'

He stopped, just at the corner, turned around, and smiled at her.

'Aye, well, in that case, you'd better keep your fingers permanently crossed,' he suggested.

And then he was gone.